Love Never Ends

by

Stacey Wilk

Big Sky Country, Book Three

The Wild Rose Press, Inc.
PO Box 708
Adams Basin, NY 14410-0708
Visit us at www.thewildrosepress.com

Publishing History
First Edition, 2024
Trade Paperback ISBN 978-1-5092-5724-9
Digital ISBN 978-1-5092-5725-6

Big Sky Country, Book Three
Published in the United States of America

Dedication

To my children. The greatest things I've ever created.

Chapter One

He told her no. Not today. Not ever, in fact. At least
not from him and not from his bank. Autumn Archer
gathered her puffy down coat, shoving it under her arm.
She reached for the financial papers that read like an
empty diary lying on the bank manager's desk. Her
shaking hands slid over the pages as if her fingers were
sharp skates on ice, and all her research on why she
should get a loan to save her land tumbled to the floor.

George Smith smirked and shook his head.
Annoyance flashed across his eyes but was gone as
quickly as it came. At least he had the decency to come
around the desk and help her. The scent of sweat and
cinnamon rolled off him, assaulting her nose. She stood
in a hurry, trying to avoid him and gather the tattered
remains of her dignity.

"I'm sorry, Autumn. I really am." George tugged the
end of his suit jacket. The material was shiny and ill-
fitting. His stomach strained against the jacket button,
and the sleeves rode above his frayed shirt cuffs.

She wanted to tell him to keep his condolences. She
had heard enough "I'm sorrys" in the past two years to
last her a lifetime. She never needed to hear it again. "It's
fine. Really. I understand. This is business. You see me
as a risk. I'll make do."

"Not you. Your ski area. This isn't personal. You
don't have enough patrons to prove you can pay the loan.

And you've already mortgaged everything else. If you can't make the next payment yourself, you should sell."

"If it were only that easy."

"I can connect you with a good realtor."

"You mean Dottie Lucier? She's already hounding me. Thanks for your time." She hurried from the office and through the bank as quickly as her boot-clad feet would carry her and before the tears started.

She would not cry in public. She would wait at least until she drove onto her property and then found a quiet place where no one would come looking for her. Not that too many people would. George was right about the lack of customers. In fact, the majority of her patrons came from her next-door neighbor—the Ryker Ranch. Which she wasn't happy about because she didn't like the Rykers. Well, one particular Ryker anyway. But that family was a package deal. If someone stood in the crosshairs of one, that person took on them all.

The tears burned behind her eyes, threatening to betray her before she could push through the glass doors that promised freedom into the damp and gray January day. A snowstorm was on its way. The heat in her house could crap out again if the temperatures dropped low enough. She didn't have enough money to solve her problems, and George Smith had squashed her last option. She couldn't fight the tears.

Do not cry.

Her palm slapped the cold metal of the door handle. She pushed with more might than needed, her frustration controlling her.

A man took hold of the door like an overeager concierge, ripping it from her hands. Her feet tangled, leaving the ground behind, and they collided.

If she hadn't seen the guy, she would have sworn she hit a stone wall. The folder of papers sprayed into the air and spun away on the antagonistic gusts of wind. Today was not her day.

She blinked, hoping her eyes would focus. Oh, she could see clearly enough but might prefer not to. Her papers twirled down Main Street like children playing a game of tag. If anyone found her tax forms lying in the gutter, every resident would know her financial situation. Who was she kidding? In Backwater, Montana, the whole town already knew.

"I'll get them."

His voice's low timbre vibrated in her gut.

She could listen to him talk all day, and that was always her problem—she couldn't shake him loose from her history. Before she could stop Jett Ryker from coming to her rescue, he took off with the grace and speed of the athlete he had always been.

She couldn't run and hide from her embarrassing escapade. He had seen her and would most likely just show up at her house, bringing the papers there if she suddenly disappeared off the sidewalk and into thin air. Better to get the humiliation over with.

He arranged the papers in a neat pile and handed them to her with a stoic look on his face. "I think I grabbed them all."

She had to tilt her chin to look up at him. Tall and handsome. Completely unfair. "Thank you."

"Crazy weather, right?" The tinge of a smile flirted with the corners of his mouth. If he allowed those lips to tilt completely, he would assault her with his charm.

"Looks that way. I have to run. Thanks again for the help. Nice to see you, Jett." Bumping into him—literally and figuratively—was anything but nice.

She avoided him whenever she could. Hard thing to do in a small town where their properties butted up against each other. But if she ever caught sight of him before he noticed her, she ducked out. It might be cowardly, but it was easier. They had to exist in town together. And for the past two decades, they had managed well enough. She had managed. He always seemed to be just fine with the way things were between them.

"Yeah. You too." He adjusted his baseball cap and darted inside the bank.

Life was full of regrets, and losing Jett Ryker was one of hers. And she had a few stacked up. She didn't risk a look back in case he was just inside the door and caught her gawking. She hurried to her truck and shut herself in its safety, where the wind couldn't get her and where she wouldn't bump into her past on the worst day of her life.

She had to find a way to save her land, and she had no idea how to do it.

A miracle would be good about now.

She didn't believe in miracles.

Chapter Two

Jett came out of the bank and spotted a white piece of paper pressed up against the side of the garbage can. He grabbed it. Page three of Autumn's tax returns. Damn, he had missed one. When those pages went flying, her face had filled with horror. Her desperation had spurred him into action. Whatever was on those pages were her private things, and he had wanted her to have them back.

He folded the paper and stuck it in his coat pocket. He would bring it to her later. Maybe he'd be better off shredding it. Autumn never took too kindly to his showing up. She had avoided him more times than he could count. She thought he didn't know.

He didn't blame her for avoiding him. He had been the reason they broke up after he had promised a life with her. But it had been so long ago now. They were different people. At least he was.

Her money was none of his business. But Backwater was the kind of place where secrets were tough to keep hidden. His family was entrenched in the town because their guest ranch employed many people, his older brother was the sheriff, and the brother who followed him in birth order was a race car driver with some notoriety. Everyone talked even when he tried not to listen. He'd heard about Autumn's troubles some time ago.

He reached his truck and slid inside. Cold filled the cabin. He kicked over the engine and turned up the heater. If Autumn ever put the property on the market, he was prepared to buy it. He wanted to expand the services his ranch offered their guests. Autumn's location was ideal, and she was already set up for downhill skiing. Every time a guest drove off his ranch to ski somewhere else, the ranch lost opportunity and—he might as well admit it—money. He didn't like losing money.

The ranch and all its acres, its views of the Montana mountains and the sky that stretched wide, had to go to the next generation of Rykers. At the moment, that was only his niece Izzy. He hoped his brothers would grow the family. He sure as hell wasn't going to be the one.

He drove through town, past the sheriff's station, and followed the road that led to the ranch.

Running a guest ranch was like running a small country. And he loved every minute of it because it was his place and his rules. Not like his sheriff brother who had to follow the rules set in place by other people and enforce them even if he didn't agree. When Jett no longer agreed with the way something went on the ranch, he changed it. Being a rancher was in his blood. He loved the horses and the land. He couldn't imagine living anywhere he couldn't see the big Montana sky. Even if the winters could be tough. Another storm was on its way tonight.

He made a quick turn for the stables that housed six horses used for guests. The ranch offered horse rides on trails all year long. And they had Silver Bell. She was as old as they came. He parked and went into the barn. The scent of hay and disinfectant met him like an old friend.

His large inhale matched his big smile. Exactly as a barn should smell.

"Hey, girl." He ran a hand over her gray snout. "You're stronger than an oak. You know that?" No one ever expected Silver Bell to live into her thirties. But here she was. He didn't know how much longer she would last. By rights, she should be long gone like her owner, but she persisted, determined to live on in his memory. His youngest brother's memory. Losing her would slice him in two.

He gave Silver Bell a carrot, checked on the other horses, then circled back toward the main house. The ranch didn't have a lot of guests right now, but that was fine. Winter in Montana scared all the East Coast tourists. The West Coasters who might want to make Montana their permanent home got wind of a snowstorm and chickened out. Once the weather evened out some, they'd all be back in force.

His family had been fortunate, mostly—if he didn't count losing his dad when he was ten or losing his youngest brother when Jett was twenty-three. He glanced toward the Archer ski area. Or losing her. But he never lingered long on that thought unless he collided with her on the sidewalk. Thinking about Autumn usually interrupted his good mood.

He went into the main house to get lunch started. His mother was already at the stove, whipping up today's menu. Karen Ryker was a small but mighty dynamo. She had raised five boys basically on her own and kept this ranch running after his father passed away. He admired his mom for her strength. And sometimes that strength looked like stubbornness and drove him up the wall.

"Howdy." He grabbed an apron off the hook.

"Oh, hi. Did everything go okay at the bank?" Mom gripped his arm as she passed him on the way to the fridge.

"Just made a deposit, Mom." And had Autumn's beautiful face planted into his chest. For the briefest of seconds, he had caught a whiff of caramel and snow. He wanted to smell her again but reminded himself that was not possible.

"You've been giving me that same line since you were a teenager and started taking the deposits for me." His mother placed a baking dish with meatloaf on the counter.

He didn't remember meatloaf on the menu. Sometimes he wasn't sure why he bothered with a menu. This ranch might be in his name and a place where he could make up his own rules, but his mother was still a force around here.

If one of his brothers or his niece asked for meatloaf, a tornado couldn't stop Mom from preparing it.

He and his three brothers all lived on the ranch in one place or another. None of Karen Ryker's children had gone far. But the ranch had the power to keep anyone rooted. As long as they were good to it, it would be good to them. If Autumn was faced with selling her land, he understood how hard that decision would be for her. She wouldn't give up easily. And she wouldn't want him as the buyer.

"Then why do you keep asking me about my time at the bank if you already know the answer?" He winked to make sure she realized he was joking.

Short answers were a habit, like walking the property. He still had chores to do, and talking was for some other time. He never knew when that time was, actually. The ranch always needed his attention, and he wasn't likely to mention Autumn today or any other. Too many webs were tangled between the Rykers and Autumn's family.

"Is that your barbecue sauce?" He hoped she wouldn't notice the subject change.

Mom swatted at him with the dish towel. "I know that trick, Jett. You and Gage learned it from your father and then taught it to Kace and Lock. But since you asked, yes, it is my famous sauce. I like to know what's going on in town. That's why I asked about the bank, smart aleck."

"If you want the town gossip, you had better ask Kace." Jett wasn't one for gossiping about who he saw at the bank or, worse, what might have been overheard.

The kitchen doors swung open. Gage strode in, commanding the room with his broad shoulders and crisp sheriff's uniform. His brother was a no-nonsense guy who believed most things were black and white. He rarely lost his temper. Thankfully, Jett had only had to pull his brother away from a fight a few times.

"Good afternoon." Gage plopped a kiss on top of their mother's head.

"Oh good. You're here. I'm making the meatloaf. It will be ready soon. Sit." Mom shooed Gage to the table as if he were still a teenager too. The fact all her sons towered over her didn't ever seem to faze her in the least.

So Gage was the one who had requested the meatloaf. Weird. Gage was more independent than that. He would've figured Lock first and then Kace before Gage asked for anything.

"Mom, I'm good. The meatloaf is for Izzy. She had a half day at school and is right behind me. I have to get back to the station. Jett, Cullum Durrell is here to see you. He walked in the same time as Izzy and me. I told him to wait in the main room. I wasn't sure if you wanted to be bothered. Figured I'd give you a way out if you need."

"Did he say what he wanted?" He wasn't expecting a visit from Cullum Durrell, the athletic director of the local nonprofit ski organization.

"I didn't ask. Probably sponsorship for the ski team again. He kind of expects it after the past three years." Gage stuck a finger in the barbecue sauce bowl. Mom swatted him too. Gage only laughed.

Jett removed the apron. "I'll be right back."

Cullum Durrell didn't usually make house calls to ask for money. He could do that with a phone call, and when Cullum wasn't feeling up to a full conversation, he emailed the request. Jett could get behind that method of communication. He preferred it, actually.

Cullum faced the stone fireplace they kept lit all winter for guests to sit by and enjoy. They also provided a coffee bar and a wall of large windows that brought in the mountain views. Cullum had a to-go cup in his hand.

"What brings you out here?" Jett extended a hand.

"Ryker." Cullum's cap-filled smile could be seen from the satellites. "I was in the neighborhood. I thought I'd stop by and say hello."

If Jett's hand were any smaller, Cullum's grip would crush it. But he gave as good as he got, and that fake white smile faltered. Cullum should have gone into politics. He played the game better than most. Instead, he had gone into real-estate development and worked his charms on the politicians to advance his interests.

But Cullum wasn't all that bad. He supported the ski

organization so kids in their area could ski competitively with a chance at college scholarships.

"The ranch isn't exactly on the way to most places. Nice to see you just the same. Do you want to join us for lunch?" That meatloaf would end up feeding twenty.

"No, thanks. I only need a minute of your time."

"You want the sponsorship again this year. I was surprised you hadn't asked before the season started." He usually gave a donation in November when the team was just starting to practice on snow. They always needed money to help fix equipment or enter competitions. He would have to run into the office and grab the checkbook if Cullum needed money today.

"About that. We always want the Ryker Ranch to sponsor our team. You and your family are more than generous with the kids. But there was a reason we waited to approach you till now."

"Yeah? Why's that?"

"We want you to be the head coach for the rest of the season."

"Excuse me?"

His brother Lock came in wearing a flannel shirt, ripped jeans—and not the fashionable kind—and a knit cap pulled down low on his big stupid head. "Jett, there's a problem out back. I need you to come and see it."

Gage picked that exact moment to come through the kitchen. "Hey, Lock. Jett, I'm heading out. I'll see you later." He patted Jett on the back. "Cullum." He nodded in Cullum's direction.

"Good to see you again, Sheriff. I was just telling Jett here that the ski organization would like him to be the head coach for the rest of the season. Our current coach, Andrew Navarro, is relocating for work. We're in a bind and could use his expertise. Don't you think Jett as coach is a good idea?"

Gage glanced between him and Cullum, then back to him. "You goin' to do it?"

"I just heard about this. I need time to think on it." He was not going to accept an offer to coach a team of high schoolers. He didn't have time to take something like that on. He had a ranch to run. Even though he shared the work with Lock, and they had a staff of people who helped out, he had to be on his ranch all day in case anything happened. No, he would turn Cullum down in an email when everyone wasn't staring at him.

"I think you should do it," Gage said. "You'd be good at it."

Jett tried to arrange his face in a way that would tell Gage to shut up. "Like I said, I'll think on it and get back to you."

"You're a great skier," Lock said, standing beside him. He brought the smell of outside with him into the big hall.

"I'm not a coach." They were going to force him into saying no right now. "Thanks, Cullum, but I think I have to pass. Our guest attendance will pick up throughout the month right through ski season. I don't have time to coach. But I'm glad to sponsor. Just send me the form. If you'll all excuse me, I have to get lunch up for the guests." He turned and hurried into the kitchen, ignoring whatever Lock was saying to his back.

His mother buzzed around the kitchen, putting the finishing touches on their lunch. "We're just about ready here. Can you bring the food out to the dining room?"

"Ask Lock to do it." He didn't want to go back out there in case Cullum was still talking to his brothers.

"Lockwood is out back fixing the broken fence."

"He's in the hall talking to Gage and Cullum." The fence must be what Lock wanted him to see. Some member of the wildlife in this area must have broken the fence again, and if he had to guess, the repair was probably going to be a pain to fix or cost him a fortune. Or both. Reasons like that were why he could not be a coach. His job was all day, every day.

"Oh, what did Cullum want?"

"Nothing. Money for the team. That's all."

His mother raised a brow over the top of her black glasses. "What aren't you telling me?"

"There is nothing to tell. I have a call in ten minutes. I need to prepare." He didn't want to talk about Cullum's real reason for being there. His mother would chime in like his brothers and give him some work-life balance excuse as to why he should do it.

"A call with whom?" His mom would not give up until he gave her a complete answer. Her stubbornness reared its unpleasant head and had its eyes on him.

"A supplier. I need to go." He couldn't come up with a better lie under pressure. She probably knew he didn't need to speak to a supplier.

"Why are you acting so strange?" Her eyes narrowed behind her glasses.

He had seconds to make a break for it, or he would have to say he'd been asked to be the ski coach and she would want to talk him into doing it.

"Because Cullum Durrell wants him to be the head coach for the ski team," Lock said, coming through the doors.

Jett hung his head. Too late. Sometimes his large family constantly being around was too much. They meant well, and he loved them for it, but when he wanted his space, he was hard pressed to find it.

"That's wonderful." Mom clapped her hands.

"I'm not going to do it." Better to make that clear and end this conversation.

"Why not?" his mother said. "You'd be a wonderful coach. All the kids will love you. You have so many skills to teach. I always thought you'd make a good coach at any of the sports you played. You have the patience for it."

"I'm too busy to coach a bunch of kids. And there's a storm coming." He turned for the office.

"What does that have to do with anything?" Lock held his big hands in the air and twisted his face into some kind of confused grimace.

"Nothing," he shouted over his shoulder and closed the door to the office.

He didn't know how to talk to kids. His family had it all wrong. He might know how to ski, even was good at it once, but he couldn't coach anyone. He had nothing to say that any of those young athletes needed to hear.

And he had a very busy ranch to run. If Gage and their other brother Kace worked on the ranch too, then sure, he could consider doing something other than working twenty hours a day. But Lock alone wasn't enough, and their mother was practically retired. She ran off at the drop of a hat sometimes. No, his priority was here. And his priority was growing his business. He couldn't do that with distractions. The ski team would have to find someone else.

He'd shoot off an email to Cullum. His mind was made up. Nothing would change it. Nothing at all.

Chapter Three

Snowfall couldn't cover disappointment with its bitter white strokes, but Autumn wished it did. She wished snow had the magic power to camouflage all her mistakes for the past two years just by dousing her poor choices in its sparkling beauty.

She pulled the plaid wool blanket around her shoulders and leaned against the porch railing of her home, a home that had been in her family for generations. And it showed. The house had been a beauty once and had operated as a ski lodge for a long time, but over the years of harsh winters and strong summer days, hand in glove with a pinch of neglect, the house wore a coat more forlorn than vibrant.

Falling snow pricked the dingy night with its white crystals. Warm lights from the Ryker Ranch reflected through the trees with a glittering luster. So close and yet so far. The Rykers had done it right. They had each other. She envied the Rykers their success and their close-knit family. She had no one to help her any longer, not since her husband Trent had died.

She could still feel the pressure of Jett's torso against hers when they collided earlier today. He didn't have an ounce of body fat thanks to his days of moving hay, raking the stables, horseback riding, and all the other things he did to keep his ranch up and running. She was terribly aware of how manly he was and wished she could wipe that awareness away as if it were nothing more than snow on a windshield.

Snow drifted down in fat, round flakes that could taunt the most wicked tongues. Cold wind whipped around her, tugging away the warmth of the blanket, but still she stayed put on the porch. Lingering outside in the elements kept problems crystal clear, no being lulled by the warmth of the fire burning inside. It also gave her an excuse to watch Jett's ranch.

She was out of options for her land, unless she found a buyer who could pull her from under the mortgage and maybe keep a few acres for her and her daughter Quinn. She didn't want a buyer coming here and taking what belonged to her daughter. Autumn had failed Quinn in the worst way.

She had also failed her family. Five generations had lived here. Her ancestors had driven through the plains on horses and with wagons to find a place to settle. They picked this spot, and then in the early nineteen hundreds, her great-grandparents turned their land into a ski area.

Each generation struggled harder to stay open as resorts popped up in many states, making competition fierce. None of her relatives wanted to expand. After her father left, her mother passed the land to Autumn. Vera was tired of owning and running the ski area. Her divorce had done her in. She handed Autumn the keys to the kingdom, failing as it was, without so much as a second glance.

Autumn ran it until she met Trent and married him. They'd operated the place together, but Trent had used the land as collateral in an unsanctioned poker game, causing them so much debt they had borrowed against the equity to pay off his mistakes.

She descended the front steps and headed in the direction of the Ryker Ranch. Something tugged her as if an unseeable force controlled her motions. Unseeable force nothing. It was the accidental meeting with Jett today. Well, the accidental contact. That was what had her so riled up. What called to her was the need to feel warm again, to feel like she belonged somewhere and wasn't so alone. What stopped her from hiking through the trees and up to his front door was bitterness.

Such an ugly emotion. Autumn brushed a snowflake from her cheek. She had made her choices. Slept in her proverbial bed. She hadn't fought for what she wanted. She had no one to blame but herself.

That didn't stop her from wondering what Jett Ryker was up to right now. She had been thinking of him all day.

How many guests had he charmed with his slow smile and flannel-clad shoulders today? How many ladies had he had in his bed all these years? A lot, according to the gossip on the small streets of Backwater. Jett had never settled down. He loved his ranch more than he loved anything else, including her. But that had been a long time ago and better forgotten. Most days she forgot just fine.

But today she'd been told she would lose her land, her ski area, and very possibly that worn-out house with its finicky heat she called a home. So, tonight, walking in the snow that came up to her shins, she rewarded herself with five minutes of self-pity and a drift down memory lane. Or more like a moment to fantasize what life would have been like if she had been able to lasso that rancher for good.

"Autumn, what in the world are you doing all the

way down there?" Her mother's shrill voice carried to her on the blast of freezing wind ripping the blanket from her grip.

With all the acres that had belonged to her family, they had decided to build their home at the bottom of the small mountain and near the edge of the property line. She wished they had been more creative and not butted up near the Ryker Ranch. The proximity allowed her mother to stand on the porch, bundled in her parka, and holler to her. Had the house been anywhere else, her mother's shouts would have fallen on the deaf ears of the wind.

Autumn didn't have the kind of mother portrayed in sweet Christmas movies who always understood and put her children's needs ahead of her own. Her mother was a bad version of the wicked stepmother.

"I'm walking in the snow." She doubted her mother could hear her response. She wasn't about to scream it back. Anyone could be in earshot on the other side of those trees and wondering what she was doing at this hour. Voices carried as easily as the snow when the wind took hold.

She retrieved the blanket from the ground and made her way back. Her mother pulled the sides of her coat closed. Using the zipper seemed like too much of an effort. Not that Autumn would bother to point it out.

"I was looking for you. The heat isn't working right," Vera Thatcher said, shivering.

Autumn assumed the visceral reaction was probably for added effect. Her mother was prone to dramatics, whether verbal or visual. Vera would employ any tactic necessary to manipulate her way.

Her mother was a petite woman, barely passing the

tape measure at five feet. But her ability to find something wrong could reach the top of a hundred-year-old oak tree. Vera still dyed her hair a chestnut brown because she was vain, and she didn't like leaving the house without makeup.

"You shouldn't be out here. It's too cold." Autumn climbed the creaking steps and stood before her mother.

"I'm only out here because that's where I found you. Why are you wandering around the yard late at night anyway? And what could you be looking for in that direction? There's nothing over there except that awful ranch with its noisy guests." Vera spit her words out as if every syllable tasted like poison.

"I'll throw another log on the fire." She would not explain the magnetic pull that could not be fought sometimes. She didn't want to talk to anyone at the ranch or even have anyone see her, but being close to the warmth that exuded from the Rykers turned her into that moth burning up in the flame. Her and Jett's flame had been hot once.

"When are you going to get the heater fixed?" Vera followed her inside. Her slippers clomped against the wood as she shuffled behind.

"When I can afford it. Until then, the wood-burning stove will do." The warmth from the stove made it up the stairs, but once the bedroom doors were closed, the rooms cooled down. By morning, she swore she could see her breath.

She needed to fix the ski lift again too. The parts were old. She couldn't risk running it and having another accident. Her money was best used there. A working lift meant money. Fixing it also meant money. Money she didn't have.

"You could ask Jay Henry for some help. He's been sweet on you for years, and he's handy." Vera hung her coat on the hook by the door.

"No, thank you." Jay was the plumber who could fix the heater, and if she had the extra cash, she would call him. But taking it out in any kind of trade was out of the question. She wasn't interested in Jay Henry in any way.

She was done with men for now. She had a daughter to finish raising and a business to save. The next time around she wanted the kind of love in those movies with the perfect mother. She wanted the man who made her head spin when he kissed her. But she wasn't sure anyone could have that twice. And she'd had it once. A long time ago with Jett. She doubted he had ever felt the same way.

"I'm just saying that Jay could get the heater to be consistent and we wouldn't freeze all the time."

"Mom, go to bed. It's late. You need your rest, and so do I. I have a group coming for some cross-country skiing." This conversation was over, at least for her. She wanted to climb into her bed, put on the electric blanket, and snuggle so far down into the mattress it would take a week to come out.

Her phone buzzed from the back pocket of her jeans. Any call at this hour probably involved an emergency room. Though she couldn't think of a soul who would call for her. Over the past two years, she had spent so much time trying to keep her head above water that each of her friends drifted away. Not that she had many to begin with. She didn't blame anyone. Her life was a reminder that things could go from bad to worse if she wasn't careful. And it might be contagious.

"Who could that be at this hour?" Vera echoed her

thoughts.

She dug out the phone and stared at the screen. The number was familiar, but she couldn't place it. "Hello?"

"Autumn, It's Dottie Lucier. I'm sorry to have called so late. But this couldn't wait until morning. I have fantastic news. You have someone who wants to buy your land. The house, the lift, everything. It's a fair offer." Dottie's voice tinkled like chimes.

"I haven't put my property up for sale yet." The meeting with George Smith still burned like a fresh wound. She hadn't accepted yet that she had to sell everything. With thirty days to come up with the money, she wanted to wait for the impossible—some kind of miracle.

"Oh, I realize that. Paperwork is just a technicality. George from the bank called me today and told me to keep an eye out just in case. I couldn't believe how lucky I was to find someone today. I just had to call to tell you. You can come to my office tomorrow, and we'll get everything settled."

"No."

"Excuse me?"

Vera looked up with her eyebrows pushing into her hairline.

"I'm not prepared to sell at this time. Please tell your buyer you made a mistake."

"Are you sure? This will take care of all your problems."

"Will it?" She doubted selling her land would result in solving anything except the money problems. Quinn's future had to be considered. If Autumn could find a way to keep her property so Quinn could inherit it, then she had to take that risk. Quinn deserved to have what was

21

rightfully hers.

"I don't mean to be rude, but you are out of options, sweetie. Why not agree to sell and enjoy your next adventure? We won't close for thirty days, and I will make sure to find you a suitable home right here in Backwater," Dottie said.

"No, thank you. Good night." She ended the call before she wavered or Dottie said another thing.

"Are you crazy not taking an offer on the land? You don't even have it up for sale, and a buyer drops into your lap? It's no wonder you ran this business into the ground and ran out of money. You have no idea what you're doing." Vera's petulant expression turned a few shades of red, and Autumn's stomach soured.

Vera never missed an opportunity to point out where Autumn had gone wrong. Any choice Autumn made, Vera was quick to state she would have done it differently.

"Good night, Mom." She brushed past Vera. She needed the safety of her bedroom, the one place she could lock out the rest of the world.

"Why aren't you taking it?"

"I'm going to bed. Please do the same." She had no desire to discuss this topic with her mother and definitely not at this hour. She was never at her best when her body ached with fatigue deep in her bones.

Dottie had been trying to help with her late-night ecstatic call, but Autumn knew how much Dottie stood to make in commission on the sale. Dottie didn't care if Autumn and Quinn had to move. In fact, their moving served Dottie better. She would make money on both the sale and the property Autumn purchased or rented, as the case might be.

For once, Vera heeded her words. Her slippers continued the plod and slog over the uneven hardwood floors downstairs as her mother went down the hall to her own bedroom and closed the door.

Autumn released a huge sigh of relief and allowed her shoulders to drop for the first time all day. She would catch a few hours of sleep, and in the morning she would decide what to do. She did have to consider a buyer at some point. Now was just too soon.

She peeked into Quinn's room. The familiar smell of sweet baby powder and old books whispered to her. Her daughter was tangled in her sheets. Quinn had been a restless sleeper since her days in the womb. Autumn absently rubbed her stomach. That time seemed like an eternity ago and like yesterday all at once.

The room was a mess with folded clothes piled on top of her dresser. She had told Quinn a hundred times to put them in the drawers. Her ski parka hung over the back of the chair near the desk. The top of the desk couldn't be seen under all the books, some open, some stacked. Quinn's discarded ski helmet cluttered the corner along with mismatched gloves, wool socks, and the random plastic water bottle.

She hoped the day would not come when she had to pull Quinn off the local ski team because she couldn't afford that either. Skiing could be Quinn's way to get a college scholarship.

Autumn stepped into the room and grabbed the picture of Quinn and Trent from the side table. They stood on the ski slope, holding their poles in one hand and making a thumbs-up in the other. Their smiles could light up the Montana sky at night.

Life had disappointed Quinn too many times in her

young fourteen years. She had lost her father at twelve, her grandmother should come with a warning label, and she was about to lose her home.

Putting the picture back with one hand, Autumn wiped the tear from her cheek with the other, then went into her own room. She wouldn't be able to give Quinn her legacy, because of too many bad decisions made through the years.

"I'm sorry." She closed the door, then climbed into bed. Sleep would not come.

Chapter Four

Jett closed his laptop and rolled his head on his painful neck and shoulders. He had completed payroll, placed an order for new linens, and reordered Silver Bell's meds. He pushed out of the chair and stretched. His body complained with pops and cracks for sitting too long. Sitting was never his thing.

The back-office stuff was not his favorite part of the job, but Lock sucked at it. He lost attention halfway through, and Jett would find him in the stables or out giving a guest archery lessons. Jett handed off what he could to his mother, but over the last few years, she had been handing a lot of it back.

He needed someone he could trust to do the banking. If he had a wife, maybe. That thought made him stop. He even checked behind him to make sure no one had said it out loud, but he was alone in the office. His only companions were the piles of papers on his desk, the Ryker Ranch mug full of pens and highlighters, and the pile of books that he meant to read some day.

A wife. His overworked brain was playing a good joke on him. The very last thing he wanted was a wife. He shook his head and laughed.

Lock trotted into the room, biting a shiny red apple. "What are you laughing at?"

"Nothing. You have apple juices running down your chin." Jett pointed in the general direction of his brother.

Lock was a slob, wearing his food as much as eating it.

Lock wiped his chin with the sleeve of his flannel shirt. Jett bit back the retort teetering on his lips about using a napkin. Lock did what Lock wanted. The rest of them had been dealing with Lock and his ways since Lock was born. But Lock was one hell of a rancher, working all hours to make sure the guests had whatever they needed. He could fix anything that broke. He handled the horses almost better than Jett did. He should tell Lock that more often, but not today.

"Your three o'clock is here." Lock wiped his chin with his sleeve again.

He couldn't take it another second and handed his brother a tissue. "You know you're part owner of this place, right?"

"I am?" Lock crowed with laughter.

"Can you stop acting like a five-year-old and at least keep from using your shirt as a napkin?"

"What has crawled up your butt today? You've been an ornery raccoon since you came back from the bank yesterday. What gives?"

"I don't know what you're talking about. And I don't have a three o'clock appointment. Who told you that?" He had been distracted, that was all. The postholiday season was always a slow time for the ranch, and he didn't like slow times. His winter income could sometimes be unreliable, another reason he wanted that ski area.

If his brother Gage wasn't renting out one of the guest cottages, he'd have more reason to be worried about this time of year. Gage provided a dependable revenue. He always paid his rent, and he always paid on time.

"Yo, Jett. Are you listening? There is a kid out there who says he's your three o'clock. He's here to talk to you about the ski team. You need to take a nap or have a beer or something. You're starting to scare me." Lock shook his head.

"Who is this kid?" He didn't have any appointment for this afternoon. He had no idea who the kid was or why he would be here to talk to him. "Can you get Mom to talk to him? She's better with kids than I am."

"She's not on the ranch. I tried to get him to tell me what he wanted because I knew you did not want to talk to some teenager, but he won't say. He also won't budge. He's in the main room. Claims he knows Izzy, though. You want me to text her?"

"Leave her out of this. If this kid ends up being trouble, I'll have to deal with him and Gage for putting his daughter in harm's way."

"Yeah. Gage would probably shoot you for that." Lock raised a brow and tore into his apple again.

He brushed past Lock without another word and weaved his way to the lobby. A couple checked in at the front desk. They were staying for a week and had booked several extra activities that weren't included in the overall price. He would make sure they had a good time and left a raving review.

A roaring fire danced in the stone fireplace that took up most of the back wall of the main room where guests could sit and drink tea or hot cocoa. Lock had most likely seen to the fire. Woodsmoke filled the air, and Jett took a deep inhale.

Standing in the corner by the double doors that led to the porch was a tall, lanky kid. His knit cap had the ski-school insignia on it. His parka was high-end, as

27

were his boots. Jett held in a sigh. He had no idea what Logan Everett wanted, but he could guess he didn't want to hear it.

"Howdy," he said, turning Logan's attention his way.

The kid flashed a million-dollar smile that creased the skin around his vibrant eyes. He yanked off a glove and stuck out his hand. "Hello, Mr. Ryker. I'm Logan Everett."

"I know. You're the captain of the ski team. I keep an eye on the teams we sponsor. Are you supposed to be at school?"

He liked to follow the local team not just because the ranch donated money, but because skiing was in his blood. He never got out on the mountain as much as he wanted to, not with all the work the ranch required of him. He usually put in eighteen-hour days. And if he expanded his business to include downhill skiing, he'd be even busier. Maybe then, though, he'd get on the slope.

When he was this kid's age, no one could beat him. Not even his brothers. Skiing was the one sport he was better at than Gage, Kace, Lock, or Ajay, though Ajay'd had a ton of potential to beat him. If only Ajay had focused on sports instead of drugs, he might have been the one asked to be the coach. Hell, Ajay would have offered without being asked.

"Uh, I have a free period before lunch. They let us leave." Logan glanced at the ground and kicked the floor.

Jett never remembered being able to leave the school property when he went there, but that was a long time ago.

"My dad said you two skied together back in the

day."

"That's right. Your dad and I were on the same team." He ignored the comment about school. Not his business if this kid skipped or not.

Markus Everett had been the one to beat back when they were kids. That rivalry had kept him up at nights. Markus had apparently shared some stories. If Jett had to guess, they were embellished with Markus always coming out ahead.

"What brings you out this way?"

"I was hoping I could talk to you about the coaching position. Mr. Durrell said you turned him down. I was wondering if I could try to convince you to change your mind." Logan flashed that smile.

That smile probably got a lot of girls to swoon, but Jett was not falling for it. "Mighty determined, huh? I can appreciate that in a man, but that's not a position for me. I'm happy to sponsor again. I'm sorry you came all the way out here. I could've saved you a trip. How about if I get you a hot chocolate for the ride back?" Giving this kid a free hot beverage was the least he could do.

Logan put his hands up as if to stop him—from doing what, he didn't know. "Mr. Ryker, please hear me out a second. I've seen all your trophies back at the school. Skiing was important to you when you were there. It's important to me too. If you don't coach the rest of the season, we have to forfeit. It's my last year. And my only chance to get a scholarship to ski in college."

"I'm not a coach. I appreciate what you're saying, but someone else would be better for the job."

"There isn't anyone else. Mr. Durrell has asked around town. Everyone has said no, including my dad. He doesn't even want me to ski. He thinks I'm wasting my time. Which I don't understand since he skied in high school too. He still does. He says it's not a future for me. Anyway, I can't lose this chance to ski. Please, Mr. Ryker. We need you." Logan unzipped that fancy parka. He was probably sweating in that thing. The fire was heating up the whole area.

"Not that I'm agreeing with your father, but a professional skier doesn't make that much. You'd have to have a second job. He's probably just preparing you for the future in something that has a better return."

"You sound just like him. I know I won't make that much unless I'm in the top three of the sport, and I'm not even going to the Olympics. But I can get a scholarship to a school in Colorado, and then I don't have to worry about my tuition. Which my father says is my responsibility." The smile slipped, and the kid failed to right it.

Jett really didn't want to take on this team. He didn't have the time or the patience. Taking care of kids was more Gage's thing. But desperation had passed over Logan's eyes, darkening them like storm clouds rolling in over the mountaintop.

The idea of doing something that Markus Everett was against had a certain appeal. They had always been rivals, and that included who would win Autumn Archer. For a while, Jett had believed Markus had captured Autumn's heart, but they didn't stay together. He never wanted to see Autumn hurt, but when news of their broken engagement had circled the town, he wouldn't deny the shot of triumph in his gut.

Just because he had sent Autumn away didn't mean he wanted her to be alone and unhappy. When she hooked up with Trent, Jett had been glad. She deserved to have what he could not give her. He never wanted to lose to Markus, was all.

"Okay, kid. I'll do it. I'll call Durrell and get the info about where and when. You drove a pretty hard bargain. I can't deny someone the chance to go to college." And if his helping annoyed Markus a little, so be it.

If he were being honest, he always saw his brother Ajay in every teenager. Ajay had needed help but hadn't asked for it until it was too late. Maybe if he had been paying better attention back then to Ajay's problems, his little brother might still be here. And he would have made one hell of a coach.

"Thank you, Mr. Ryker." Logan stuck his hand out again. "You won't regret this. We're a great team."

Jett slid his hand into the kid's sweaty one. "Yeah, okay." He needed to get back to work before he changed his mind. He had no idea how he was going to pull this off.

"There's one more thing." Logan dropped his hand and his gaze.

"What do you mean 'one more thing'?" This kid had set him up, playing on his guilt and now clobbering him with another request.

"We need a new place to practice. The ski area we were using closed down. You'll have to help us find somewhere."

"Did Mr. Durrell send you here because he thought I had some connection with a ski mountain? I know the same people he knows. Someone else is going to have to find your practice spot." He did know someone who had space. He didn't want to ask her.

"Mr. Durrell doesn't know I'm here. I thought I could convince you better than he could. Does this mean without a practice location you won't be the coach?"

"Nah. I said I'd do it, and I will." He couldn't go back on his word now. He'd said he would, and those words were his bond.

"Thanks again. The team is going to be thrilled. I'll text everyone. Can I have your cell? I can put you on the group chat." Logan held out a hand.

"I'll get everyone's number from Durrell. When is your next practice?" He ignored the gesture. When he was ready, he would input those numbers, after his head accepted the fact he agreed to coach. For now, regret was a possibility.

"It's supposed to be tomorrow, if we have a place to go. We really need the time on the slope. The team is mostly freshmen this year. They aren't very good, and we have a competition on Saturday."

Yeah, he was already regretting this. He would have to talk it out with his brothers and see if they could cover him some of the time. But he did have an idea about where to take that practice.

"You should get back to school before you're late, and I have to get back to work. I'll see you tomorrow."

"Thanks again, Mr. Ryker. You won't regret this."

Famous last words.

Chapter Five

Autumn ended the call and shoved her phone into her back pocket. She leaned her forehead against the wall in the kitchen. The buyer who only hours earlier wanted to buy her ski area had already changed his mind. She had barely said the words that she agreed to Dottie Lucier before Dottie cut her off.

"Sorry, Autumn," Dottie said.

"It's fine." Which it was far from.

"Do you want me to continue looking?"

"Yes, please." She had ended the call then. If Dottie couldn't find a buyer in the next thirty days, the bank would take the land and she would have to move out of her house. Losing the ski area killed her, but she had to hang on to the house.

Just that much, please. For Quinn. She had no idea who she was asking that favor from. In the meantime, she would continue to cater to the few guests she had and make this last winter on the Backwater Ski Area the best they'd ever had—as long as it didn't cost any money.

She put the last of the dinner dishes in the dishwasher. Quinn was upstairs in her room doing homework. Vera, thankfully, was tucked in her room for the night. She hadn't been feeling well and had retired right after dinner.

The ski slope was closed too. She had managed to get the lift fixed this morning in time for the first run. But she didn't offer night skiing. Everyone was gone by five.

Now she would pour herself a glass of wine and soak in her tub. She had earned a few hours to herself.

The knock at the door stopped her hand midair over the dishwasher. She never received guests anymore. She had no time to entertain these days. She could ignore it and hope they would go away, but her mother's door opened.

"Autumn, who's at the door?" Vera said in her bad stage whisper.

"How would I know? Go back to bed, Mom. I'll take care of it." She glanced at her mother in her pink flannel nightgown.

"Fine." Her mom huffed and closed the door.

Her mother definitely didn't want guests to see her in her nightgown. Autumn was grateful for Vera's vanity at the moment. She would be less likely to get involved in the conversation, and Autumn could send whoever it was away quickly so she could soak in that tub waiting for her.

She pulled the door open, and the air froze in her lungs. She could blame it on the freezing temperatures outside, but she would have struggled to breathe on a perfect seventy-five-degree day with not a cloud in the sky.

Jett Ryker stood on her porch. His tall frame and wide shoulders took up most of the doorframe. His hands were shoved into the pockets of his shearling barn coat, but when his gaze registered hers, he tipped his black cowboy hat.

His face was passive and absent of any smile. His dark eyes could stare down a grizzly. He had probably shaved this morning, but his strong jaw was dusted with a day-old beard. His facial hair had always grown in quickly, and she hated that she remembered that.

"Howdy," he said. "I'm sorry to bother you so late. May I speak to you a moment?"

He was forever formal. In all the years they were nothing more than neighbors, he had not once treated her without kindness. Unfortunately, he had treated her like any other stranger he would encounter. He was always polite. She had wished just once he would get angry at her or allow her to express her anger. But that wasn't the stoic Jett Ryker. She hadn't fallen for the brother with a more uneven emotional tilt. Not that any of the Ryker men were ever that emotional. But Jett held his emotions closer than the others.

"Is there a problem?" Maybe his truck had broken down at the edge of her driveway and his cell phone was out of service.

"Nothing like that. I have a proposition for you. I thought it better to speak about in person than over the phone. I couldn't break away from the ranch until now. Could you come outside?"

Her curiosity was piqued, though she'd be hard-pressed to tell him that. And she would not invite him in. Her mother probably had her ear against the bedroom door, listening for whoever would be at the front door.

"What kind of proposition?" No matter what he might offer, it would be all business. Jett wasn't the kind of man to show up out of the blue with anything on his mind other than business, even if deep down she might entertain the idea of his proposition being a little more seductive. No, if Jett were ever interested in her in any way other than professional, he would not show up at her door unannounced and proposition her.

"A business one."

Like she figured. "Can you elaborate? It's late." And the cold air was penetrating her sweatshirt and flannel pants.

"Can you come outside? I don't want to wait to do this in the morning or ask you to meet me somewhere else because I don't have a lot of time. I know my presence makes your mother uncomfortable. But I'm asking, as a neighbor, if you would come outside and listen to me for a minute."

And ever the straightforward one. "Let me get my coat."

She grabbed the old quilted coat off the hook by the door. It had been Trent's once. She should get rid of it, but it was warm and easy to grab in a hurry. It didn't smell like him anymore. It didn't smell like anything except dust.

Closing the door behind her, she faced Jett. "Okay. What's up?"

The night air was as crisp as a fresh crease in a new piece of notebook paper. It was a lovely night for a sleigh ride or a horseback ride. The sky was clear, and the moonlight drifted over the untouched snow, setting off its blue-diamond blaze. She pulled the coat a little closer, but sitting outside with a hot drink and a fire would do wonders for the stress knotted through her tired muscles. She might have to forgo the bath and come back out here to relax after Jett left.

He shoved his hands in his pockets again and leaned against the railing. "I'd like to rent your ski slope through March."

"What do you mean 'rent'? You already send your guests over here to ski. You've been doing it for years.

Why the change now?" Was he trying to partner with her in some way? He had better come up with another crazy idea because she would not partner with him. That was totally out of the question. She couldn't afford to lose the revenue those guests brought by splitting it. The money was what kept the lights on.

"The local ski organization needs a place to practice. Their slope closed. You're in a good location, and the rent would be added income. Every business in town could use the extra money these days."

Her cheeks heated up. She hoped if they were red, he would think the cold was the culprit and not the embarrassment of him knowing her predicament. At least he had the decency not to mention he knew she needed money.

"Why are you here asking me and not someone from the ski school?" And she wasn't sure why he couldn't have called about this. But she was glad he had come by. Even with their tattered past and the distance they had kept over the years, she still enjoyed seeing him.

He was an incredible-looking man with his dark skin and darker hair that flipped a little at the ends. She had always believed he was the best-looking Ryker with his narrow nose and close-set, steamy black eyes. His thick biceps pressed against the fabric of his coat. Working the ranch wore well on him. A sigh fought its way to her lips, but in the end she pushed it back.

He removed his hat and scratched his head. The hint of a smile shifted his lips. "I'm the new coach. It's the coach's responsibility to find a new practice spot. Your place came to mind. I won't have to drive far for the practices. That will save me a lot of time."

"You're coaching? I wasn't expecting to hear that."

Not from the man who lived to work.

"Why not?" His shoulders snapped straight.

"Anything besides the ranch isn't exactly your thing. You're not known to have a lot of hobbies."

"Who says that about me?" He shoved his hat back on his head.

"I don't know, Jett. It's just talk. You know how this town is. Anyway, what I think about you coaching isn't important." She wanted to tell him no way. She did not need him on her property every afternoon. Living next door was bad enough. Bumping into him in town was more than bad enough. But to have him on the land every day? How much pain could one woman take?

"Will you allow the ski school to come? They would be here every day from three till five. Longer if the daylight allows. The school is prepared to pay a hefty price."

"Are you the only coach?"

"Yes, you'll have to deal with me. I don't like it any better than you do, but we've managed to coexist in this town all these years. We should be fine. This is all business. Nothing personal. I'll stay out of your way. And you can stay out of ours."

"Stay out of yours? Do you think you'll come onto my ski area and just ignore me?" She tried to keep her voice from rising, but she didn't do a very good job of it. This man was the epitome of arrogant. What did he think? That she would hang on him like some groupie? She had walked away from him all those years ago and had not once asked him to come back. Not once.

"I'm not trying to argue with you. I wouldn't ignore you. Have I ever?"

She crossed her arms over her chest to ward off the

cold and to protect herself from his direct attention to detail. "We have always been able to be polite. And I thank you for that."

"Then you'll rent it to the school? Name your price, Autumn. This arrangement will be good for you."

"I wouldn't dream of overcharging the ski school. Quinn is a part of it. The school is a great opportunity for these kids. Some of them really need it. And actually, they are lucky to have you as a coach. You were a very good skier once." She dropped her gaze. Looking into his intense stare while she paid him a compliment made eye contact difficult.

"You remember that?"

She remembered too much. She had never forgotten how agile he was on the slope. He could slice through the snow as if he weren't even touching it. She remembered his tender way with the horses on his ranch and how his face lit up when he allowed something to set loose that laugh he kept hidden. She could still feel his rough hands against her skin. Every part of her body would tingle when he touched her.

"Sure. You were the captain of the team when we were young. You beat Markus in every race."

"Not every race." His lip curled up, and his eyes smoldered.

She was pretty sure she knew what he was getting at, but she wasn't asking. He had effectively ended their relationship. Life had become too hard for both of them, and Jett didn't or couldn't get near his emotions. She had tried not to blame him. When they broke up, he had recently lost his brother in a violent crime. But together they had lost so much too. She had needed him then, and he had abandoned her.

"You were the best skier. That much I remember. The school can rent the slope. I'll send an invoice over there. But a fair one. I'm not doing this for the money. I'm doing it for my daughter who loves to ski." And might not be able to on this very mountain any longer.

"You should do it for the money. Having extra money isn't all that bad."

"I don't need the extra money." She struggled to hold his gaze again. She wasn't a good liar, and she would never dream of lying to him. She might omit a few things but never lie.

He leaned in. She caught a whiff of woodsmoke and cedar and bit her lip to keep her tongue from shooting out of her mouth and licking him. She was a disaster. She still had a lifetime crush on the one man she couldn't keep and who had never wanted her. How pathetic.

But she had been alone these past two years with plenty of time to think about loneliness and lack of romance. Romance wasn't Jett's strong suit, but he was a generous lover. At least he had been.

"I know the money will help you." His breath was warm against her skin. "There's no shame in that." He pulled back, and his warmth disappeared into the cold night as if it were never there.

His words shook her. He knew. Of course, he knew. The whole damn town knew she had failed. But to have failed with Jett's obvious knowledge sliced her in two. He had been a success at everything. Even though he suffered so much loss, he still had come out on top. And she had been flapping in the wind ever since.

"I don't know what you're talking about. I'll call the school in the morning. Good night." She hurried inside and closed the door before she could rethink her choices.

"Why was Jett Ryker here?" Vera stood at the end of the hall with her hands on her hips.

"Were you listening?"

"Hard not to. The walls around here are pretty thin. He didn't come here looking for anything, did he? Because if he did, you just tell him this family doesn't need anything from the Rykers."

"The ski school wants to rent the slope for their practices."

"You're going to do it, right, Mom?" Quinn bounded down the steps in her stocking feet. Her hair was pulled up on her head with long strands framing her young face. The smile bursting open made her look like Trent in that moment.

"Mr. Durrell said we had a new coach and had a new place to practice. I didn't know it was going to be here. That's really cool. I can't wait to tell Emily. Can she come home with me right after school? We can grab a quick snack here before practice. That would be great."

Quinn had that strange teenage ability to speak as fast as an express train without losing the air in her lungs, all the while bouncing on her toes. Oh, how Autumn envied that much energy.

"Were you listening too?" She tucked a piece of hair behind her daughter's ear. Quinn usually shied away from affection like that now that she was fourteen, but her need to touch her daughter had outweighed the need to also give her daughter what she wanted.

She glanced at her own mother. How was it that Vera never seemed to understand she had a daughter who had needs too? Who had often needed a mother to lean on in difficult times.

"Of course, your mother isn't going to do it.

Montana is full of places to ski. The ski school doesn't have to come here." Vera huffed. Probably for added effect.

Autumn needed to intercept any more talk before Vera spilled all the beans on the past. "In fact, I already agreed." She turned to Quinn. "I told Mr. Ryker that the school could practice here. We could use the extra money."

"You're making a mistake," Vera said.

"It will be fine." It had to be. Besides, it was temporary. By March, the season would be over, and she and Jett would go back to barely acquaintances. And the full truth was by March they wouldn't own the slope anyway. But at least she could tell a buyer—should one ever show up—that the ski school had the space until the end of the season. It was the least she could do for Quinn.

"Well, it if were me—"

"It's not you, Mom. The decision has been made."

Quinn gave her an unexpected hug. "Thanks, Mom. This is going to be the best season ever. I have to text Emily." Quinn ran up the steps, her feet pounding on each one.

Vera returned to her room. The door closed with a definitive click.

Alone at last.

She poured herself a glass of wine and drew a bath. When she sank into the hot water, she promised herself she would not think about Jett and how good he looked tonight.

At least she'd stop thinking about him when the water grew cold.

Chapter Six

Jett called an emergency family meeting. He had brewed up a big urn of coffee since the sun was barely up over the mountain. But this couldn't wait, and with everyone's busy schedule, he didn't want to hear they couldn't come.

He also had grabbed donuts and muffins from the bakery in town. He might as well drug his siblings with sugar this early too.

Lock stumbled into the kitchen from the family side of the building. His hair was pointing in various directions. He bellowed a yawn and scratched at his chest. "Morning." He reached for a mug.

"Rough night?"

Lock looked down with confusion across his brow as if he had recently noticed his state of poor dress. "Not rough. Late. I need to grab a shower. But you said this was life or death."

"I said it was important."

"Same thing with you." Lock poured coffee into his big mug.

"You are annoying." Jett tossed a crumpled napkin at Lock.

"That's what happens when you're the youngest." Lock threw it back.

"Ajay is the youngest."

"Ajay gave me the job."

He couldn't argue with that. Lock had only been nineteen when Ajay passed. Maybe if his tragic death had been from an illness, Lock would behave differently, but Ajay had died in a gang war, fully aware of his decisions, just too young and dumb to know how to get out of them.

Gage sauntered into the kitchen, his appearance the exact opposite of Lock's. Gage was always put together, even in his zip-up sweatshirt, jeans, and sneakers. He had already shaved and smelled like soap. "Good morning. I didn't think you'd beat me here." He punched Lock on the shoulder.

"I didn't want Jett to get his panties all tangled up. I dragged myself out of bed to make sure I wasn't late."

Gage gave Lock the once-over. "I can tell."

"Shut up." Lock grabbed a donut.

"Good morning, family." Kace bounded into the kitchen at full speed. He high-fived each of them but went back to Gage for an additional fist bump. Kace also seemed ready for his day in his mechanic's overalls. He was the brother right after Jett and the family race car driver until recently. Now Kace worked on race cars. "Is Mom coming?" He looked around the kitchen.

Jett pushed away from the counter. "No. I told her I'd catch her up. Now that we're all here, I can tell you what's going on." He held the donut box out to them.

Kace took one. Gage shook his head.

"Are you sick?" Kace said to Jett. "If you're sick, I'll go to the doctor with you."

"Will you let me talk?"

"Yeah, Kace, let him tell it." Gage put a hand on Kace's shoulder. Gage was forever their referee and their stand-in father. They all looked to Gage for guidance, and he had always taken that role very seriously. Too seriously sometimes.

"The ski school asked me to coach. I said yes. I'm hoping for the next few months I can ask you all to help me out here at the ranch. I will have practice every afternoon. I won't be able to tend to the horses in the afternoon or take care of the guests or put out any fires."

"Isn't that what Lock's for?" Kace bit into the donut.

"Lock has his work to worry about. I need some help with mine."

"You do realize we all have jobs," Kace said.

"Kace, man, ease up." Gage stood to his full height and stared Kace down before turning to Jett. "Of course, we'll help out. You let us know what needs to be done, and we'll do it. You don't have to ask."

"Yeah, I kind of do, because the hotshot race car driver thinks he doesn't have to help out here."

"I don't work here," Kace said.

"No, but you own a fifth of this land, and you're living here. At a discount, I might add."

"Not this again." Lock rolled his eyes. "I thought you two had buried the hatchet already. Look, I can handle whatever Jett can't get to. If I get stuck, I'll call. Otherwise, go about your businesses."

"I want their help." He didn't want Lock overriding what he said. He wanted his brothers to be there because he needed to know his ranch would be taken care of. Sure, they all had a part share in ownership, but he ran the ranch. He made sure everything worked the way it should. Lock helped out a lot, and he couldn't do it without Lock, but Lock slacked off whenever he could.

"I just said we'd help," Gage said.

"No, you said you would help. I'm busy." Kace

poured himself some coffee, then leaned against the counter. His lips disappeared into a thin line.

"Why don't you want to help?" Gage shoved his hands on his hips.

"Because I'm not the rancher." Kace narrowed his eyes.

Lock shoved a donut in Kace's face, smooshing it until the pieces fell to the ground.

"What the hell?" Kace wiped the sugar from his eyes. "Are you nuts?" He lunged for Lock. Coffee went everywhere.

Gage jumped in and pushed Kace out of the way. "Enough. You're still acting like kids."

"Why did you shove a donut in my face?" Kace splashed water on his face.

"Because Gage won't and you're acting like a prick. How often does Jett ever ask for anything? Tell him you'll do it even though I don't need you to." Lock turned to Jett. "I can handle your share of the workload, or we can ask one of the employees to do some of the grunt work, but if you want Gage and Kace involved, then I'm in. I always have your back. Even when this prick doesn't." He pointed a thumb in Kace's direction. "I need a shower." He grabbed another donut and his coffee and left the kitchen.

"Jett, you hurt his feelings." Gage wiped up the mess on the floor. "He wants you to think you need him."

"I'll talk to him later and apologize." Lock always had his back. Hurting his feelings hadn't been his intention, and Jett often forgot how sensitive Lock could be. Extra help around the ranch was always welcome. The pain that had passed over Lock's eyes, too quickly for anyone who didn't know him to notice, should have been enough for Jett to realize Lock would want to be the one to decide if he needed help. He was grateful for everything he and Lock shared even if he didn't say it much.

Jett always wanted to run this ranch with all his brothers, but Gage and Kace had other plans. By rights, Gage should be in charge here since he was the oldest, but he had decided a long time ago he didn't want to die like their father, alone in the fields and overworked. Jett had become that man—overworked and alone.

The realization he had turned into his father when he wasn't looking was a cold bucket of water on his head. And part of the reason he had agreed to coach. He did need a hobby. Autumn had said as much last night. He had been surprised about her revelation. He didn't think she paid any attention to him anymore.

"Just tell us what you need, and we'll do it," Gage said.

"We will?" Kace poured more coffee.

"Yes, we will because we're brothers, and the Rykers always stick together. Not everyone is as fortunate as we are. We have each other. And I, for one, am glad I have my brothers around." Gage patted his shoulder and then shoved Kace.

"Fine. I'll help." Kace pouted just like when he was a kid.

"Thanks." Jett was glad for his brothers too. Even when one of them was being a jerk.

"Where will you be practicing?" Gage asked. "I heard the slope the school used shut down."

"Backwater Ski Area. It's close by." Having a reason to talk to Autumn more often wouldn't hurt. He had always wanted to try and build a friendship, but every time he thought he might try, she would see him on the street, shoot him a death glare, and he would keep walking. That woman held a grudge like no one's business. He had made mistakes back then, but he had been hurt too. She hadn't been the only one.

"Does any of this coaching have to do with one Autumn Archer? Her daughter is on the ski team," Kace said.

"Why would you think that? I'm helping out the school because no one will coach. And yes, I asked Autumn for the use of her slope because it's close."

"The word at the diner is she has to sell her land by the end of the month or the bank takes it." Kace dropped into the kitchen chair. "Are you trying to save her or something?"

He hadn't gotten word she was that desperate. He figured she was short on cash because her attendance was down and she had taken a while to fix that lift. He had sent guests to another downhill slope a little farther away for the past month. But sell entirely? He wanted a chance at that land.

"If she ran her business into the ground, I can't help her." But he could buy her land from her and expand the activities the ranch offered. He was sorry she hadn't been able to make her ski area work after Trent died, but losing sales was not a knock on her. She would probably be glad to be out from under the stress even if he was the buyer. He would run the ski operation the right way.

"He wants to help her," Kace said to Gage.

"I'm not getting in the middle of this. I have to get to work. Jett, call or text me with what you need. And if I can't do it, I'll send Izzy over."

"Thanks." He stuck out his hand, but Gage pulled him into a hug.

"Don't you have to get to work too?" he asked Kace after Gage left.

"In a minute. You didn't know Autumn needed to sell." Kace's eyes narrowed.

"Nope." If he had, he would have made an offer last night on her porch. She had looked adorable in those silly cow slippers and that oversized coat that hung on her. She hadn't aged at all through the years. She was more beautiful now than when they were younger.

"Are you going to put in an offer?" Kace finished off the donut and grabbed a muffin.

At least someone was eating. He was starting to think like his mother. When had he become his parents? "Maybe."

"She'll never sell to you."

"You don't know that." She was a smart lady. She would take the best offer, and he would make sure it was from him. He'd have to find out which realtor was handling the deal. Then again, Autumn might turn him down if he made an offer directly. She was smart, but she was stubborn. And her mother could influence her. Vera had never liked him since he and Autumn broke up. And then after what his mother had done, well, Vera could hold a grudge too.

"I don't know that she would turn your offer down, but she hates you." Kace smirked.

"I'm aware." Painfully so.

"What is it with you and Gage and those women from your past?"

He and Gage had been in relationships when Ajay died. Their brother's death had rocked their family. Gage and Calista had broken up because her sister died too that night. After Ajay's death, Jett couldn't be with anyone. He hadn't meant to hurt Autumn, but loving her was too painful. She was better off without him. And she had proved him right. She had eventually married Trent and built a nice life and had a child. Jett could never give her that. He had tried.

He had promised to build a future with her when they were twenty and she became pregnant. They had lost their child, and he had not left her. He had been the rock she needed even though he was suffering too. But after Ajay died three years later, he had fallen apart. He couldn't be anything to anyone back then. And Autumn blamed him.

"Let's leave the past where it belongs. We can't all be in love like you and Tara."

"I never thought I'd find a woman like her. Speaking of which, I need to ask Mom if she'll babysit Royce for a couple of days. Tara and I want to get away. Good luck with this Autumn thing." Kace paused at the kitchen door.

"There's nothing going on with me and Autumn. I just want to use her slope." And feed her bank account a little. And do one little thing—buy her property.

"Yeah, keep telling yourself that, bro. I'll see ya." Kace pushed through the door, leaving him alone again.

He had some time before he had to get breakfast started. He could leave a message at the realtor's office for a call back. He had a ski slope to own.

Chapter Seven

Autumn stared out the window. She couldn't keep her gaze off him. Damn him. Jett looked all rugged and manly in his ski jacket and knit cap. He held a clipboard and spoke to the kids standing in a half circle around him. She could spot Quinn in her pink jacket with a smile as wide as the sky. All the kids looked on with anticipation as Jett spoke. Even Logan Everett, Markus's son.

Markus. Another one of her big mistakes. Thankfully, she had figured out he was a shady business person and a cheat before they walked down the aisle. She hadn't even loved Markus. She had only agreed to marry him hoping that Jett would get word of it and come running back. A lot of good that did. Jett had never said one word to her about her relationship with Markus.

Logan was the result of Markus's affair when they were together. She was glad the boy had been born. He was a sweet boy. Judging from the rumors she heard around town, Markus didn't know how lucky he was to have that son. Markus was obsessed with work, much like Jett. But Jett loved his family fiercely and made time for them. Markus had no concept of that, and she knew it firsthand. Markus didn't give his son the attention he deserved, and since Logan lost his mom some years ago, Markus was all that kid had. Well, now Jett would coach him, and that would be good for Logan and all the kids.

The timer on the oven dinged. She thought the kids

would like a snack when they took a practice break. She had mixed up her special hot-chocolate recipe in a big urn and baked seven dozen cutout cookies in the shape of mittens. She pulled out the tray and allowed the sweet smell of sugar and butter to snuggle up against her nose.

She'd had a son once. The thought wormed in as it often did when her defenses were down—like now with Jett in sight and thoughts of her past sneaking up on her. For the briefest of moments, she'd had a little boy. Jett's boy. But they had lost him right after they found out the sex. She'd believed with her whole heart that if they survived that, they could survive anything. But three years later his brother had died a senseless death, and Jett imploded. She'd been a victim of that. She'd blamed him for a very long time. That anger had sent her straight into Markus's arms. She'd wanted Jett to react to something. He'd reacted, all right. He'd relegated her to the neighbor zone.

"Are you baking cookies?" Vera shuffled into the kitchen. The color of her face matched the parchment paper lining the cookie sheets. The thin skin around her eyes was the color of a bruise. Her mother had probably been up all night with her friend, spewing about Jett and the ski team on the slope.

"Would you like one? I made them for the ski school."

Vera huffed and pressed her lips into a tight line. "No, thank you. Sugar isn't good for me."

"One cookie won't hurt." She placed a cookie on a plate and slid it down the counter. Her mother had no issues with sugar. She was as healthy as a horse, but Vera would say anything to get attention.

"Are you trying to kill me?"

Right on cue. Vera's timing for cutting statements was on a professional level. If she were even an ounce amusing, her mother should have considered a career in comedy. The ridiculous thought triggered a snicker at the back of Autumn's throat. She had to swallow it down.

"Hardly. How about a cup of tea? I have that chamomile you like. I went into Bozeman earlier to that cute little tea shop." If she had made different choices, she would have a little bakery with a wall full of different loose-leaf teas in glass jars for customers to sample. She would mix her own leaves and share her knowledge of tea and baking instead of trying to keep a failing ski area afloat. She had clearly failed at that.

She suspected the real reason her mother didn't want a cookie was because her acquiescing might be interpreted as her somehow being okay with Jett on the property.

"What time does the practice end?" Vera looked out the window.

The team had dispersed, but Jett remained. The kids had probably gone back to the top for another run. He would time the kids as they came down. He was looking for speed. Quinn wouldn't be one of the first. She was too slow, though she had been practicing. Autumn was proud of her determination but hoped she wouldn't be too disappointed when Jett had to put his faster skiers in for the tough competition.

He looked at his phone. The clipboard was tucked under his arm. He turned his gaze toward the sky, shook his head, and marched in the direction of the house.

Oh boy.

"He's coming this way," her mother said.

"I see that." She quickly put the warm cookies on a

plate, grabbed her coat, and went to meet him halfway.

When she approached, he stopped. A frown furrowed his brows, but his face returned to neutral by the time she reached him.

"Hi. I made some cookies." She held out the platter. *Smooth, Autumn. Goofy much?*

"That's nice. The team should be down in about five to ten minutes. Can you stay here and write down their times? I have a problem at the ranch and have to get back." He handed her the clipboard.

"You want me to help you?"

"Not me. The team. Just this once. My staff is still getting used to me not being there. No one can find Lock or my mother. Kace isn't due for another hour, and Gage is in the middle of arresting a tourist for disorderly conduct. It seems no one can make a decision without a Ryker present. Please?" He flashed a hint of a smile, as if to tease her. Or to taunt her.

"It's simple. The stopwatch is going." He handed her that too.

She juggled to hold everything.

"Just write down the kid and the time. If you don't know their names, just write what they're wearing and then ask after everyone is down. I don't know their names at all. I'll come back as soon as I can. Just end the practice when they're all down."

"I have a business to run too, you know."

"I know. Except your last customer just came through thirty minutes ago. No one is going to start a run this late in the day with the sun setting. The only people on the slope are the kids from the team. Please, Autumn? I really have to get back."

"Okay. For the team. Take a cookie." She held the

plate out again. "Sounds like you'll need the sugar boost."

"Thanks." He took two and trotted off. His long legs carried him with ease and grace.

She needed to stop paying so much attention to him. The behavior was unhealthy. She trudged to the spot where the team would come down and placed the plate of cookies on the ground.

A few minutes later, swooshing skis against snow interrupted the quiet blanketed around her. Logan was the first one down. He turned to stop with perfect precision. Snow glided up in an arc. The smile on his face said everything his eyes couldn't because they were covered by the sun-blocking visor. He must know how good he was. And of course he was. Markus wouldn't stand for second best from his kid.

She jotted the time down. The rest of the team came through. All of them finished fairly well. She did a quick head count. One person hadn't returned. She offered the team the cookies, and they inhaled them all.

"Save one for Quinn," Emily, Quinn's best friend, said.

Ten minutes after the last team member had crossed the line, Quinn came through. Her cheeks were red, and she sucked down long breaths.

"Great job, Quinn." Autumn handed her the last cookie.

"I suck, Mom. And where's Coach?"

"Coach Ryker had an emergency back at the ranch. He said practice was over and he would see you all tomorrow."

"Are you his assistant now?" Logan asked.

"His assistant? No, of course not. I happened to be

out here when he had to go." Being Jett's assistant coach was a preposterous idea. She would never. She didn't have the time, the inclination.

"You should be," Logan said. "We can use all the help we can get."

Not from her. She caught a glimpse of a face in the window back at the house. The house that had once been a lodge filled with customers wanting to warm up with her hot cocoa and cookies after a long run on the slope. Her mother watched them.

Her mother would hate the idea of her helping Jett.

"I'll talk to Coach Ryker. If he wants help, I'll do it."

****

Autumn kicked the furnace. That move always worked in the movies, but it never worked in real life. She couldn't figure out what was wrong this time, but it had stopped working, and the house was turning into a fishing shack. She would have to call Jay Henry and see if he could bring his plumber's toolbox or whatever the heck he used to fix things. She hoped he didn't try to ask her out again.

She climbed the basement steps to find her mother and Quinn waiting for her. Quinn wore her pink pom-pom hat, matching fingerless gloves, and a striped scarf around her neck. Vera stood beside Quinn with a scowl on her face and her down coat zipped up to her neck.

"Well, is it working?" Vera said.

"I wish."

"Mom, it's freezing. Can we go to a hotel?"

"I don't think so, honey. We'll have to put more logs on the fire and camp out in the living room." The living room was an oversized open room with high ceilings and wood beams. It doubled as the common area for the ski guests during the day.

The room had a leather sofa that faced the fireplace and another that faced the windows. During the daylight hours the view out of those windows took most people's breath away even when the branches were dressed in nothing more than layers of snow.

"I'm not sleeping on that couch. It will kill my back," Vera said.

"Then sleep in your room. You can use the electric space heater. I'll come in and turn it off after you fall asleep. With all those blankets on your bed, you'll be fine."

"Do you want to set the house on fire and kill me?"

"Mom, stop being so melodramatic." She couldn't handle Vera's theatrics tonight. That woman always thought everyone and everything in the world wanted her dead.

"Didn't you hear about that family last year up on the county road? They left their space heater on all night and burned the house to the ground. They all died."

"No one died in that fire," Quinn said.

"Quinnie, Grandma knows. Don't correct me."

Quinn showed Vera her phone. "The article says everyone survived."

Vera humphed, obviously caught in one of her exaggerations. "The pipes are going to freeze." She sneered, changing the subject.

"I'm aware. I'll have to try and run hot water every hour." Autumn wasn't even sure that would work. But she couldn't afford to have the pipes burst. "I'll turn on the oven too." The oven ran on electricity. She could heat it up and leave the door open. At least while they were awake. But by morning the house would be one big ice pop.

"I'm going to get Dad's old sleeping bags out of the attic. He used to say he could sleep in a blizzard in one of those. Is it okay, Mom?" Quinn looked at her with wide eyes. Trent was in her eyes, the shape of her face, and the dimple in her chin.

"Sure. Just be careful."

Quinn hurried off. Autumn wished she had asked more questions of Trent when he had run the ski area, but she had allowed herself to believe he was different and would take care of them. She wouldn't be in this mess if she had paid better attention.

"Why do you let that girl play in the attic?"

"She's not playing."

"It's not safe up there. Not that you would ever listen to me. No one listens to me. I'm going to bed." Vera stomped out of the kitchen.

She grabbed her phone off the kitchen table to call the plumber. A knock at the door startled her, and she dropped the phone.

"I'll get it," Quinn shouted from the front of the house.

She had no idea who would be calling at this hour, but whoever it was would know the lodge and her family. She didn't have to worry about strangers knocking or intruders. Not a damn thing here was worth stealing.

Her fingers fumbled over her contact list until she found Jay Henry's name. An emergency call would cost extra, but she was out of options. Hopefully, she had some room on her credit card to cover the expenses.

"Mom, Coach Ryker is here. He'd like to speak with you."

Jett was here? What was he doing here? Hopefully, Vera hadn't heard the knock at the door.

The call to Jay connected to his voicemail. She left a message and hurried to the front door. Sure enough, Jett stood there.

He had traded his parka for the brown quilted jacket again. The jacket hugged him nicely, accenting his broad arms. He had swapped his knit cap for a baseball cap. The man was meant to wear hats. She looked like a tiny rat in hats.

"Sorry to come by so late. I needed my clipboard back. Were you able to write down those times?"

"I got them all." Autumn grabbed the clipboard off the hall table and handed it to him, and their fingers grazed. A warm jolt shot up her arm and into her chest. She snatched her hand away.

He narrowed his eyes as if he wondered what had her jumpy. "Thanks. Great job today, Quinn."

"Thanks, Coach."

"You're dressed like you're freezing." Jett's gaze bounced between her and Quinn.

Autumn had forgotten she wore one of Trent's old fleece-lined flannels over her fuzzy sweatshirt and her cozy flannel pants tucked into her shearling boots. "We were outside."

"The heat's not working," Quinn said at the same time.

She prayed her cheeks weren't turning red or that at least he believed her rosy cheeks were because she was cold. But wouldn't her lips be blue and not her cheeks red? Geez, she was a mess.

"What happened to the heat?" Jett said.

"I don't know. I have a call in to Jay Henry."

"You can't stay here."

"We'll be fine." They didn't have any other options, anyway. And they would be fine because she would see to it.

"It's too cold, and the temps are supposed to drop more overnight. Is there somewhere else you can go till Jay can get here?"

"Mom says a hotel is out."

"Quinn." She hoped the look in her eyes would stop her daughter from telling more of their family secrets. She didn't know what had gotten into Quinn. She knew better than to discuss money with anyone outside these walls.

Quinn shrugged. "It's true."

"Come to the ranch."

"No, thank you. I would rather not spend the extra money right now." That much was true, even if she had other reasons to decline.

"I'm not asking you to check in like a guest. I'm asking you to come as a friend. I don't charge my friends. I have an extra room in the main house for the next two nights. Pack a few things. I'll drive you all over."

"I'm not staying on your ranch." Vera crossed her arms over her chest.

Autumn hadn't noticed her mother's return from her bedroom, but Vera had ditched the nightgown for her pearls and a black sweater. The hallway light reflected in her newly applied lip gloss too.

"Hello, Vera. I think it would be in everyone's best interests to come with me. If you're uncomfortable in my truck, drive with Autumn."

"I'm not going to stay anywhere you are." Vera spit out every word.

Jett's face remained impassive. Autumn had to give it to him. Her mother could test the patience of the most devout saint. He didn't seem to be affected at all.

"Your choice, then." He turned to Autumn. "The offer stands for you and Quinn. I don't think your mother will budge. If you don't want her to be alone, I can have my mother try to get her."

"I can hear you. And you will do no such thing. Your mother is the very last person I would go anywhere with." Vera clutched her pearls. Her face contorted as if she might cry, but Vera did not have the skill to cry on command. Thank God for small favors.

"Here we go," Autumn said.

"What is Gram talking about?" Quinn said.

"Grab your stuff," she said to Quinn, ignoring her question. Now wasn't the time. The time might never come to explain to her daughter what had happened between Karen Ryker and Autumn's dad that had turned Vera into a bitter, impossible woman. The past could stick up its withered hand right from the grave and latch on to any innocent bystander close enough to get sucked in.

"We're going to the ranch?" Quinn said, as if Vera and her declaration had never happened.

"Yes. Coach Ryker's offer is very kind." She must be out of her mind for accepting Jett's offer to stay for free on his ranch. At least now, Quinn would think of something other than Vera and her complaints of Karen Ryker.

"I'll be right back. This is going to be fun." Quinn pounded up the steps with the energy and enthusiasm reserved for teenagers.

Fighting all her battles alone exhausted her. The

world was against her at the moment, and she just wanted to sink into someone, almost anyone, who could carry the burden for her a little while. Sleeping in a warm bed would be one way to release some of the stress.

In the morning, with a good night's sleep— something she wouldn't get on the living room floor or in the arctic temperatures of her room—she would have a clearer head and the fortitude to continue her battles. For tonight, she was willing to allow Jett, of all people, to give her a hand. She wouldn't have believed it possible even one day ago.

"Autumn, he's going to make a fool of you." Vera's voice shook with what had to be loss of control as she watched her daughter and granddaughter conspire with the enemy.

"Mom, enough. If you want to stay here and freeze all night, so be it. But Quinn and I are going to the Ryker Ranch."

"I'd rather freeze to death." She pursed her lips. Her fingers tangled in that defenseless necklace.

"Have it your way." Autumn turned to Jett. "I'm ready to go."

"Wait, don't go. My back has been giving me trouble all day. What if it goes out?" Vera took two large steps toward them.

"Call me. I'll come back." She turned away from her mother to make her point clear. Quinn and she would not be staying.

"I can't believe you'd leave your mother all alone. What kind of daughter does that?"

Jett took a step forward. "Vera, with all due respect, you are more than welcome to stay in my home where you'll be warm and comfortable. If you choose not to, that's up to you. Autumn and Quinn are coming with me."

Autumn wanted to throw herself in his arms for that. "Thank you," she whispered.

He leaned in. Her body warmed for the first time in hours.

"You don't deserve all those accusations from your mother," he said.

Quinn bounded down the steps with her backpack, pillow, and blanket.

"Darlin', I've got plenty of pillows and blankets." Jett flashed his full-wattage smile at Quinn. It lit up his whole face and danced in his dark eyes. He took the items from Quinn and tucked them under his arm. "But I will make sure they are brought to your room for the night. I want you to be comfortable while you stay with us."

Autumn's heart needed a jump start. He was charming when he wanted to be.

"Those are my favorites," Quinn said.

"I can't sleep without my favorite pillow either. I just don't want you thinking the Ryker Ranch doesn't cater to its guests." He winked at Quinn, then shifted his gaze to Autumn.

"No way. I know that." Quinn swiped the air with her hand as if Jett had said the most ridiculous thing. How nice to be so young and innocent, believing that Jett would never think of leaving her high and dry.

Autumn, however, still gazed at Jett with some skepticism. The heart rarely forgot the moment it broke. She had no reason to believe his intentions to help them weren't honorable. If Jett were anything, it was that. But the wounded part of her wanted more information before she completely let her guard down around him.

"Vera, you're certain?" Jett said over his shoulder.

Her mother only huffed in reply and returned to her room. The bedroom door seemed to have closed with the extra force of a stiff wind.

"Don't you need to grab anything?" Jett held her gaze.

"I have everything I need." She collected her purse from the table. "We'll drive over in my truck."

"Fair enough."

Chapter Eight

"You did what?"

Jett held his mother's confused gaze. He couldn't believe it himself, actually. He had said the words to Autumn before he realized he uttered them aloud. Sure, he had thought about asking her to spend the night but hadn't meant to actually say the words. Somehow his mouth had betrayed him. He was afraid another part of his anatomy had been the instigator.

"The heat is broken, and Jay Henry hasn't called her back yet. I couldn't let them stay there all night. The wind is going to pick up to thirty-mile gusts. It's only one night."

Autumn's old house would creak and moan all night. Cold wind would leak through every crack and crevice. The fireplaces would never keep them warm enough.

If he hadn't shown up to retrieve his clipboard and the skiing times, he wouldn't have known. But once he had the knowledge, he wouldn't have allowed anyone to sleep in a cold house. Of course, he couldn't force her, but she had caved pretty quickly. He had expected her to react much the way Vera had.

"And you said Vera stayed behind." His mother grabbed clean towels from the linen closet.

"You know Vera."

When Vera tried to make Autumn feel guilty for

wanting to sleep where there was heat, he hadn't been able to stop himself from saying something. He never liked the way Vera always tried to manipulate Autumn into doing her bidding, and then the woman would get angry when Autumn listened to someone else.

"Unfortunately, I know how stubborn that woman is. She would rather catch pneumonia than be anywhere near me after all these years."

"What's that saying about a scorned woman?" He took the towels from her.

One of the things Mom had taught them all was that people made mistakes and shouldn't be judged by their mistakes only. She would never allow anyone to say a bad thing about Ajay, who had made some pretty big mistakes. But that wasn't who Ajay was at his core. And she did not want to be judged by her worst moments. Jett had to thank his mother for that lesson. He wished Autumn would stop judging him for his worst day too. And he sure as hell had had plenty of days filled with mistakes.

"You'd think that Vera would feel some kind of satisfaction. It wasn't as if Ives and I fell in love and lived happily ever after. It was only a couple of sweaty afternoons designed to bring a little relief."

"Mom, easy on the details." He looked away. Making eye contact with his mother while she spoke about having sex turned his stomach.

"Oh, please. Don't be ridiculous. You know what sex is." She grabbed the towels from him. "I'll take these to Autumn and Quinn."

"I'll take them." He grabbed them back. "And I do know what sex is. I've been having it since I was sixteen. That doesn't mean I want the visual of my mother doing it." He kissed her on the cheek.

"You had sex at sixteen? How come I didn't know that? And with whom?" She followed him down the hall.

"I don't tell you everything." He laughed at the puzzled look on her face. She was probably trying to go back in time and remember who his high school girlfriend was.

"You did not," she said.

"Did not what?"

"You slept with that sweet Carla. The one Kace liked." She pointed a finger at him.

"He was fourteen at the time. Carla was never going to be interested in him. She was a year older than me." And way more experienced than he was.

Mom shook her head. "Raising boys was no easy feat. Please tell Autumn whatever she needs I'm just down the hall. Good night, Jett."

" 'Night, Mom." He waited until she turned the corner where her en suite was before knocking on Autumn's door.

The door opened, and Autumn stuck out her head. She was beautiful even with fatigue weighing on her lids. He didn't know how she was handling running that ski area all alone for the past two years, except that she was one tough lady. She had to be after all she had lived through, including loving him once. He had never made anything easy even when he wanted to.

At least he had Lock and his mother for the tough stuff on the ranch. And when anything got out of control, Kace and Gage always jumped in. Even if Kace complained while doing it.

"These are for you." He handed over the towels.

She pressed the towels against her face and sniffed.

"These smell divine."

Splashes of red spread across her cheeks, which only made her more adorable in her oversized sweatshirt and fuzzy pants.

"I'm sorry. I can't believe I just sniffed your towels in front of you."

He tried not to laugh, but a little snuck out before he could stop himself.

"You don't have to laugh at me." She arched a brow.

"I'm not laughing at you. I think it was...never mind. If you need anything, my mom is just around that corner." He had been reminded of all the times she would stop to smell honeysuckles. Her face would light up, and she would pick them right off the branches to carry with her and use in a recipe.

"Where do you sleep?" she said, interrupting his visit to the past.

"I'm upstairs. I have our old apartment we lived in when we were kids." It was the length of the building and sometimes more space than he needed, but Mom had wanted him to take it when he officially became the head of the ranch. She preferred her small suite of rooms that had once been a bridal suite. Lock had built a guest cottage that they used for brides and grooms now.

"Oh. Okay. Thanks again for this. Quinn is already asleep. I wish my mother would've come."

"She had the chance. If she changes her mind during the night, come get me. I'll drive over and get her."

"You would do that?"

"Of course, I would."

"My mom isn't very nice to you or your family." She leaned against the wall and clutched the towels to her chest.

"That won't stop me from doing the right thing. She shouldn't stay there, but we can't force her. If she changes her mind, she'll have a ride. Good night, Autumn."

He turned away, needing some space to breathe. She captivated his attention too much with the flecks of gold in her light eyes and the way her hair fell around her face in soft waves, taunting him to put his hands in it. She smelled like iced pears too. He wanted to taste her to see if her skin was as cool as frozen fruit or as hot as his. He shouldn't have these thoughts about her. They had no chance together. If they had, it would have happened by now.

"Jett?" Her voice drifted toward him.

"Yeah?" He looked back. She had stepped away from the wall but still clutched the towels as if to protect her from something. Maybe him.

"Thank you for being such a decent man."

It wasn't the compliment he would have preferred. "That's me. I'm the decent one."

She shut you down, Ryker. He had been right about there never being a chance between them.

And he hadn't even known he was trying for another.

****

Autumn couldn't sleep. The wind whipped around the house, whining as if it were a banshee coming for her. She threw the blankets off because the room was warm. Instead of wanting to cool her body down, she should snuggle under all the blankets and sweat as a way to appreciate the fact that she was in a warm house and not the icebox she owned.

This room was lovely too with its two full-size beds.

The mattresses were stuff dreams were made from. Quinn took full advantage of the comfy bed. She was sprawled out on her belly, legs stretching in two directions. The girl practically snored with each breath.

Autumn had audibly sighed when Jett first showed them to their sleeping quarters. The white clapboard walls decorated in simple farmhouse design and long, wide windows that gave a view of the mountains would entice even the most determined city dweller. The room was decorated in creams and greens. The wood floors were washed oak. The space welcomed a guest and brought the outdoors in, complementing nature in a soft and cozy way. She could stay here for a lot longer than one night.

But that was not remotely possible. In a few hours, she would return to her broken and neglected house. Though she did love that old lodge. It had plenty of charm and sat brilliantly on the end of the mountain. Once the sale of the property went through, if she ever found a buyer and she was out from under the pressures of the ski area, maybe they could fix up the house a little. But who was going to allow her to keep the house? It made the perfect lodge for the skiers.

She hopped out of bed and grabbed her sweatshirt. Lying there thinking about all the things she couldn't have, including Jett Ryker, was doing her no good. If she wasn't going to get any sleep, she might as well move around. She could find her way to the kitchen. The Rykers must have a teapot and a few bags of tea lying around.

Back when she and Jett were together, Karen had kept part of the kitchen open for guests who, like her, wanted a midnight snack. To Karen, this was a home away from home for all who stayed here. Autumn suspected that hadn't changed.

She'd always liked Karen Ryker and had often wished her own mother was more like Karen. She adored her boys, always hugging them or putting a hand on their arm when one of them was nearby, never saying a cross word to them. She had raised them to be confident, strong men with a moral compass that always pointed north. Ironic that Karen had been the one who committed an indiscretion with Autumn's father. Truthfully, she didn't blame Karen. Ajay had just died. The woman could not have been in her right mind. And her father was always willing.

The hallway was lit with soft white lights along the baseboard and a small table lamp at the end where another hallway turned, offering more rooms for guests to stay. The temperature dropped a few degrees cooler out there, and Autumn relished the cool air against her clammy skin.

She pushed through the doors that led to the main lobby. The great room was dark at this hour, but the smell of woodsmoke still clung to the air. The wailing of the wind was less obvious at this end of the building, but she still pulled her sweatshirt closer.

The kitchen was dark too, except for the lighting under the cabinets. They had been updated since she was in here. Dark wood glimmered even in the dim light. She ran her hand over the quartz countertop. Her kitchen was almost thirty years old. Her parents had updated it after a big ski season. Instead of saving the rest of their annual profits that year, her father had gambled it all away, leaving them broke.

A sign on the refrigerator read *Clean up your mess*

if you make one. She chuckled. That sign had hung there years ago too—on a white fridge instead of the pretty double-doored stainless steel one. Karen Ryker had never minded if someone came in for a midnight snack. She only wanted it cleaned up by morning. Probably because having five boys equaled a seriously messy kitchen. Autumn ran her fingers over the wooden sign. She was glad some things never changed.

She found the teapot in the corner of the counter and a box of teas nearby it. A warm cup of White Christmas Vanilla might hit the spot.

While the water heated up, she glanced out the front windows that faced the parking lot and the activity area. Her stomach clenched with the unwanted pang of jealousy. Shame heated her cheeks. She should be happy for the Rykers. She just wanted a little of this success for her and Quinn. Especially Quinn.

"Couldn't sleep either?" Jett's deep voice turned her from the window. He wiped a hand over his face. His jaw was dotted with a thicker beard than earlier.

His T-shirt pulled across his pecs, but it was the way that his sweatpants sat low on his hips and defined his thighs that had the breath stuck in her throat.

She swallowed a couple of times to be able to speak. "You know how it is in a new place. It always takes me a day or two to get used to a new bed." Why had she said that? Now it sounded as if she wanted to stay longer.

"You can stay until your heat is fixed. I don't mind."

She wanted to smack her head or tie her mouth shut with twine. "No. We can't. I didn't mean to sound like I was looking for a handout or anything. I was just making an observation about new beds. Your bed is great, by the way."

And foot in mouth again. *Get it together.*

He choked out a laugh. "Top-of-the-line mattresses. Lock insisted on them because he wanted one for himself."

The teakettle interrupted them with a whistle. Jett grabbed it off the burner and poured the water into the mug she had located as well. He grabbed a second for himself.

"Thank you for that. I would've done it."

"I know. I was standing closer. That's all. I'm glad you made yourself at home." He tossed her a sideways smile while he poured.

"I remembered you always left some things out for guests who couldn't sleep. What has you wandering the halls so late? Don't you have a kitchen upstairs?"

"I do. When I can't sleep, I come down to check around. Make sure everything is the way it should be." He handed her the mug.

"Still paying attention to every detail." She had to grab for the handle because the mug was hot. Their hands tangled as he let go and she took over. Her body sizzled from the touch of his skin on hers.

"Sorry about that. You didn't burn yourself, did you?" He took a step closer.

She took a step back and held the mug in front of her like a shield. "No, I'm good. The place looks great."

"Thanks. It's a labor of love. But you know about that." He slid onto the chair at the island and blew on his tea.

The moment of embarrassment for her and most likely confusion for him was over. And still she might melt in her spot. He had to be the most rugged and manly man she knew, from his cowboy hats to the way he looked poised on the top of a horse, to the way he could throw a bale of hay, and here he was blowing on a cup of tea. So much for getting it together.

"The ski area has been more of a chore than anything these past two years." She couldn't believe she had said that to him, revealing a part of her heart better left hidden. He would never understand the way she felt. Running his ranch was in his blood, and he had the kind of help she dreamed about. His life was easy.

"Have you thought about—"

She needed to cut him off before he asked more questions. "How is the ski team looking?"

He narrowed his eyes for a split second, but he rearranged his face before she could be sure of what she saw.

"I'm still getting to know them, but I like what I see so far. I won't change anything for the next competition. After that, I'll have to reevaluate. I think we need to switch a few things."

"Quinn loves it. She would ski all day if I let her." She moved closer to him as if another force directed her.

"She's got a ton of heart. I could tell from the very first run." He held out the other stool and motioned for her to sit.

"Thanks for noticing." She shook her head and stayed put, trying to focus on her reality and not some crazy fantasy brought on by a sleepless stress-filled night. Being in his presence under his roof fried her brain. His gesture meant nothing more than he was a guy who did the right thing and could be counted on to help out when needed. Just like him taking on the coaching job.

"She's a tough kid. She's been through a lot," he

said.

"She has. And now…never mind. It's late and my mouth has a mind of its own. You probably want to get back to sleep."

"Finish what you were going to say."

Maybe because it was late and the kitchen was dark, protecting her from a harsh reality, or maybe it was the way he looked at her with those eyes as dark as coal and full of something that could be confused with smoldering fire, but she wanted to tell him.

"I have to sell the ski area. I have less than thirty days to find a buyer, or the bank takes it." She dropped her gaze to the tea. Heat filled her cheeks.

He came around the island and took the mug from her. His large, warm hand rested on her shoulder. His touch and the nearness of his body aroused her, shocking her. Her gaze shot up to meet his. A slow smile spread across his face.

"I'm sorry things didn't work out."

"Me too. I have to tell Quinn. I guess I'm still hoping for a miracle."

"Miracles rarely happen in business. We make our own luck." He dropped his hand and retreated.

She stepped farther back. The temperature in the room cooled. "Are you saying it's my fault that I have to sell?"

He put his hands on his hips. "I'm only saying luck doesn't just happen. We have to work for it. Businesses go under all the time. It's got nothing to do with you as a person."

"In other words, it's not personal."

"Exactly." He flashed another smile as if his petulant student finally understood a simple math problem.

She wanted to smack the look off his face. Instead she tilted up her chin. "Don't you think if you lost this ranch, it would feel personal? Your father did pass away right in your field."

A darkness crossed over his eyes. The smoldering was gone. "Our family business has been around for decades."

"So was mine."

"It's not the same. You let Trent run your business while he was alive. You might own it, but you handed the day-to-day to him."

"I helped." She had Quinn to raise, but she had checked in guests, made coffee all day, made sure the ski lift worked. But Jett was right. She had that similar thought not so long ago.

"You did help. That's not what I meant."

"Really, Jett? What did you mean exactly?" Even if he was right, she didn't like his implications. Or maybe he had hit too close to the truth and that stung.

"You're twisting my words. The guest ranch and the ski area are two very different businesses with a different business model. But business changes. Yours ran its course. That's all."

"How convenient for you to judge me from your spot at the top of the heap. Do you ever come down off that throne to see how the rest of us live?"

"You're kidding me with this. I shovel horse manure just like the guy who works for me, and you know it."

"What I know is you like your neat little life as king of the ranch. And you don't want anything coming along that might mess that up. And when it did, you did what you do best. You shoved me away." Her throat burned from the words she vomited. She hadn't planned to say anything about their past, and somehow she had dragged them back to their old fight.

He stared at her with his eyebrows up near his hairline.

"I'm sorry." She turned to run, but he gripped her arm.

"Autumn, what's going on here?"

"Nothing. I don't know. It's late. And I'm tired. Please let me go."

He released her and held his hands up in surrender.

She bolted from the kitchen, ran to the room, and locked the door behind her.

If Quinn weren't sleeping like the dead, she would grab her daughter and race back to her cold house and have herself a good cry.

What else could she do after completely humiliating herself?

Chapter Nine

Jett would never understand women. He sure as hell hadn't expected Autumn to make a reference to their relationship last night while standing in his kitchen. She had snagged his breath when he found her staring out the window into the night. She had only become more beautiful with age.

He waited for the ski team to come down after their final run of the day. The sun was setting, and an icy wind had picked up. He wanted to get indoors and off Autumn's mountain so he could stop thinking about her. His mind hadn't been on practice, and he was almost certain the kids had noticed.

When Autumn's and his relationship ended years ago, she had agreed it was for the best. He had believed she was telling the truth because he needed to, and she had never lied to him. He might have believed anything said to him in order to stop the unbearable hurt of losing his brother. He couldn't risk Autumn leaving too, so he pushed her far away.

Since then, she had practically ignored him, and he had given her the space she seemed to want. Her complete retreat from his life had only proved he had been right about the breakup.

He checked his stopwatch. Where was the team? Were they goofing off? He hoped not. He would can them all if they were. He had better things to do than freeze his butt off, standing still.

But after last night, just those few words falling from her lips about driving her away seemed to imply she was still upset at him. He didn't understand how that could be. She had agreed, damn it. She had said he should get on with his life without her, that he wasn't in the right space for a relationship.

It wasn't every day his brother got shot, killed someone else in the process, and died in the arms of their oldest brother. And it wasn't every day he lost a child of his own even if that child hadn't been near ready to be born. He couldn't handle a relationship back then. Hell, he hadn't been much older than the kids on this ski team.

He wiped a hand over his face. He needed to focus. What happened all those years ago was in the past. He and Autumn were in the past. And as far as he was concerned, that was where they would stay.

He stole another glance at Autumn's house. He hadn't been able to stop doing that either. Jay Henry's truck had been in the drive the whole two hours of practice today. Jett didn't think it would actually take that long to fix the heat. If he were in there, he'd have her furnace working in no time. Was Jay trying to finally get Autumn to go out with him? Jett hoped not. Jay was a good guy, but Autumn needed a man who wasn't afraid to look someone in the eye when they spoke.

He hadn't seen her since the kitchen last night. He had woken early, but she had been long gone by the time he knocked on her door to tell her breakfast was ready.

He had hoped she would still be there, and maybe they could talk or smooth over what happened, but the beds had been made, and she had left a thank-you note. Polite as always.

Finally, the kids plowed in, expertly turning on their skis to stop. Some laughed. Others high-fived. Most were out of breath with flushed cheeks and giant smiles.

Once again, Quinn was the last one in. He was going to have to figure out what to do about that. He could take a run down with her and see where her hesitation was. She could need more body strength. The skiers with more strength often skied the fastest. Or it was her leg work.

But if she didn't pick up speed, he might have to cut her. He would be doing Autumn a favor and saving her the money it cost to keep Quinn in the school. There had to be a free after-school activity she could get involved with at the high school. Quinn could always ski for fun. She was a good skier. But a professional career or a scholarship wouldn't happen. No point in putting off the inevitable. It would kill him to cut her. Autumn would kill him too.

"Okay, guys. That's it for today," he said, drawing their attention his way. "Great job. You're all doing good work. I'll see you all tomorrow."

The kids popped off their skis and chatted in small groups. Quinn stood off to the side alone. A look of sadness or frustration masked her face. She resembled her mother at that age. Jett had seen that same expression on Autumn's face. Oftentimes directed right at him. He could talk to Quinn tomorrow about her spot on the team.

He needed to get back to the ranch anyway. He had a late delivery coming, and he wanted to be there for it. He turned for his truck.

Quinn ran up alongside him. "Coach, I need some help with my edging. Can we take a run together?"

He hesitated. He couldn't let this young woman

down. He was going to have to find a way to help her. "You bet. But not today. I'm sorry about that. I have to return to work. Let's practice on Saturday. I'll check with your mom that we aren't going to be in the way of any of her customers." And it would give him a reason to talk to Autumn since he hadn't been able to come up with one for the past two hours.

"We don't have anyone scheduled for Saturday. I probably shouldn't have told you that. My mom will be mad I said something."

"I won't say anything." He would keep the secret and allow Autumn to keep her pride. He wasn't trying to rub her nose in anything, especially not last night when he'd said businesses made their own luck. But that stubborn woman would have to come to terms with her situation sooner or later. That miracle she had talked about wasn't going to be anything more than a buyer for her property.

"Thanks, Coach. Mom's pretty private."

"I can respect that. Let's say Saturday around eight."

"In the morning?" Quinn's eyes grew two sizes.

"If the sun was up at six, we'd be on the slope then. If you want to improve, you need to put in the time. In or out?"

She gnawed on her bottom lip for a second. "Yeah. I'm in. I'll see you then. Thanks again, Coach." Quinn trotted away.

He would have to rearrange some things Saturday morning and see if Gage could take out a group who wanted to ride horses on the snowed-over trail for the great photo ops this time of year. The group couldn't get pushed off to Sunday because another snowstorm was due, which would cause too many safety issues.

Quinn revealing the ski area had no customers for Saturday stuck with him. Autumn needed someone on the slope every day. She needed the money to pay for more than just fixing the heat. Taxes would be due, and the price of the oil used to heat the place was always on the rise. That lift of hers broke on a regular basis. She should really give up and let someone take over. Taking a buyer sooner rather than later was in her best interest. He planned on being that buyer.

Jay Henry trudged out of the house with Autumn behind him. She was wrapped in the old coat that hung to her knees, and he loved seeing her in it for some reason. She and Jay were talking because Autumn tilted her head back and laughed, even though Jett only caught the ends of her tinkling laughter and nothing more. The wind had done him no favors and carried her voice away from him. His blood burned. Jay turned away from Autumn's laughter and ducked his head.

Of course, he did. *Look her in the eye, man. Or better yet—don't.* This newfound prickly feeling in his gut came out of nowhere. Autumn could talk to and spend time with whomever she liked. She was not his business. Autumn folded Jay into a hug. The feeling in his gut climbed into his diaphragm and stifled a breath. Jett took a step forward.

"Hey, Coach, can I talk to you a second?" Logan Everett approached him, carrying his skis over his shoulder.

The kid had an apprehensive look on his face as if he were debating with himself about talking to Jett. He could remember feeling that way at Logan's age—old enough to make decisions on his own but still too young to trust those decisions. Having someone to bounce them off usually helped. Logan probably wanted to know what Jett thought about signing up for a race or two.

"Sure, what's up?" He stole a quick glance at Autumn, who had let go of Jay. Thankfully. Jay turned his plumber's van around in the driveway and honked a goodbye. Autumn turned without another wave and paused, looking in his direction now. He raised a hand, and she did the same but continued back into the house.

He glanced at his phone. He had about ten minutes before he needed to get to the ranch. Whatever Logan had to say, Jett hoped it wouldn't take long.

"It's kind of...well, I could use some advice." Logan looked around.

This might be more than just asking about which race he should tackle. Except for Quinn, who was still making her way back to the house, they were alone now.

"You're killing it on the slope, kid. You should be giving me advice."

"It's not about skiing." Logan's gaze dropped to his boots.

"Oh." His phone vibrated in his hand. Paula, who worked for him in the afternoons, sent a text. The delivery of saddles had arrived, and she didn't know where to put them.

"Hey, Logan, I really want to hear what this is all about, but I have to race back to the ranch. There's something going on only I can handle. I'm sorry. Can you come to practice early tomorrow? We can talk then."

"Yeah. Sure." The smile slipped off the kid's face.

"Thanks for understanding. You going to be okay till then?" He didn't know the first thing about handling a teenager's problems. He tried to think about how Gage would handle someone coming to him for advice. When in doubt, pretend to be his big brother.

"Yeah. Yeah. I can wait. See you tomorrow." Logan hefted his skis onto his shoulder and trudged down the mountain.

The boy looked defeated. If he had a problem at home, Jett was the last person who could help him. But then maybe he should be the first person to do it. If Markus Everett wasn't there for his kid, someone should be.

"Hey, Logan."

The kid turned back.

"Give me five minutes, and we can talk." He pulled his phone back out.

"Great. Thanks." The smile reformed on his young face.

Yeah, Gage would have put down whatever he was doing and listened. Jett had seen it a million times when they were teens and one of them wanted to talk. Gage always felt like he had to be the man of the house after their dad died. His brother always got it right. Jett sent a text to Paula with instructions, then dialed Lock.

"What's up?" Lock said with what seemed to be a mouthful of food. What else was new? Lock was always eating.

"The new saddles are at the ranch. Where are you?" He glanced back toward Autumn's house, but she was nowhere in sight now. The sun dipped into the treetops, and the temperature fell with it. The moon would be full tonight. A clear crisp night for a horseback ride.

"Not at the ranch." More chomping.

"Can you get there? I've got to help out a ski student for a little while. I told Paula to put the new saddles in the tack room and wrap them in fleece, but she wasn't sure she could handle them all. And the tack room door seems to be stuck again."

"I'll text her to leave them right outside the door. I'll take care of it when I get back. I'll fix the door too."

"I just spent a fortune on those saddles. Is there a reason why you can't get back to the ranch now and take care of it?"

"Can't, big bro. I'll be home in an hour. Or call Kace and see if he'll do it. I think he's home with Tara and Royce."

"Where are you again?"

"Out." Lock ended the call.

Jett stared at the screen. His brother could send his blood pressure right over the mountaintop. When Lock decided he didn't want to tell what he was up to, he wasn't talking and nothing would drag it out of him. He could be with a woman, at the diner having a late lunch, or he could have driven three hours away to get a view of the snow on another mountain because he saw a post on social media about it. Lockwood only heard his own drum beating in that head of his.

Jett sent a quick text to Kace and shoved his phone in his pocket. "Okay, Logan. Do you want to talk here, or do you want to come back to the ranch and get something hot to drink?" He was ready for something hot after being outside for hours. And he was starving. His mother might have prepped a dinner for the family to share. He hoped, anyway. The ranch didn't offer dinner to the guests, but the Rykers still needed to eat.

"I don't want anyone to hear us."

"That sun is about to say good night. I don't know about you, but I'm cold through my bones about now and could use some soup or a hot coffee. How about if I drive us next door, and I promise no one will bother us."

"Well, if you think it will be private." Logan checked his phone.

An expensive foreign car drove up Autumn's drive and blocked in his truck. The car was sweet to look at but mostly impractical here on the base of the mountain or on his ranch. He could appreciate a nice vehicle, especially with a race car driver for a brother, but Jett preferred his worn and weathered pickup.

He motioned for Logan to follow him, but Logan stood still. "You okay?"

"That's my dad." Logan's face matched the snow.

"We can talk another time." He didn't have to be a genius to figure out the kid didn't want to have any discussion in front of his father and most likely hadn't known Markus would show up here.

Markus slid from the shiny sedan. The black paint glistened in the remaining rays of the sun. Markus was tall, like him, but slender because he preferred running and skiing to anything involving weights. Markus's wavy light-brown hair was always slicked into place. Jett often wanted to rough it up a bit just to see if it moved when touched and because it would probably drive the pretentious Markus with his wire-rimmed glasses crazy.

"Logan," Markus called, waving his hand, but didn't move from his spot beside the vehicle. "There you are. I was looking all over town for you."

"Where else would I be?" Logan said under his breath.

Together they walked over to Markus and his shiny car that matched his shiny shoes. Maybe those expensive, useless-in-the-snow shoes were the reason why Markus had stayed put. The suit was a giveaway too. He would get those suit pants wet from the snow.

"Hello, Jett. Nice to see you." Markus gave a curt nod with a stiff lip.

"Markus." He turned to Logan. "Great practice today. Don't forget that practice starts thirty minutes early tomorrow, okay?"

"Yeah. I got it. No problem, Coach. Thanks." The smile spread wide on the kid's face.

Jett nodded to the kid and his father. He was ready to get in his truck and get out of there.

"How's my boy doing, Ryker?"

"He's doing just fine. Our best skier. The schools will be looking at him."

"I tell him never to half-ass it. Don't you let him get away with anything less than his absolute best out there. One hundred and ten percent for him. You have my permission to push him past his limits." Markus pounded Logan on the back.

Logan's cheeks turned pink.

"I provide a safe and fun environment for all my skiers. They work to their potential. And hopefully, they'll grow, but at their own pace." He might not be great with kids, but he sure as hell knew what a good coach was. And he would never threaten a kid or demean someone to push them. And absolutely never push them to do things they weren't ready for on the slopes. What the hell was wrong with this guy?

Jett suspected he knew. Markus had a thick competitive streak, and he was strangling his son with it. He glanced at Logan, who stood there shifting from one foot to the other. Was the kid going to tell him he wanted off the team? That would suck. But whatever the kid wanted. Jett would have to let him go.

"Sure. Safety first. I get it, but Logan is special. I want him to have every opportunity to surpass the others. His future is bright, my boy." More pounding on the kid's back.

"Since when do you care?" Logan said with a snarl. "You keep telling me I'm wasting my time."

Markus shot a death glare at his son.

"Logan, you're doing a great job out there. You're a real leader. The other skiers look up to you. Keep doing what you're doing. Everything else will fall into place." He didn't know what exactly was going on between son and father, but he wouldn't allow Markus to use his son as a showpiece just to get at Jett.

"Thanks, Coach. Dad, I have my car. I'll meet you at home," Logan said.

"I'm not going home. That's what I came to tell you. Honestly, I'd forgotten about practice. Got my days turned around." Markus leaned toward Jett with some kind of conspiratorial laugh.

Jett remained still and shot Markus a glance he hoped would shut him up.

"Anyway…" Markus coughed into his hand. "I have to go out of town for two nights. You'll be on your own. Just order takeout. I didn't get a chance to grocery shop."

"Fine. Whatever."

The tension between son and father would snap if Jett reached out to touch it.

Markus grabbed his wallet from inside his coat and handed Logan a wad of cash. "This should hold you over."

Logan's cheeks turned pink again, but he shoved the money in his pocket. Jett wasn't sure a teenager should have that much cash on him. At Logan's age, he might have been tempted to spend it on beer and girls. Until Gage found out anyway.

"Thanks, Dad. I'll see you tomorrow, Coach."

"Sure thing."

Logan slid into his car and drove down the drive.

"Listen, I'd like to stand here all day with you, but I need to get back to work. The ranch doesn't run itself. Could you move your car?" The driveway was big enough Markus could have parked anywhere and given the pickup plenty of room to get out. He suspected Markus knew exactly where Logan had been and had decided he would remind Jett that he was important too.

As if Markus ever let anyone forget. He did not care about Markus, but Markus seemed to think Jett still did.

"No problem. Did you hear that Autumn is selling this land? A real shame she can't hold on to it. But it would make a sweet development deal. Maybe even bring a little competition to that monopoly your family has going on over there." Markus hitched his chin in the direction of the ranch.

"Are you planning on trying to buy it?"

"Maybe."

"Why don't you loan her the money instead of stealing her land from her for another of your questionable deals?"

"It's not stealing if it's for sale. Besides, this is business. Nothing personal. Autumn is a great girl. Always has been. She just doesn't have the business mind her husband had."

When he told Autumn that buying her land wasn't personal, he hadn't thought much of it. But when Markus said it, the words turned slimy like scum on a pond. "She isn't a girl, Markus. You should know better than that."

"Girl. Woman. You know what I mean. I'll let you get back to your horses." Markus eased into his vehicle and made his way down the drive too.

Jett stood there until the car was out of sight. He turned, finally able to leave. And bumped into Autumn.

She braced herself from falling by grabbing his arm. "What did he want?"

Even through his parka, the heat from her touch shot up his arm. "To tell Logan he was on his own for a few days." He was glad to see her up close even if the reason for her presence had nothing to do with him.

"That poor thing is going to be all alone in that big house?" She released his arm.

He wanted her touch back.

His thoughts headed into dangerous territory. An old flame shouldn't mean this much. "Looks that way."

"Can you do anything about it?" She stared up at him with wide, hopeful eyes.

"What would you like me to do?" He couldn't change the kid's life. But her asking made him want to come up with an idea.

"I don't know. Give him a place to stay." The wind blew her hair across her face. She brushed it away.

"He has a place to stay. A very nice one at that. And he probably has a staff of people ready to give him anything he needs." He might want to assist Logan because she had asked Jett for help, but he couldn't tell the kid to stay on the ranch. He wasn't in the business of sparring with Markus any longer. They stayed on opposite sides of town, the way Jett liked it.

"It must be lonely being Markus's son."

"I wouldn't know." He had an idea.

"Your family is very lucky to have each other.

There's always someone around to lean on."

"We are lucky. And I think we know that. Most of the time, anyway. Did you come out here to find out what Markus wanted, or did you have another reason?" He hoped for another reason. Maybe she wanted to talk about last night again.

"I don't like him around my place. I don't know why it bothers me after all these years, but he can't be trusted. He's always up to no good."

Autumn had that right. Markus could not be trusted. No one could prove it, but in a town like Backwater, the gossip was as thick as the snow on a mountain, and the gossip said Markus made his money in ways better not to know about. How Markus had such a good kid like Logan escaped Jett every day.

"He was just here for Logan. Don't worry." No point in tipping her off about Markus's eye on her place. He wanted a chance to approach her first. At least with him, her land would be preserved as a ski area and she could continue to live in her home because he didn't need a lodge when the ranch was right next door.

"The heat's fixed," she said.

"I saw Jay Henry here earlier. He still sweet on you?"

Autumn rolled her eyes. "The whole town knows about that man's crush on me like we're still in the seventh grade. I have no interest in Jay Henry as anything more than a friend. And a plumber."

"I'm not sure he knows that."

"I feel bad for him. He's all alone." She shoved him with a smile on her lips and play in her eyes.

The sun grabbed the last of the daylight, leaving everything around them muted. Dusk settled against the trees and the mountain, blurring their edges. He could watch her smile all night as if she didn't have a care in the world. He wanted to take her cares away.

"Why did you leave so early this morning?" He wished he could yank the words right back after he said them. He hadn't planned on bringing up her leaving so early. She had left, and that was that. But it wasn't, was it?

"Quinn needed to get ready for school. Thanks again." She pulled that oversized coat closer.

"Anytime. How's business?" He wanted to keep the conversation going even in the cold, but he didn't want to come right out and say he knew her schedule was empty.

"Same. Slow. Word got out my lift was broken. People rescheduled at other places." She sighed and turned toward the lift and then looked back at him with hurt in her eyes. "This kind of small mountain isn't a draw anymore. People want the whole ski-resort experience. I can't give them that."

"It's not your fault." He stepped closer to her. The heat rolled off her even in the dipping temperatures.

"It feels that way." She dropped her gaze.

He tilted her chin so she had to look up at him. Her misty gaze punched him in the gut. He had to swallow to find his words. She was doing things to him he had thought were long gone between them. "You're a smart woman, Autumn. You did everything you could to save this place."

She put a hand on his arm again. "I wish I could've done more. It isn't fair to lose everything when I've already lost so much."

Those words held a lot of meaning. They had lost

their child. She had lost him, a husband, and now her land. He wanted to wrap her in his arms and protect her from the harsh realities of the world, at least for a little while. Until morning, maybe when the sun came back out and gave hope to the day. For now, when the air was still but dry and bone-deep cold, he wanted to hold her and tell her he'd take care of everything.

"Can I ask you something?" She still stood inches from him with a hand on his arm as if she had done that very thing a million times before.

"Sure."

"Why does it feel so right when I'm standing here with you and you have barely spoken to me in the longest time?" Her words were a whisper.

"I don't know." Muscle memory for him. He had never forgotten her gentle touch or her sweet smell. The way she would curl in on him when they slept together. She was always running a hand or her fingers over some part of him when she went past. He could pull memories at the drop of his cowboy hat of her laugh and the way she'd squeeze her eyes shut when she really got going.

"Do you want to kiss me, Jett Ryker?"

"Hell yes, ma'am. I do."

And so he did.

Chapter Ten

Autumn's head spun. She was kissing Jett. And not just a little friendly peck on the cheek either, but a full-on tongue-in-mouth messy kiss. For the first time in almost twenty years, she was locked in an embrace with him.

She wasn't sure what had come over her, but when she saw him talking to Markus, she had to come outside and find out what was going on. Something had dragged her out of the house and down the driveway. The same something that often had her peering through the trees at his ranch. The same something that had her kissing him now.

The two men had been in a standoff. She was pretty sure neither of them had even known they were staring the other down as if a gunfight at the O.K. Corral were about to take place. But she'd recognized that stance of Jett's. He had squared his shoulders and fisted his hands on his hips. His legs had stood shoulder width apart, and he most likely had that glare in his eye that could make a grizzly stutter. She hadn't been able to tell from her spot at the window, but she had seen it plenty of times before.

Jett was a force when he wanted to be. She had always felt safe in his arms, as if the world could not come in and harm her. And even though she and Trent had a good life for a long time, only with Jett could she be completely vulnerable.

She had wanted some of his sexy confidence today. Because after last night in his house, all the ways she had loved him had seeped into her heart and cracked it open. Her damn heart had not forgotten how good it had been with Jett even when she tried so hard to make her mind forget.

And her body remembered now. He cupped her face and drew her in. His mouth expertly devoured hers as if he too had been missing something for a long time and had finally found it. She tangled her fingers into the ends of his hair that flipped out of the bottom of his knit cap. She tugged because she wanted more of him.

He seemed to know what she meant and ran his hands down her arms and slid them inside her coat. She should be freezing out here with her coat unzipped and her thin shirt doing nothing to block the cold, but she was as hot as a bonfire now.

His lips released hers and moved to the spot below her ear. "You still taste so sweet," he said against her skin.

His breath was warm but sent shivers over her. She fumbled with the zipper of his parka. She had to feel more than nylon and down. His mouth returned to hers. He sucked on her lips and ran his tongue over the places where his teeth left little nips. Her lips might end up swollen if he kept it up, but the tiny pricks of pain were delicious.

Her hands dove inside his coat and warmed up immediately. His body was like a furnace, and she wanted to fold in against him and stay there. Instead, her hands explored his strong and muscular back.

"Autumn, what are you doing?" Her mother's shrill

shriek shoved her away from Jett.

She stumbled. Jett gripped her arm to steady her.

"Looks like we got busted." The smirk on his face said he didn't care. He ran a thumb over her lip.

"Autumn." Vera pounded her fists on the porch railing. If her mother continued, she'd end up breaking a hand and needing the hospital.

"I should go." She tried to step around him, but he blocked her with his muscular body. She couldn't see her mother's flailing now.

"Don't let her bully you." He held her gaze. "We're not kids anymore."

"I know how old I am. I don't want to deal with her. If I go inside, she'll run out of steam soon and I can get on with my evening."

"It's time to start—"

"Vera isn't like your mother. She doesn't understand how to behave. She holds grudges. I wish she didn't. I wish she were anyone else most days, but she's her. I have to go." She dodged him, or he stepped out of the way to let her by. She wasn't sure which, but if she knew Jett, he wasn't likely to stop her again.

She hurried up the drive, past her mother without saying a word, and into the house. Vera was fast on her heels. As fast as Vera could go.

"I can't believe my eyes. How could you?" Vera sucked in a few deep breaths and held her side.

"Do you need some oxygen?" A ridiculous question, considering she had none, but her mother probably would be screaming for the emergency room in minutes.

"I'm fine. What were you thinking? What is wrong with you?"

"Mom, drop it."

"Answer me. I'm your mother. Why were you kissing that Ryker? Haven't you learned anything about that family? All they do is use people for what they want and then toss them aside when they're done. He's using you."

The anger burst through her. "What is it that he could be using me for? My money? I don't have any. Sex? Jett Ryker can have sex anytime he wants. There are plenty of willing women in this town and every surrounding one that would be happy to jump into bed with him. He's a catch. I don't have anything he wants."

"I don't know what he's up to, but you mark my words. He's after something you have. You're a fool. You always were so gullible like your father. He fell for the wiles of Karen Ryker. She turned his head without any effort, making him think he was some kind of big man."

"That was almost twenty years ago. When are you going to let it go? You and Daddy never got along. Your divorce wasn't Karen's fault." Her father would have left her mother anyway. He had been a serial cheater, but in moments like this she didn't blame him. Trying to get any emotional support from Vera was like cuddling a porcupine.

"She had no right to sleep with my husband," Vera huffed and shuffled out of the room.

Autumn flopped onto the couch and held her head in her hands. Her mother's angry voice echoed in her head. She didn't know how to get it out.

Jett wouldn't use her. He had no reason to. But why had he kissed her now? She had wanted him to. She had leaned into that kiss as if a life preserver were thrown her way. She was pathetic, holding on to her crush for him.

He would never want a relationship. Commitment wasn't his thing. The man was in his forties and had never even been engaged. He liked his bachelor life too much, it seemed. Maybe he was just looking for sex. Familiar sex. Well, she wouldn't be a winter booty call. Not even for him.

She pushed off the couch, hung up her coat, and went into the bathroom to splash water on her face. She could still feel Jett's lips on her skin. He had seemed into the kiss as much as she was. She didn't remember him being a very good actor. Jett always said what was on his mind, regardless of the consequence. His face often confirmed the story. He was never mean, but he was direct. He had to be in his line of work. Too many people and animals relied on him to get his point across.

She did remember, however, how great he was in bed. They might have been young, and she was never sure how many girls had been with him before her, but in his early twenties he'd taken his time, making sure she always felt good. He had never rushed her. In fact, he would linger in places for so long that she would be the one to push things along. The man had patience.

Could all of that have changed over the years? Was he trying to get back at her finally for losing their child or walking away when Ajay had died even though he had been clear that was what he wanted?

No. She wouldn't allow her mother to ruin that wonderful kiss. She would put it on her memory shelf for visiting. Even though she liked kissing him more than she should, she couldn't get involved with him. Too much water under the proverbial bridge. She couldn't listen to Vera yelling about her betrayal to their family by taking up with a Ryker. Not when she had to deal with her land issue. She could only solve one major problem at a time. And if in the future, when she was settled into a new life with a new career and Jett wanted to kiss her again, she might let him.

****

The air smelled of snow. Jett slid open the stable doors. The night sky was absent of light. Clouds covered the stars and the sliver of moon that hung on a tilt this time of the month. They were due to get a few feet of the white stuff tonight. The extra snow would be good for practice tomorrow.

He paused outside the stables and breathed in the damp air. He loved this time of year, when everything was covered in white and a stillness blanketed the land in warm wool. Wildlife was tucked in for the season. Birds had flown to warmer weather. He strained to hear, but only the ripple of the creek in the distance came back to him.

He couldn't imagine being anywhere except on his land, surrounded by mountains that reached for the big sky. He could think in the quiet night. And after that kiss earlier, thinking seemed out of the question.

He walked through the stable to check on the horses. The new saddles had been placed inside the tack room. The stalls had been cleaned. The horses were warm and bedded down for the night. He should go to bed too, but he was too wired to sleep. Coming down here usually calmed him when his mind raced, but he hadn't been tangled up over Autumn before. Well, not in a long time anyway. He had thought he'd put that to rest when they broke up. Obviously, they still had some unfinished business left if that kiss said anything.

"Hey, girl." He stopped at Silver Bell's stall. She

whinnied while he petted her head. "You doing okay?"

She nodded as if to answer him. Silver Bell had been Ajay's horse, a gift from their parents when Ajay was born. Each son had been given a horse at birth, but for whatever reason Silver Bell had lived a long life. Gage believed Silver Bell hung in there all these years because Ajay hadn't. As if she wanted him to live on and she would do it for him because he couldn't. Ajay had loved Silver Bell more than anything else.

"What are we going to do without you?" Her time was coming. She moved slower. Wasn't eating as much. She slept longer and longer. "I bet Ajay is ready to see you. It's okay if you're too tired to keep going. We'll all understand."

Except maybe Gage. When Silver Bell went, he would be hit the hardest. He had taken over caring for Silver Bell as if she were his. He thought he owed it to Ajay. Gage thought he owed all of them. But Gage owed no one. He had done more than his fair share of taking care of the whole family.

"What are you doing down here?" Gage appeared in the stable doorway as if Jett had willed him to the stable. The snow fell behind him in the light above the door. He wore a knit cap pulled low on his head and his sheriff's coat with his jeans tucked into his snow boots.

"I was just thinking about you. That's strange." Was his brother reading his mind or something? He looked at Silver Bell. She only stared back as if to say, "I didn't send him, stupid."

"What is? That you were thinking about something other than this ranch and that horse or that you were thinking about me?" Gage sauntered to him and ran his hand over Silver Bell's snout. "Hey, girl."

"Weird that I thought about you and you showed up. Mom would say I made it happen or something bizarre like that." He turned over the feed bucket and took a seat. The day had been long, and he was ready to get up in his apartment and have a beer and shut down. Another busy day would begin at dawn.

"Yeah, and Calista would agree with her." Gage leaned against the stall door and rested his foot on it.

"You believe in that voodoo stuff yet?" He had spent his life trying to be practical and logical. His mother might believe in magic, but he didn't.

"No way. I might love Calista with my whole heart, but I prefer facts. Black and white. No shades of gray for this sheriff. I leave that other stuff to her and her yoga mat."

"Good. I don't want you going and changing on me now." He expected his brother to be the stable person he could count on. Calista had softened Gage, had reminded him to open his heart again, and he would be grateful for that, but he didn't want Gage putting those crystal things around his house and believing if he thought hard enough about something, it would just appear. The world wasn't ready for Gage to start burning incense, and he sure wasn't either.

"I saw you go past the guest cottages. I figured you'd come down this way. I thought I'd catch up with you," Gage said.

"Just doing my nightly rounds." And trying to get Autumn out of his head before he did something dumb like throw rocks at her window and beg her to come down and make out with him.

"How's Silver Bell doing?" Gage ran a hand over her snout again. Silver Bell nudged him, making Gage laugh.

"Well, the arthritis seems to be getting worse. She's got dental issues now. I'm concerned about her weight loss." He wanted to spare Gage, but his brother knew about horses as well as he did. Trying to smooth over the truth would only hurt more because Gage could check for himself and see Bell's issues now.

"Do you think she'll last the winter?"

"I didn't think she'd last this long. She might be stubborn enough to keep going."

"I want to be here when it happens."

He stood and met his brother's watery gaze. "She might choose to go when you're not here. She knows how you feel about her."

"I thought you didn't believe in things like that?" Gage swatted at his eyes.

He didn't care that his brother could cry over this horse. Hell, he would bawl like a baby when Silver Bell took her last breath, but watching Gage cry was something different altogether. Gage was his rock.

"I believe this horse is smarter than you." He shoved Gage like he did when they were kids trying to work out their feelings.

Gage choked out a laugh. "True enough." He straightened his face into something neutral, as if they had been talking about nothing more than the weather. "How's the coaching going?"

Grateful for the change in subject, Jett headed for the door. They could talk and walk back to their homes. "Good. For now."

He told Gage about Logan and Markus and filled him in on Quinn's skills and what could happen if he couldn't get to the bottom of it.

"You need any help with talking to either of them? I could take Quinn for a run or watch the team if you want to go with her." Gage walked beside him, always ready to help one of them.

The snow continued to fall, coating everything with its touch in regal white. The ranch spread out before him, and the warm glow of lights in and around the buildings puddled on the ground. Someone laughed in the distance. This place was in his blood. He didn't know what he would do if he lost it. Just this fall Kace had considered selling his share, and that nearly killed him. No stranger would own what belonged to the Rykers if he could help it.

He suspected Autumn felt the same way about her land, and she was about to lose it.

"I might take you up on it. I can't be in two places at once. That happened today when the saddles arrived and I couldn't get Lock to take care of it. Thanks again for dealing with that."

"That's what I'm here for. You ever find out where Lock was?" They followed the walk toward the guest houses where Gage lived with Izzy and had since Izzy was a baby.

"He's not telling me." He had tried to pin Lock down again after dinner, but he wasn't saying where he was. He could have found a casino and gambled his inheritance, or he could have helped some family in need build a house. With Lock, it was always up in the air.

"He wouldn't tell me either. He got to the barn right as I was finishing with covering them. He apologized, but he said he had stuff to do. I let it go. I've had more than my fair share of conversations with Lock about his disappearing acts. In the end, he always pulls through.

It's just Lock being Lock." Gage stopped at the bottom of the walk to his house.

"If he's not telling you, then he's not telling. You still scare him. He can't lie to you."

Gage roared with laughter. "He might be the youngest, but he's the biggest. I'm not about to fight him."

"Ajay is the youngest."

"You know what I mean, Jett." Gage lasered a stare on him.

"When you give me that look, you can scare me. So I know you scare Lock." He hadn't meant to step on Gage's pride with that Ajay comment. He never wanted his baby brother to be forgotten. Gage would never forget Ajay. It was just late, he was tired, and that kiss had his head on backward. "Sorry. I shouldn't have said that thing about Ajay."

"Forget it. Listen, there's one more thing before I go inside. I bumped into Betty Mason at the grocery store. She mentioned you and Autumn were going at it hot and heavy out in public today."

"Betty Mason is losing her mind." Betty Mason was one of the town gossips. Her sister was Margie who happened to be best friends with Vera Thatcher—Autumn's mother.

"So Betty got it wrong when Margie called her with the news?"

"Why are you asking me about this?" He would not kiss and tell. Autumn deserved better than that, but the gossips had grabbed on to a tiny morsel and would spread it all over town by morning. He shouldn't have kissed her right in front of her house with any sign of daylight left. But he had lost his head when she stood so close, smelling so good. And that hug she had given Jay Henry had his blood boiling.

"Because if it's true, Mom is going to find out."

"She isn't going to say anything. Besides, she likes Autumn." At least his mother could separate her life from his. Vera Thatcher seemed to think Autumn's life should be entwined with hers, as if Autumn owed Vera all of her happiness.

"Autumn slept here the other night." He might as well tell Gage before he bumped into another town storyteller.

"What did you say?"

"I was doing her a favor. Her heat was out, and I couldn't let her and Quinn sleep in that old house. They took the extra room. She was gone before I was up. Mom was totally aware."

Gage ran a hand over his head. "Okay, I didn't see that one coming. Is it true, though? You kissed Autumn and got caught?"

"I hadn't planned on it." He hadn't even been thinking about it until the very last second. Spending time with her had opened up that box everyone said should be kept shut because nothing good came from opening it. And now it was opened and causing trouble.

"If you wanted to kiss her, you should've at least waited until nightfall and taken her out into the woods like when we were kids."

"I think we're a little old for that." He had never taken Autumn into the woods for a make-out session. They had been nineteen when they started dating. And twenty when they got pregnant. He had believed he was too mature to drive his truck into the woods and pull a girl over the gear shift and onto his lap. Mature was the last thing he had been back then.

"Just be careful. I know you've always held a torch for Autumn. I don't want her trying to manipulate you," Gage said, dragging him back to the present moment and the snow falling around them.

"Why would she do that?"

"Because you can help her out of her jam. She could ask you to lend her money."

"You think she's using me?" That kiss had seemed genuine.

She had responded to him in the way he remembered. She had even let out that little moan he liked so much. And she was far too proud to ask for a handout. She would go to the bank and ask for a loan, which she must have done and been turned down since she needed to sell. But put out her hand and ask him to give her money? Not the woman he had been in love with. No way. But was she still the woman he had loved once? How well did he really know her now? She had her back up against the wall. Desperate people could do desperate things. How far would she go to keep her land?

"I don't know if she's actually using you. She doesn't seem the type. She might even still have feelings for you too. She might just want to get back with you. But go slow, okay?"

Go slow? He wasn't even planning on kissing her again. They could never be together. Not with her mother hell-bent and determined to stir up trouble. He didn't do drama. Not even for Autumn. And if her intentions were less than honest… He didn't want to think it.

"I want to buy her land. I'm going to see what she's selling for and make an offer."

"Did she ask you to do that?" Gage's eyebrows

climbed under the rim of his knit cap.

"Are you kidding? When she finds out I want to buy her land, she'll probably punch me. She's too proud and stubborn to sell to me." That alone would stop any more kissing. She would probably hate him for taking her land, but it was business, even if Markus had said those same words. For Jett, the words were true. He would never deliberately hurt Autumn. Markus, on the other hand, was capable of anything.

"But you'll be the one to keep her land intact." Gage pointed out what he had thought.

"You're damn right I will. And I'll let her stay in that house that needs major repairs. Anyone else is going to come in, divide it up, and develop on it. I don't want the competition either."

"Maybe kissing her wasn't such a great idea."

"It was one of my worst." But that didn't mean he didn't like it.

Chapter Eleven

Autumn stared at the computer screen on her desk in her office that doubled as the laundry room. The washer and dryer provided a white noise to drown out her mother in the kitchen, but not the noise in Autumn's head while they worked hard to wash the sheets and towels.

She willed the numbers in her bank account to change. They only stared back, mocking her. She was almost out of money. Fixing the heater had drained her account. But the house had to have heat, or she would have even bigger problems she couldn't afford to pay for.

She was going to need another source of income to keep the lights on for the next month. And what would they do when the bank foreclosed on her land because there was no buyer? Where would she take Quinn and go? She would need money for that too. Hotel rooms weren't rented on good looks. Well, some were, but she wasn't that desperate. Yet.

Backwater wasn't exactly swimming in job opportunities. And she still had to be around to run the lift and deal with the occasional guest who still came for the skiing. At least the ski school was renting her space. To think she had tried to turn that money down because Jett had come with his hand on that check. They would already be out on their backsides if it wasn't for the school.

She hadn't spoken to Jett since their kiss the other day. He had shown up for practice, but each day he had run out in a hurry at the end. Quinn said there was always something on the ranch that needed his attention. Autumn commended him for his work ethic and commitment to these kids. She didn't know how he juggled it all. He did have help. She needed to remember that. Help she didn't have.

She pushed out of the chair and checked the dryer. Nope. The sheets were still wet. Hopefully, the machines didn't pick any time in the near future to die on her.

Jett was out on the slope now doing runs with Quinn to help her speed improve. No one had ever done that for Quinn. Autumn didn't want to read too much into the gesture. Jett was the kind of coach who would teach by example because he was that kind of decent man. But her heart still took notice that he was helping her child.

She slammed the dryer door shut and went outside for a little reprieve. The sky was clear, and the snow was bright against the sun. She squinted to cut down the glare, but the air was crisp and clean. She could breathe deeply when she was outside. She wasn't going to be able to give this place up. The mountain was her backyard. The pines dotted the landscape like little gifts for her. If they hiked a couple of miles to the north, the creek was back there for fishing. The Ryker Ranch was to her west, and that land went on for miles. There was so much space around her. She couldn't imagine living somewhere closed in. Even the five acres she desperately wanted to keep seemed like nothing, but at least she'd still have the view of the mountain.

A car drove up the drive. A white Buick with its shiny grill parked in one of the spots by the front. She went down the steps to meet this unexpected guest. Hopefully, they wanted to ski today and tomorrow. All month, maybe.

Only this wasn't a customer. It was Dottie Lucier, the real estate agent. Dottie was tall and big boned with sprayed stiff long blond hair that fell below her shoulders. Her winter-white coat had a thick shawl fur collar and a belt that fought its way around her waist.

"Hello, Autumn." Dottie waved as she navigated the asphalt in her heeled snow boots. "I'm so glad I caught you. I know I could have called, but I was in the neighborhood and wanted to say hello anyway."

The neighborhood was a long country road that snaked and climbed on its way to somewhere else. Her neighbors were the Rykers and the mountain drop-off. She wasn't exactly in town. Dottie was probably on her way here.

"This is a surprise. Do you want to go inside?" She preferred that Quinn not notice Dottie standing in the driveway in her winter-white glory. Autumn would explain the need to sell soon enough. She also didn't want Jett to take notice either.

"Sure. It's freezing out here." Dottie shivered and laughed. "You think I'd be used to winter in Montana after the twenty years I've lived here."

"Cold is cold. How about my homemade hot cocoa? I made up a batch for the ski team, but only Quinn had practice, it seemed." She hadn't realized it would only be Quinn. Jett had come specifically to help Quinn. Another reason to like him when she shouldn't.

"I would love some." Dottie followed her inside and took a seat in the kitchen nook.

Autumn poured two oversized mugs and joined her

at the table. "So, what brings you by?"

"I have an offer for your property." Dottie clapped her hands, almost knocking the mug over in the process. "Ooh. Sorry. I get so excited about a possible sale."

She bet Dottie did. Even though she needed the sale, didn't see any other options unless a suitcase full of money fell out of the sky, her stomach still hollowed out. Once she asked who the buyer was or what the amount was, the offer would be real and she would have to seriously consider it or risk losing everything to the bank.

"I suppose it was a fair offer." She focused on the hot chocolate, taking a sip and burning her tongue.

"It's below what I would ask for the ski area, but it's not insulting."

"If it doesn't cover what's left on the mortgage with a little left over for me to live on for a while, then the answer is no." She didn't want to give up her home and not even have a penny left. She'd rather take her chances with the bank and force them to remove her from the property. That could take months. And maybe give her time to find a new career.

"We can negotiate, but I don't know if the buyer will come up much higher. At least I didn't get that impression. Because of my experience, I can read people well."

What she figured Dottie could read was the dollar signs this sale would mean for her. She would get her commission regardless of whether Autumn paid off her mortgage and ended up living in her car with her mother and her teenage daughter. She was going to have to hold firm and wait it out for another buyer.

The hot cocoa had grown cold. She met Dottie's animated gaze. "I'm sorry. It's a no for now. I'd like to see if any other offers come in."

Dottie's mouth fell open. That animated look was replaced with something dark and a little cold. "I think you're making a big mistake. You don't know when the next offer will be in. You can't stay here forever. If you sell today, you get the money. If you wait until the bank has possession, you'll get nothing. You're better off cutting your losses now and getting out as painlessly as possible."

"If the amount of the offer doesn't cover my debt, then I get nothing anyway. If the bank is going to end up with my land, then they can wait until the last possible second to have it. Thank you, Dottie. But it's still a no. For now." She stood, hoping Dottie would get the hint that their little gathering was over.

"I understand." Dottie pushed out of the chair and retightened her coat belt. "I still think you're making a huge mistake."

"Duly noted." She walked Dottie to the door.

The cold air swooped in and circled around her ankles, freezing her skin as she opened the door.

Even though she didn't want the sale, the mystery of the buyer piqued her interest. "Who was the offer from?"

Pounding footsteps on the front porch interrupted them. Dottie looked between her and the arrival of Jett and Quinn. Quinn's smile was radiant. Jett seemed to have a triumphant look too. The practice must have gone well.

"Oh." Dottie pointed at Jett. "The offer was from him."

****

"Let me explain," Jett said.

She didn't need to hear it. She would never sell to

him. Never. He had kissed her with an ulterior motive. She couldn't believe her mother had been right. She didn't want to believe anything Vera said because it always came with a score to settle. And she also couldn't believe what a fool she had been to think the man was attracted to her still or again. She wanted to scream.

"Get out." She pointed at the front door. Dottie had left on her innocent or not-so-innocent declaration that the Ryker Ranch was making an official offer. Not Jett personally, but the business. Quinn had read the tension in the space and ran for the safety of her room.

"Autumn, will you just listen to me?" He tucked his knit cap into the pocket of his parka.

"No, I will not. You don't have anything to say that I want to hear." She needed him to go because her emotions were on the crest of the wave and about to crash all over her.

"You're being unreasonable. My business wants to b—"

"Stop." She resisted the urge to put her hands over her ears like a toddler who couldn't stand the taunting of a fire truck's siren. "I don't care. I won't sell to you."

"Why not?" He reached for her, but she swung her arm out of his way.

She couldn't because the humiliation would eat her alive. From the moment they broke up, she had wanted to prove to Jett that she didn't need him. He could not become the person to save her now. Living with the knowledge that he'd swooped in with her solution would be the end of her. Not him. Anyone but him. Tears burned the backs of her eyes. She hated the fact he even knew about her predicament. She might be spiting herself because of her stupid pride, but that was that.

"I have to ask you one thing." She needed to know even though asking was going to cost her too much. "The kiss the other day, was it real or did you do it to prime me for the offer? You know—if you gave me a good time, maybe you even get a little lucky, then I would be more likely to accept your money."

His face twisted with hurt, and she regretted the words, but she had to know. He stared at her for a full minute. "You think I wanted to sleep with you and then leave payment on the bedside table? Shit, woman. What kind of a man do you think I am? I thought you knew me well enough to know I would never insult you or any woman that way." He marched out of the house without looking back.

She slammed the door on his retreating hind end.

"I told you. The Rykers are always thinking about themselves and what they can take from everyone else," her mother said from her perch at the end of the hallway. Vera must have been listening again.

She regretted ever allowing her mother to live with her. When she took control of the property, she had moved home. Living here had made the most sense at the time. The house had plenty of space. But over the years, she'd realized how wrong that decision was and she could never figure out how to tell her mother to move out.

Autumn ignored Vera, went upstairs to her own bedroom, and locked the door behind her. She grabbed a pillow off the bed, shoved it against her mouth, and finally screamed.

Chapter Twelve

Jett paced his apartment. He wanted to hit or throw something, but that wouldn't solve any of his problems. He needed to get out of there and hurried toward the stables. It was dinnertime, and the ranch was quiet. The few guests they had would be going into town for dinner and not needing anything. Most of the employees had gone home for the day because the nighttime activities were limited in the winter. Basically, only the spa was open now. And he wasn't interested in a massage by Kace's girlfriend. Of course, he liked Tara. She was fantastic. She was a great employee, and the guests loved her, but he couldn't lie still on a massage table if his life depended on it.

He had to do something with all the anger in his veins. Autumn's implying he saw himself as some kind of pimp to buy her land turned him into knots. Hell, he could have sex anytime he wanted for free. He didn't need to pay for it. And not at that price.

His boots pounded the frozen ground. The cold air did nothing to cool him off. Only one thing could take the edge off for him. Okay, there was more than one thing, but this was the best one. He slid open the barn door.

The horses were in for the night. The ranch didn't have an evening ride scheduled on Saturday nights mainly because no one wanted to work on a Saturday night. But that was fine with him. Now he wouldn't have to deal with anyone or explain what he was doing.

He saddled up Butterfly. He liked riding her and always took her out. Tonight would be no different. Before he rode off, he made a quick stop by Silver Bell's stall.

"Hey, girl. I'm too wrangled up to stick around tonight. You don't need any of me right now. I'll come back and sit with you later."

Silver Bell pushed his hand with her nose. He looked into the horse's eyes and thought for a brief second she could read his mind.

"I know. She's hurting, and I make that pain worse for her. I always have." But tonight he didn't care about that. Even though he should. He was angry because she had swung and hit him square in the bullseye. He prided himself on doing the right thing. That was how he and his brothers were raised. He didn't stray far from that line. He had left all the straying to Lock and Ajay. Even to Kace with his reckless career that had almost killed him.

But him, he followed so close to Gage's tutelage that sometimes he wasn't sure where his own principles stopped or started. Gage had been the compass he followed. And Gage never strayed. He was a tough one to live up to, and yet Jett had been trying for over forty years. For Autumn to imply otherwise had cut him clean through.

He hopped on Butterfly. They trotted out toward the easy hiking path. It was basically flat and soft when the grass was in. He didn't take chances on a night ride. Even with his eyes adjusted, he could miss something and risk himself and the horse. He wouldn't do that, but he had been riding on this land his entire life. He knew it inside and out.

Now the snow had been packed down, but Butterfly could handle it. He would ride out to the creek and back. By then, the heat in his veins should be placid enough he could be around other people.

The cold air swirled on every side of him but didn't cool him. The anger held on with both hands. Butterfly's hooves clomped against the hard ground. He could smell pine and snow in the air. But all he could think about was Autumn. She had believed he would use her, as if she were the prize in all of this. He cared about her too much for that.

That kiss had been real enough to shake him from his head to his toes. No woman had lit him up like Autumn. Being with her had always been different. Special. And when their lips touched, his brain and his body remembered as if no time had passed.

Did Vera have anything to do with Autumn's refusal to accept his offer? Even if Autumn said no, he had to consider her mother would put negative thoughts in her head. And Vera was vindictive enough to try and convince Autumn that Ryker money was dirty. Vera would allow her daughter to suffer because of her own bitterness.

Butterfly followed the path. She knew the way better than he did. He took this ride at least once a week. More if he could swing it. But the ranch kept him busy. And if he could take over the ski area, he'd be even busier.

The business needed the expansion if they were going to continue to compete in the guest ranch world. Every day other guest ranches in Colorado or Utah offered bigger and better activities and adventures right in their backyards. Hell, he had read an internet article about a ranch right in Montana that doubled as the location of a very popular television show and that now offered guests a chance to rent their cabins. Everyone in the industry was going to suffer from that one.

The path turned, leading them deeper into the woods. The pine branches offered some coverage. The ground had little snow here. In the daylight, the sun shone through the branches and glistened against the snow layered on the pine leaves. The first deep breath since arguing with Autumn filled his lungs. Gage had warned him about making an offer on her land. He should have listened.

But if he didn't buy it, someone else would. And they wouldn't take care of it the way he would. He planned to expand what she was already doing with the backing of his business and reputation.

She just hadn't been able to run her business well enough to stay in the black. She didn't have the help. And he also knew, though he probably shouldn't, they had lost a lot of money because Trent had gambling problems. That had been years ago, but they never recovered, and then the tanking economy forced people to stay home. Plus, she didn't offer enough activities for the skiers. People wanted the big resorts now with a restaurant and tubing. They wanted the town at the end of the hill if the facility didn't offer a ski-on, ski-off option because after a long day of skiing, they didn't want to have to go far. They didn't want to come for the day. Maybe in smaller states where getting to a mountain was easy enough for a day trip, but in Montana everything was spread far and wide.

He and Butterfly came upon the creek with its quiet

gurgling. This very water ran behind Autumn's property too. He could follow it, if he wanted, and end up in her backyard. He wasn't sure why he was thinking about that particular path or what it might be like to knock on her door at this hour and have her come out in her cute pajama pants. She had made herself clear when she threw him out today. She didn't want him or his help. He wasn't about to try to convince her he wasn't up to no good when she should already know that about him. He had shown her his true self more than enough times.

He turned around and headed back toward the barn. Butterfly took her time as if she knew he was in no rush, that nothing waited for him when he returned. Not a complete truth. Plenty waited for him. His ranch, his guests, his family—his empty bed. Was he finally ready to have a woman in his bed every night? He hadn't thought so. But Gage and Kace had done it. The look was good on both of them.

Lights from the ranch's buildings cast their warm glow against the fallen snow. Fatigue spread through his body as he approached the barn. He might actually get some sleep tonight. He would keep his offer to buy Autumn's place on the table. And if Autumn changed her mind about selling to him, or found herself out of options, he would be there to help her. Whether she liked it or not.

****

Autumn couldn't sleep. She threw back the covers, shoved her feet in her boots, and grabbed her coat from the hook by the front door. Quinn and her mother were asleep. At least, she assumed they were.

Her mother had been doing a lot of coughing today. She had complained about not feeling well, the flu or some such thing. But Vera had looked well enough. Every time Autumn's mind had drifted off, thinking about Jett of all things, Vera would bring on a dry hacking cough that sounded more like a novice acting student failing at their first performance.

If Vera was actually sick, Autumn wasn't sure she could handle dealing with her mother and the possibility of being homeless all at once.

Cold air hit in her the face as she rushed outside. Air froze in her lungs. She had no idea where she was going or what she was even doing out at this hour, but she couldn't stay still in that house any longer.

Her legs propelled her through the snow of their own volition. She couldn't stop them even if she wanted to, and she should want to. In about five minutes, she'd be in the tree line that separated her property from Ryker Ranch.

"I'm out of my mind," she muttered to herself, but that didn't stop her. Branches poked at her, catching her jacket and yanking her back. She tripped over a branch and fell on her hands. She brushed herself off and shoved aside the brush and pine leaves, ignoring the cedar scent she always loved and cherished.

Her gaze fell on Jett climbing the steps to the front porch. She hadn't expected to see him. She hoped she would burn off a little steam, get near the main building, and turn around and go home. Instead, he took the steps two at a time, halting her in her tracks. Denim wrapped his long muscular legs like a gift. His barn coat filled out with his strong arms, and that adorable knit hat slid up his head as if being pulled by an invisible string.

She should run back. He hadn't seen her, wouldn't know she was there. She could hold on to what was left of her dignity and slip into the trees.

Dried leaves crackled under her foot and broke the silent night as if they were shattered glass.

He turned. "Autumn."

She could still run. But she would look like a bigger fool than she already was. She had kissed him, had liked it the way a child liked making snow angels, and he had only kissed her to prime her to accept his offer.

She needed his offer. Needed to sell the land she had fallen in love with as a little girl when dreams were still made of castles and kings who could share a life with her.

But selling to Jett stole all the wind from her lungs. She had pretended for years that she didn't need him, didn't care that he had broken her heart. She had laughed at the people of this town when anyone even implied Jett was the one who got away. How ridiculous, she would say with a forced chuckle. We were kids. Young and stupid. Nothing that could last a lifetime. But that love had resided deep in her heart, living on even when she told it to die a certain death. She had pretended she hadn't loved Jett because she had loved Trent. But the heart had room for more than one love. It was sneaky that way. And her heart had loved Jett from the moment he walked across the schoolyard toward her.

He walked toward her now too. She had missed her chance to make a break for it. She would have to explain her appearance on his property, in a spot that suggested she had entered through the trees like a stalker. The time of night played against her too. She had no good excuse to be where she was.

"Autumn, what are you doing here? Is everything okay?" He stopped inches from her, narrowed his eyes, and took her elbow in his hand. Concern touched the features of his face.

He must think something awful had happened and she had run here in her pajamas seeking help. Jett was always ready to help. When someone in town needed anything, he would bring food, a strong back to repair or rebuild, and a steady presence. But he had a shrewd business mind too. She couldn't forget that.

She willed her voice to cooperate. "Nothing is okay, if you must know the truth. Nothing has been okay in a very long time."

"Did something happen to your mother? Is it Quinn? Do you need me to get Gage?"

"They're fine. It's me...and you." Saying those words hurt, but now was the time for honesty. She had risked a lot by coming here and getting caught. She might as well jump into the deep end with her eyes wide open.

"I never meant to hurt you with my offer to buy your land, but if you're going to sell it, why not to me?" His hand remained at her elbow.

She should step back, but she wanted his touch. "You don't understand."

"So make me. Because all I can see is a stubborn woman holding on to a grudge. I don't understand why you hate me still."

Still? "I don't hate you. I have never hated you." She had been angry from her toes to her scalp. She had cried for months after they broke up. But she had never hated him. She had wanted to, only to make the pain go away, but hate wasn't possible. She had loved him too much.

"That's not what it feels like." His hand moved from her elbow up her arm. The heat from his touch penetrated the nylon of her coat and scorched her skin.

She resisted the urge to run her fingers through the hair coming out of the back of his hat. "Now I don't understand." She tried to read his expression, unable to figure out what he was thinking. "You and I have managed to get along fine through the years. Why do you think I hate you?"

She had only pretended to be fine with bumping into him in town or the diner or the bank. The smile she plastered on when she saw him had cost her, not because she disliked him, but because of exactly the opposite. Inside, her nerve endings frazzled and her stomach turned in on itself. He had ended their time together without consulting her, forcing her to move on and find love elsewhere. She had believed they were in it for the long haul.

And she had moved on. But she hadn't wanted to.

"Come on." He arched a brow. "You avoid me at all costs. I thought it was because of Trent. When you first started dating him, I figured he asked you to keep your distance from me. I didn't like it, but I'm a man. I can understand not wanting your woman continuing any kind of relationship with someone from her past. But after he passed, you didn't thaw out toward me. It wasn't until I stepped foot on your land as the coach of the ski team that you even smiled at me."

"What are you talking about? I always smile at you." She avoided his gaze because she didn't want him to see her soul in her eyes. After Trent died and she was ready to date again, she'd had to continue to pretend she was no longer interested in Jett. He had never so much as hinted in a joke that he thought of her as anything except the neighbor.

She had believed he had put their relationship in the rearview mirror and never looked back. He made moving on look so easy. She had to make him think she had too.

He shook his head. A hint of a smile tilted his lips. "Sorry, sweetheart. You haven't smiled at me in almost twenty years."

"That can't be true. Why would I do something like that?"

"Because you hate me." His hand drifted to her shoulder.

She stepped closer to him. Heat rolled off him in waves, and she was cold in her bones. She wanted to sink into him and let his warmth seep into her. "I don't hate you, Jett Ryker."

He tilted her chin with his strong finger. "Look at me when you say that."

Her heart climbed into her throat and blocked the air. She swallowed to breathe again. "I don't hate you." But her voice was nothing more than a whisper swept away by the winter wind and blown to the tops of the cedars.

A breeze picked up and lifted her hair. His hand cupped the back of her neck. "Are you sure about that?" His gaze fell on her mouth. Desire flashed in his eyes.

The electrical charge in the space between them could heat her house for a year. How easy it would be to run her fingers over his jaw, letting the rough stubble of his beard prick her fingers and stir up those old wants. She might never get a chance to touch him again. Leaving would be the wise and safe choice, but she couldn't bring herself to go.

"I'm very sure. I don't hate you."

His mouth met hers. He kissed her as if he had a

hunger he couldn't satiate.

His lips were cold, but she wasn't cold any longer. She had wanted this for so long. He tasted like fresh air and mint and the promise of something better. Wrapping her arms around his neck, she pulled him against her. That electric charge was overpowering. She was helpless to it.

His hand moved to cup her face, tilting her chin up and taking the kiss deeper. If anyone had told her she would be kissing Jett Ryker a month ago, she would have had herself a good old laugh. She couldn't believe what was happening, but she wouldn't stop it.

His mouth moved to the soft spot below her ear. His breath was warm against her skin. This time she shivered while her lips found his neck. She caught a whiff of his bourbon-vanilla-scented soap and wanted to lick the man all over his muscled body.

Something that sounded like logic fought its way to the front of her lust-filled brain. She couldn't be with Jett. He wanted to buy her land, and though it was a good, practical choice, she needed another buyer. She couldn't explain to her mother that the Rykers would own the land. Vera would see it as the Rykers throwing them out and taking something that didn't belong to them simply because they could and had. Vera believed Karen had stolen her husband. The land would be an easy steal.

With enough regret to stop a train, she eased out of the kiss. Jett stared down at her with glassy eyes and a smirk on his lips.

"We shouldn't do this." She stepped back, putting him out of her reach so she wasn't tempted to grab him and kiss him again.

The smile dropped. "You seemed like you were

enjoying it. I was."

"I was too. I'm sorry. I'm not trying to lead you on. I guess…I guess I'm still attracted to you. But I meant what I said. I don't want to sell my land to you. And I don't want you trying to convince me with sex."

"You still think I'm a pimp." He threw his hands in the air. "Unbelievable. You are the most stubborn woman I have ever met."

"Jett, I wish you would try and understand."

"I understand that you have held a grudge for a long time. That you never actually understood the pain I was going through when Ajay died. For the briefest of moments these past weeks, I thought maybe we could try again. That I was far enough away from the man I was that I could be in a serious relationship. And then there you were standing by the trees as if you had been delivered to me. But you standing there must be some kind of joke on me."

"I wasn't trying to hurt you. I needed to see you." She was making a mess of things, trying to keep control of her emotions and her property.

"You're going to lose your land one way or the other. The bank isn't going to care what happens to it. And neither will some big-time developer. But I would take care of it. I would see to that, and you could live in that house or move to New Jersey or whatever state if you wanted. But you go and spite yourself by turning me down because you think I'd play some kind of awful game." He pointed at her, then turned on his heel.

She stood frozen until he hurried into the house, never looking back. How could she have a relationship with him no matter how much she wanted to try? Her mother would never let her hear the end of how she had betrayed their family by siding with a Ryker.

Her pride reared its head too. She didn't want Jett to be the person who saved her. She would rather see the bank sell the land to a stranger and she and Quinn and Vera leave Backwater and start over somewhere else than know that Jett Ryker whose touch was gold owned the land that had been in her family for generations.

She pushed back through the trees and returned home. Her feet were numb, and so was her heart, but her lips still vibrated from that incredible kiss. She put the teakettle on and sank into the chair. Sleep wouldn't come for a long while now. And neither would solace.

Chapter Thirteen

Jett had barely slept after his run-in with Autumn out in the yard of all places. That kiss replayed in his mind as if it had been a tight call in the end zone. When he kissed her, he wanted to take her clothes off and make love to her until neither of them could handle another minute. She was going to allow her pride to be the end of them before they even started and the reason she lost her land to a stranger. Why wouldn't she want a Backwater lifer to own it?

He ran a hand over his face. He had to stop thinking about it. The morning had started off on the wrong foot when one of the guests couldn't get hot water in their bathroom. He had to move them to another location, refund them a night's stay, and threaten Lock to fix it. They had to shut down the shooting range today too, because another guest refused to follow the simple rule of keeping the damn gun pointed downrange. The guy continued to do it, as if on purpose, after Jett had told him twice and Gage told him once.

Now he waited by his truck where Autumn's driveway met the road. Logan had asked to talk to him again, and Jett didn't want to run into Autumn. He wasn't sure she was even home. He hadn't seen her truck during practice, but he had tried not to look in the direction of her old lodge.

He had suggested to Logan they go into town, but

Logan expressed the desire to avoid his dad. Jett wasn't ready for whatever this conversation held. He didn't understand why Logan would entrust him with this secret, and once he knew, what would he be obligated to share with another adult?

Logan's car came down the drive and parked on the road in front of Jett's truck. Logan shuffled over with his hands shoved in his pants pockets and his shoulders slumped and head down.

"Hey, Coach."

"Howdy. Are you sure you don't want to go somewhere inside? It would be a lot warmer."

"Nah. Here, if anyone sees us, I can say we were talking about skiing or the team or whatever. We go anywhere else and people start asking questions."

The boy was smart about that. "Okay, what's on your mind?" He shoved his own hands into the pockets of his parka. Evening soaked up what was left of the sunset, throwing everything into a washed-out gray. Frosted air stung what skin he had exposed.

"I have a problem, and I need a guy's perspective."

Jett bit back the words asking where his friends were. At Logan's age, he would have been hesitant to confide in his friends about much, but he had his brothers always there to help him. He was lucky that way.

"What kind of a problem?"

"With a girl." Logan's gaze searched the road as if he were waiting for someone to come around the bend.

"Well, I've dated a few. Are you having trouble asking someone out?" Now that was a problem he could handle. He hadn't heard Logan talk about a special girl during practice or on the bus at their last competition, which Logan had won.

Logan shook his head and smirked. "I already asked her out."

"So what's the problem? Does she want to get serious?" He would tell Logan to take his time about that. College was in the near future. He had plenty of time to settle down with anyone.

Of course, Jett had believed that about himself. When he broke it off with Autumn all those years ago, he had believed there would be plenty of time to fall in love again. And now he was in his forties, still in love with the same woman. He could never reveal his true feelings to her after what they had been through recently. She didn't want to hear that the guy she thought was a pimp was also in love with her. She would believe he made it up to get the land.

"Honestly, I don't know if she wants to be serious with me. I think she loves me. But I'm not sure it matters."

"Listen, kid, I can't guess what's going on with you and this girl. But if you want some advice, you're going to have to tell me more. Did she cheat on you?"

"She's pregnant."

He wasn't expecting that one and needed a second to figure out what to say next. "Are you sure?"

"Yeah."

"Don't kids your age know about birth control? I thought they taught that stuff in gym class or wherever." His niece, Izzy, who was the same age as Logan… A frightening idea slammed into him. "It's not my niece, is it?"

He didn't want to have to pummel a kid if he had gotten his niece pregnant. And he sure as hell didn't want to see what Gage would do if his little girl was.

"What? No." Logan held up his hands. "Izzy and I are just friends. My girlfriend lives in the next town over. We met at camp over the summer where we were both counselors. And did you forget Izzy dates Justin Crow?"

"You scared me for a second. I did forget. My protective uncle instincts kicked in before logic. Sorry. Izzy told me about a program at school run by the students that teaches safe sex. Did you miss that one?"

"I thought if I pulled out in time, it would be okay. That was pretty dumb, huh?" Logan pressed his lips into a thin line.

"Not the surest of methods. Can I ask why you're telling me and not your dad?"

"I don't know what to do. What if she wants to keep it? I can't be a dad. And my dad is going to go ballistic when he finds out. He's going to tell me I ruined my whole future and what a screwup I am. I can't tell him. Please promise me you won't."

Jett didn't know the rules on this. He would have to investigate where his responsibilities lay. But the fear in Logan's eyes said he was begging for secrecy. The last thing Jett wanted was to keep a secret like this from Markus Everett. They already had a huge competitive streak between them, mostly because Markus wouldn't let anything go. If Markus found out that Jett was helping his kid behind his back, the war would be on.

"I can't tell you what to do. You and your girl are going to have to work this out. If you want me to be there when you tell your dad, I'll do that. I can even come when she tells hers, but it's not my place as your coach."

"Please, Coach Ryker, you have to help me." Logan swatted at the tear running down his face.

His heart went out to the kid. He could imagine how

scared Logan was. When Autumn had come to him and told him she was pregnant, he hadn't been able to eat for a week because his stomach was so twisted. And they had been three years older than Logan and his girlfriend.

He had gone to Gage first with the news. Gage had put a hand on his shoulder and said whatever Jett decided, Gage was in his corner. No matter what Jett's decision had been, they'd figure it out and Gage would be right by his side. Nature had decided for them. And he had been relieved. Foolishly.

"Listen, Logan, don't rush into a decision. Make sure to consider all your options."

"But I'm too young. I want to go to school." Logan's words came out on a squeak as if to prove that he was, in fact, too young to handle this very adult problem.

"Then that might be your decision." He couldn't put ideas like adoption or abortion into this kid's head. Logan and his girlfriend would have to come up with their own plan.

"What would you do?"

"Oh no. I can't tell you that. This one is on you and your girl. You two made the baby. You two have to make the lifetime decision. But I'm here if you want to bounce thoughts off me, or like I said, I'll come with you when you tell your dad. Which I think you should."

"No way. He's going to be the last to know." Logan threw up his hands.

"I think that's a mistake."

"It was a mistake telling you. I thought you would help me. You're my coach."

"I am helping you the best way I can. I can't tell you what to do. No one can." He didn't want to be in this position. Coaching was enough, but stand-in parent too?

He hadn't signed up for this.

"Whatever." Logan stomped off, jumped into the car, and drove away.

Okay, so much for handling that one the right way. Seemed like he was making everyone mad.

Now he was in the awkward position of what to do with this information. Did he keep it to himself, or did he find Markus and tell him?

Jett slid into his truck and kicked over the engine. He would give Logan some time to figure out his next move before he said anything to Markus. Logan needed to know he could trust Jett. The kid seemed to believe he was alone in the world, and maybe he was. Why not let Logan know someone was in his corner? Even if Jett didn't have the answers and even if he hadn't planned to be anything more than ski coach, being there for Logan was a small thing to do.

With that behind him for now, he was ready for a quiet night. He pulled up to the main building. His mother came out the front door, waving her hands.

Now what? He grabbed his keys and contemplated making a run for it. "What's up, Mom?"

"Can you make a quick run to the general store and grab me two pounds of butter?"

"Now?"

"No, tomorrow. Yes, now. I've been watching for you to come back. I'm baking my pecan cookies, and I don't have enough butter. They're on tomorrow's menu, and I'm bringing them to the ladies' auxiliary meeting tomorrow. They've been asking for them."

"Do I dare ask why you didn't go?"

"I didn't have time. The Wi-Fi crapped out today, and I couldn't figure out how to get it working. Lock had to help me. I was late starting to bake when I saw I was low on butter. Lock isn't here. I can't drive at night as well as I used to. It's supposed to snow too. Would you mind? I didn't want to bother Gage. He worked all day. And Kace isn't back yet."

"Wait a second. What do you think I did today? I worked and coached that ski team."

Mom put a hand on his cheek and gave him her soft smile. "I know how busy you are, and I'm so proud of you and all that you do. Your father would be proud too. He looks down on you and beams with pride for his second son. You've turned his business into something bigger than he had dreamed."

"Thanks, Mom."

"Since the cookies are for your guests, you're the unlucky one who has to go. Thank you." Karen poked a finger into the air, turned on her feisty heel, and marched back inside.

He was a sucker for his mother. She had played him. She knew how to play all of them. But she hadn't lied. His mother would never do that. Not even when she had been caught having an affair with Autumn's father. Karen Ryker had owned it with her head held high. She had made a mistake. She was human, and she owned every bit of it. She had taught them to do the same. Most of the time they listened.

He jumped back into his truck and headed for town. He glanced over in Autumn's direction on his way out. What would she say about the revelation Logan had dropped on him? He wouldn't ask even if she was the best person to discuss the problem with. It was too late for them.

****

Autumn's last stop was the grocery store. She had run errands most of the afternoon just to not be at the house when the ski team had practice. She didn't want to look out the window and see Jett there in all his male glory, looking sexy in his ski parka and helping the kids do their best.

Quinn had told her about the way Jett had skied the mountain with her last Saturday. He had given her pointers, told her how to turn her skis, encouraged her, and applauded her improvement. Quinn said she was still on the slow side, but the coach had really helped her. Of course he had. The damn man was too kind and too good at everything.

Especially kissing. Her body heated up as the memories of his expert mouth working her over played in her head. If they had gone on for much longer, she would have rid him of his clothes right there outside in the freezing cold and had her way with him.

She had gone too long without sex. That was her problem. She was lonely. A simple romp in the hay would do her some good. Too bad there wasn't a single man in Backwater who interested her—except, of course, for Jett.

She parked the truck and ran inside. She only needed a few things for dinner. Her mother had already texted her three times, wanting to know when she would be home. Soon was all she could say.

She ran down the produce aisle, tossing in what looked good and vibrant for winter. She wasn't much for cabbage stew, and this time of year vegetables were either a fortune or not to her liking. She didn't have much money on her. She would have to be choosy. She really needed to find herself a job.

"Well, hello there."

She turned at the sound of the male voice coming from her side. Her gaze fell on Markus Everett, and her stomach dropped. She wasn't up for another one of Markus's strolls down his success trail. He always exaggerated his accomplishments. The truth resided there somewhere, but anyone who knew him had to dig deep to find it.

He flashed her his cap-filled fake white smile. His skin tone looked as if he might have visited a tanning salon recently. Or he had just returned from some Caribbean vacation.

"Hello, Markus. Nice to see you." Lie. She hoped her smile was planted firmly on her face. The smile Jett accused her of never giving him.

"How are you?"

"I'm great. How about you?" *Here it comes.* She braced herself for the onslaught of good news he would throw at her.

"Good. Business is good. Keeps me out of the house." He paused but didn't say more.

She had expected him to go on for ten minutes.

"How's Logan?" She really did want to know, never begrudging Markus his son, even though that son had been born to the woman Markus had an affair with. When Logan's mother passed away years ago, Autumn's heart had broken for the boy.

"He's a typical teenager. Sulky. Doesn't talk. Gives one-word answers when forced." Markus grabbed an apple and turned it in circles.

Quinn was starting to be like that too, a teenager who kept to herself more and more, who sought out her friends instead of her mother, but Autumn wasn't going to share that. Let him think what he wanted. He would anyway.

"He'll outgrow it. At least that's what I hear happens." She had even heard the stubborn teen would come back to the parent someday. She would have to wait and see.

He choked out a laugh. "I sure hope so. I heard about you putting your land up for sale. I'm really sorry. That must be hard."

She didn't want to talk about that with him. She didn't want to share any of her fears or worries with him. He had never been good at the support-person role. She had failed to notice soon enough. Well, maybe she had. She had never walked down the aisle with him.

The tears burned her eyes for all her recent problems and missed opportunities of the past. She would die if she cried in the produce aisle in front of Markus.

He was one of her huge mistakes. She had run to Markus's arms when Jett dumped her. Markus had made her feel special, like a princess. He had spent money on her, taken her places, showed her off. When he had proposed with a three-carat diamond, she had jumped at the chance to live a comfortable life with a man who might not totally support her dreams but could afford to make them come true. Or so she thought.

"Everything works out as it should. You don't have to feel sorry for me," she said, wanting to believe her own words.

"I don't pity you, Autumn. I know how hard selling must be. I'm sure your mother hasn't let you hear the end of it." He tossed the apple again.

"No surprise there."

"What are you going to do once the sale goes

through?"

"I have no idea. I've been thinking about that." Her phone vibrated in her coat pocket. She dug it out to find another text from her mother asking for her whereabouts. She powered down the phone. She was tired of explaining herself to Vera.

"Everything okay?" Markus gazed at her with what appeared to be genuine concern. But she had better remember he was a con artist at best. He had made most of his money that way. What could look like concern might be the snake ready to bite its prey.

"It was nothing. I do have to go. It was nice seeing you."

"You too. And if you need anything at all, don't hesitate to call me. The number is still the same."

She had no intention of asking Markus for help. But he did know a lot of people. She could regret what she was about to do, but she was desperate. She couldn't afford another major appliance breaking. She worried about choosing to pay for ski school or groceries.

"You know, maybe there is something you could do. If you hear of any part-time jobs, let me know. I'm working on reinventing myself." She left out the part about needing extra cash. Let him think it was only about a career change. If he even believed her. She wasn't a good liar.

"This is going to sound crazy." He came around the apple display and took a step closer to her. "I could use a little help around the house. I know you're overqualified to be a cleaning person, but I also need a cook. Someone who could plan out a few dinners for me and Logan. He eats everything in the house. I'm always here trying to fill the fridge back up. It's probably not what you're looking for, but think about it at least." He flashed a small watery smile.

She took a good look at him for the first time. His dress shirt was open at the collar and limp from a full day's wear. His eyes were hooded as if sleep had eluded him recently. Even pieces of hair hung loose over his forehead when normally he wore it tightly groomed.

Was life getting to him too? Did everyone get to a point in their lives when reality hit a little too hard and getting back up wasn't as easy as it used to be?

"I'll think about it. Thanks." She would consider the offer, even though she wanted to be anywhere besides Markus's house. Logan needed someone to fuss over him. She could make large meals and split them for her house and his. And if she had to run a dust cloth over a couple of surfaces, so be it. She would be doing honest work for a man she had cared for once. Worst jobs existed.

They parted at the apples, and she hurried to the dairy aisle. Her house was out of milk, butter, and eggs. She tossed the items into her basket, turned for the registers, and crashed into another shopper who let out a low moan. Her basket tumbled into the air. Eggs splattered on the tile. Milk rolled out of reach. Her butt smacked the floor.

"Sorry."

She closed her eyes because when she opened them, the man who could make one word rumble rich and full and delicious would be looking down on her with his wicked smirk. If she kept her eyes closed, maybe he would disappear.

"Are you okay?" he said.

Nope. Not gone. She opened one eye at a time. Jett

held a hand out to her. She ignored the gesture and climbed to stand, attempting to tuck the frayed edges of her dignity inside her coat.

She soaked him in. His barn coat hung open, revealing a navy-blue sweater molded to his torso. His faded jeans hung loosely over his legs. He still had on the snow boots he wore on the slope. His jaw was dotted with a thicker beard than usual. He must have skipped shaving today, and that rugged-mountain-man look only made her want him more. Damn her libido.

She also took in the mess in the aisle. She bent to pick up the items.

"Let me." Jett held up a hand as if to stop her.

She was too tired to fight. Fatigue from another long day and pretending with Markus and now seeing Jett again wiped her out. He put the items in the basket and gave it back to her.

"You never answered me. Are you okay?" he said.

"I'm fine. I didn't see you there. Sorry about bumping into you. Are you okay?"

"Don't worry about me. You seemed like you were in a big hurry."

"I am. Now I need to get someone to clean up the aisle, and I'm late getting home. Excuse me." She tried to duck around him, but he blocked her path.

"Autumn, I'm sorry about last night."

"About what you said or kissing me?"

"I shouldn't have kissed you." He gripped two boxes of butter in one hand and shoved the other hand in his pocket.

Even though she believed the kiss was a mistake too, the words still stung as if her skin was stuck to ice.

"We can both agree it won't happen again. We'll

blame it on the late hour. Now, if you'll excuse me, I need to get home. I'm sure you do too." She pointed to his items, wanting to be free of this awkward moment.

She could have gone on living in Backwater for the rest of her life the way she and Jett had interacted for the past decade plus. But now that they'd kissed, twice, and the kiss had resonated in her soul, she wouldn't be able to simply be polite when she bumped into him in the grocery store. The constant reminder of what she had lost, would never have again, kept the wound open and bleeding. She might have to consider moving away. Far away to the East Coast, as he had suggested.

He glanced down at his hand as if he had forgotten he was even holding the butter. "Yeah. My mother is waiting for these."

A man who ran errands for his mother. Could she possibly be in love with him more? And therein lay the biggest problem. Kissing him had stirred up the love like a pot of boiling water.

"Please say hello to Karen." She hurried past him before he could say or do anything else.

Paying for her groceries, and hoping her credit card still had space on it, she stole one last glance behind her. Jett was in the next checkout line, talking with Barbara, the cashier. He had said something that made Barbara laugh.

Autumn shoved her wallet in her bag and ran-walked to her truck. She couldn't bear to witness the way he fit everywhere he went. Everyone liked him and his whole family. And though Autumn was no pariah, Vera made their station in town unbalanced. Moving was looking better and better.

She powered up her phone before she pulled out.

Three more calls from Vera and another text. Autumn swiped to read it.

—*Where are you? Hurry home. We have a guest.*—

A guest? The last thing she needed was someone to entertain tonight.

She texted back.

—*Is it Dottie?*—

She would haul that overprocessed woman right out of her house. Even if Dottie had another buyer, which Autumn doubted, the news could wait for dawn when the sun's bright rays and attempt at warmth would push away the demons lurking in the dark.

Chapter Fourteen

Autumn didn't recognize the car parked near the house. Well, at least it wasn't Dottie's. She grabbed her small bag of groceries and headed inside.

"I'm home," she called out, kicking off her boots, and hoped whoever was over might stick their head around the kitchen doorway.

The main living room was empty. She always loved that room with its high ceiling and stone fireplace that someone in her ancestry had built. When they had an influx of skiers on the mountain, that fireplace roared eighteen hours a day and the room was filled with people, laughing and getting warm with hot cocoa or hot toddies.

When she was a little girl, she would watch sometimes from upstairs when her parents thought she had gone to bed. Men and women dressed in cable-knit sweaters and ski boots had sat in the oversized chairs. For some reason, they all had looked like movie stars to her. She'd had plans for this place back then. She hadn't planned on her father's inability to stick around or her husband's interest in gambling money that wasn't his.

"Finally." Vera peered around the wall. The color had returned to her cheeks, and her smile was bright. She had fussed with her hair, and gloss painted her lips.

Autumn didn't want to go into the kitchen. She wanted to put her boots back on and go anywhere else.

Vera only fussed for one person. And Autumn didn't want to see him.

"Mom, look who's here." Quinn came around the corner, dragging Ives Thatcher with her. Quinn's smile could light up the biggest Christmas tree.

Autumn hadn't seen her father in almost a year. He had the sense to at least appear sheepish when Quinn introduced him. He had been her hero once. The tall man who could put her on his thin shoulders so she could see the floats in the town parade. He was always lanky, but he was strong and handsome. He also possessed charm in spades, charm he had spread around to as many women who would lap it up.

Ives was a con artist a lot like Markus Everett. Talk about almost marrying her father. Hell, she had married her father. Trent had tried to con the casinos. No one conquered that foe.

"Hi, honey," Ives said.

"What are you doing here?" She hung her coat up by the door. She kissed Quinn on the side of her head, dodged her father's outstretched hands, and began unloading the groceries.

The kitchen was warm, as if the oven had been on. A pile of fresh brownies were stacked on her mother's best cake plate. Two mugs sat abandoned at the table.

She would not ask how long Ives had been sitting in her house. Instead, she would get dinner started. The sooner she found out what her father wanted now, the better. Because he had to want something. He only came around when he did. When life for Ives was going well, no one heard from him. After he said his piece, then she could quickly tell him no way and send him along.

If she knew her mother, though, Vera had probably

asked him to stay for dinner and promised some huge, involved meal too. Vera always held out hope that her ex-husband would return to her. She never seemed to understand that Ives wasn't someone who stuck around.

"Your mother invited me." Ives tugged on the end of his sweater.

Her hand paused in midair. *Her mother?* She glanced at Vera, who busied herself with washing out the mugs.

"Mom, I'm going to run and do some homework. Will you call me when dinner is ready? You're staying for dinner. Right, Grandpa?"

"If your mom says it's okay."

He didn't miss a chance to make her the bad guy. "As long as we have enough." Dinner would have to be pasta and jarred sauce. A pound of spaghetti could feed four. Or she could say she wasn't hungry and make do with an egg. If she had one. She had never grabbed another carton after bumping into Jett and breaking the eggs in her basket.

"Perfect." Vera clapped her hands.

Quinn skipped out of the room.

With her daughter out of earshot, she could investigate the reason for this unexpected—and for her, unwanted—visit. "Why are you really here, Ives? What did my mother promise you?" She stole another glance at Vera, who only stared back stone-faced. She couldn't imagine what had possessed Vera to call Ives. Most of the time her mother verbalized her dislike for her ex-husband, but Autumn knew deep down that Vera held a torch for the man.

"Can't a guy come and visit his family?" Ives did a shuffle in place. His body always seemed to move of its own volition. She chalked it up to nerves.

"You're such a cynic, Autumn," Vera said, pulling down dinner dishes from the cabinet. "Your dad said he missed us when I called. I had to extend a simple invite for one dinner, didn't I?"

"But why did you call?" She could feel in her bones that Vera was up to something.

"Mom said you're selling the mountain."

Selling wasn't exactly a secret, but why did her mother feel a call to Ives was necessary? It wasn't as if he had the bankroll to give her the money. And he would never simply hand over a sum of that size. A very large, thick string would come attached.

"I'm selling the land that butts up to the mountain where we ski. No one owns the mountain." The mountain wasn't good for a whole lot except skiing and hiking in the warmer months. That's what made her property exceptional for a ski area and why one of her ancestors had purchased it long ago. Nothing could last forever. She only wished she hadn't been the one to lose it all.

"Why are you selling?" Ives took the last plate from Vera and placed it on the table.

Vera's cheeks bloomed red.

Autumn tried not to roll her eyes. "Because my father and my late husband didn't have a way with money. I'm out of options." She busied herself with putting up the water and gathering spices to add to the jarred sauce.

No point in sugarcoating her problems. When her parents were married, Ives had created large credit-card bills and stuck Vera with them. He claimed he had his reasons but eventually came back around and begged for forgiveness. Vera had obliged without much hesitation. He'd racked up debt two more times after. Vera had forgiven each one. Only after Ives had the affair with Karen Ryker had Vera sent him to the curb.

"Your money problems aren't because of me." Shock contorted his face. "I've been living on my own a long time now."

"Seriously? You think your wife dug herself out of your debt that quickly? We're still paying for your choices." She had to wonder if the shock on his face was legit or not. She turned back to the water in the pot for fear she might throw something.

"Let's not argue," Vera said. "Tonight let's have a family dinner like we used to. Tomorrow we can air out the dirty laundry."

"Tomorrow Ives is going to be long gone."

"I was thinking of staying in town a few days." He performed his little shuffle dance like a puppet on a string.

"Really? Where? The hotel out on the highway? The Hartman Bed-and-Breakfast?"

"Right here." Ives held her gaze. "You have the space. Unless your old mom here wants to share a bed again." He pulled Vera into a hug, pressing her against him.

Vera cackled with laughter and pushed Ives away.

If Autumn had been hungry at the grocery store, she wasn't now. Between Jett and her parents' nauseating display of affection, food had lost its appeal. "No way. You are not staying here."

"Come on, Autumn. It's only for a couple of nights. You can't hate your old dad that much. And Quinnie is excited I'm here. I'd like to spend some time with my granddaughter."

"Why are you really here? What did Vera promise you?" She had to get to the bottom of this unexpected visit. When her father was around, he only disrupted things for her by either asking for money or needing a place to stay until the turmoil of his life calmed down. Once, he'd put her house as his place of residence and had to live with her until his community service was up. He wasn't like other dads who helped and supported. He rarely cheered her on unless someone else was buying the booze.

Ives broke hearts and made promises he didn't keep. But boy, did she understand what women saw in him. Her dad was funny and smart. Scary smart. He had deep blue eyes that looked right through her. When she was a kid, she'd sworn her father could read her mind. Confidence rolled off him like a calm wave.

She had loved her father so much once. Until he left and broke her heart. He hadn't come back for her, didn't send her cards, didn't miss her, and that was too much to bear.

He knew what to say to a woman to make her soften—even if she started out skeptical—and open her arms, her bed, and often her wallet to him. She had witnessed her father, with lust-filled eyes, pull a wallflower onto the dance floor and sway with her. In the morning, that shy thing would ease out of his bedroom, emboldened.

Ives had gunned for Karen Ryker for years. Autumn had watched him make up reasons to go next door to pay a visit. When Jett was around, Ives always asked probing questions about Karen. She had paid no attention to him and his advances. At first, she'd had boys to raise. As those boys became men, she'd still had a business to run. But when that woman's world crashed down on her like a crumbling skyscraper, she hadn't been able to resist the polished charms of Ives Thatcher. He was a pro, and poor Karen had been broken and alone.

"Why can't I just invite your father to dinner?" Vera fisted her hands on her hips.

"Because he wouldn't come unless there was something in it for him. He never shows up without a motive."

"You're hurting your poor old dad's heart." Ives put his hands on his chest.

The man should have been in theater.

"I missed my daughter and granddaughter. Mom happened to call at the exact moment I was looking at old photos. Figured it was some kind of sign or some such thing. I have a few days between jobs. I decided to take a ride. But this place is so far out of the way I thought I'd stay and do some catching up. Maybe even a little skiing."

The truth would resemble something closer to he had time in between some big poker game or his next scam. She tried to picture him looking at photos of good times in the past. As much as she hated to admit it, they had shared a few good moments. Ice around her heart splintered a little, but she forced her guard to stay up. Trusting Ives could be dangerous. And she would pay for it, dearly. She also didn't want him disappointing Quinn. Her girl had enough of her own heartache.

"Come on. It's only for a couple of days. I promise to be on my best behavior." He held his palm up and cracked his most handsome smile.

She hated that he knew her so well, that she would

fall victim to his charm because she would always be that little girl wanting her daddy to love her.

"One night."

"One night it is," Ives said.

She was going to regret this.

****

Jett knocked on Gage's door. He didn't know what to do about the bomb Logan had dropped, and he needed some direction. Gage had moved into the guest cottage when Izzy was an infant and had never left. Raising a child wasn't easy, and Gage did it alone. Having his brothers and mother in shouting distance had helped him get on his feet.

Gage opened the door in his sweats and a pullover hoodie with *Backwater Police* on the chest. He and Gage were the same height with the same dark hair, though Gage's was streaked with a little gray. He wasn't sure when that had happened. He didn't like the idea of his brother aging. He needed Gage around forever.

"Hey, man. What are you doing here?" Gage stepped aside and waved him in.

Jett pulled off his knit cap and twisted it in his pocket. "Sorry to barge in. I was hoping to talk to you about something. Is anyone home?" He took a quick glance around but didn't see Izzy or Calista.

"Izzy is in her room, and Calista is at the B and B. She's sleeping there tonight to help her dad out. They have a full house. You want a beer?" Gage headed to the open kitchen.

All the guest houses were laid out with the same open-floor plan, fireplace in the living area, and two bedrooms down a hall. He always loved these cottages with their walls made of logs and the rustic feel of them against the mountain's backdrop.

"Is coffee too much trouble? It's too damn cold for a beer. I walked over." He slipped out of his coat and sank into the leather sofa. His shoulders sagged under the day's weight. He could really use the beer to relax a little, but his decision to hoof it had proved to be colder than he thought.

"Walked? Why didn't you drive?" Gage narrowed his eyes.

"Yeah, not my wisest of choices. I needed to clear my head." He needed to get Autumn off his mind. Bumping into her at the store brought back the memory of the kiss and how his body woke up when she wrapped her arms around his neck and kissed him as if her life depended on it. He would have kissed her all night if she hadn't pushed him away.

The accidental meeting also brought back the fact she believed he was using her. She didn't know him at all. She'd had her share of bad experiences with men. Markus Everett hadn't worked out. Her father was a shyster. And even her husband had let her down.

But he wasn't like all those men. If she didn't know that, then they could never be together. It had been a fool's mission to think for even a second he wanted another chance with a woman who believed all men were the same.

"What's clogging up that brain of yours?" Gage grabbed mugs and coffee pods.

"I have a kid on my ski team who came to me with a personal problem and wanted my advice. I'm not sure how to handle it." Talking about Logan would be easier than vocalizing his confusion about Autumn. In the end, they wouldn't be together. He needed to stop giving her so much of his time. Time he had little of.

"What kind of problem?" Gage handed him the mug of hot black coffee and went back to make another.

"Is this decaf?"

"You want caffeine at this hour?"

"I don't plan on sleeping." He hoped for some sleep tonight, but if he didn't get his mind straight, he'd be up walking the floorboards until the sun came up high enough he could go to the stables.

"Give me that." Gage took the mug back. "I won't ask who the kid is yet, but what was his problem? It was a him, wasn't it?"

"It's a him. He knocked up a girl."

"Oh boy. Are they the same age?" Gage handed him a new mug and took the seat opposite him. Gage would be the one worried about an age difference because of the statutory rape laws in Montana.

"Yeah. Consensual and old enough to know better. Just stupid. No condom." He took a sip, and bitter coffee burned his tongue. He drank more.

"In this day and age? I thought kids today were supposed to be smarter than us." Gage eyed him over his mug.

"They're smarter than Lock." Lock was a pretty smart guy, and the comment was only a joke. One he would make right in front of his brother, who might punch him in response, but that was how they communicated. He wouldn't change a thing about how he related to his brothers. Well, maybe when he got pretty pissed off at Kace this past fall, he could have handled that time better.

"True enough." Gage barked out a laugh. "What did you say to this athlete of yours?"

"I told him I would support whatever he did, but I couldn't tell him what to do."

"Well done. That's all you can do. You handled yourself the way you should have as a coach. Did he need something else?" Gage kicked up his socked feet on the coffee table.

"I think he was hoping I would give him a straight answer. You know, tell him exactly what to do. But after we talked for a while, I think he might have come around to the idea I can't say more than I did."

"I don't see the problem, then," Gage said.

"He also asked me not to tell his father."

Logan's request gnawed at him. He could understand wanting to keep secrets from his father. Everyone was entitled to their secrets. But Logan was a kid, and so was this girl. They needed their parents.

"You can't keep that secret. And if she tells her parents, his are bound to find out. Better he be the one to come clean before someone stops his father or mother on Main Street and congratulates them for becoming a grandparent." Gage pushed off the chair and went to the mantel. He grabbed a framed picture of all five Ryker boys on a Mother's Day about twenty-four years ago.

He had the same picture in his place. And Kace and Lock had one in theirs.

"It's hard to believe he's gone sometimes." Gage held the frame in his hand and glanced over his shoulder toward him.

He joined Gage and took the picture from his brother. They had worn white T-shirts and jeans and hired a photographer—all Gage's idea. He had hated every minute of the posing and Ajay's goofing around the whole time, but their mom had cried and hugged

153

them when she saw the photo. If he had known that Ajay would be gone shortly thereafter, Jett would have appreciated the moment more.

"Sometimes I'm going along doing my thing, minding my business, and the grief hits me like a truck out of nowhere. As if he just died, and it isn't two decades ago." Grief could rock him straight to his core. Sometimes, in ways he couldn't explain, the loss of his and Autumn's unborn child would sucker punch him too. He had never asked her if that happened to her. He never asked her about that time at all.

"Ajay kept secrets from us. It got him in a lot of trouble. The worst kind of trouble," Gage said.

"His secrets were bigger than getting his girlfriend pregnant. That one Mom would've stepped in and handled. She would've helped Ajay make the best choice he could at the time, and she would've loved him regardless of his decision. Dying at a gang initiation and taking Ava Hartman with him was far worse." He put the picture back on the mantel.

If his kid brother had come clean about his problems, he might still be alive. Knowing that Ajay could have chosen differently didn't mean Jett was in a position to decide how Logan should handle his issue. What if making the wrong choice ruined his life too?

If he could go back in time with the information he had now, would he make better choices than he had? Would he beg Autumn to stay with him instead of breaking it off? He had come to terms with the fact he could never have changed Ajay. Nothing he could have done differently would have saved his brother. Did that mean if he had begged Autumn to stay, she would still think the worst of him now?

"A secret is a secret. They serve no one well. He should tell his father. The dad is the best suited to help him." Gage returned to the sofa and grabbed his coffee.

"What if the dad isn't exactly the best one for the project?" He sat, too tired to keep standing. Even the caffeine wasn't doing its job.

"You know the dad?"

"Don't we know everyone?"

"It's a local kid, then. Not someone on the team from a surrounding town. What about the mom?"

He stared at Gage and hoped his on-the-ball brother would connect the dots himself. Gage had to know who most of the kids on the ski team were. And he did know just about every single family because he was the sheriff and he thought it was his job to help and protect those families as if they were his own.

"It's Logan Everett," Gage said without question.

"If I confirm it, do you promise to keep the secret?"

"Since you came here as my younger brother and not as a citizen reporting a crime, then yes, I can keep the secret."

"Thank you. It's Logan. I don't know who the girl is." But finding out wouldn't be too hard. He could probably ask Izzy to keep her ears open. Gossip like that didn't stay hidden. His limited experience with teens had taught him they expressed every thought they had.

"You can't tell Markus. At least not yet," Gage said.

"That's what I was thinking." He would encourage Logan to do it. Whenever Markus found out, he was pretty sure Markus would blow up. Markus had plans for his only son. A man who sought approval through the objects he collected would not approve of a detour like a baby. And if the girl's parents were religious and required her to have the baby or keep the baby, Markus would do everything in his power to sway the decision in his favor.

Markus would be the one to go so far as to sleep with someone for the outcome he wanted. Anger washed over him again. He stood up because sitting was out of the question.

"Thanks, man. I'm gonna go. I have to get up early. I have a group scheduled for a sunrise hike."

"Lock's not doing it?"

"He wants to do the fire-making workshop that runs almost at the same time. He's better at that than I am."

Gage walked him to the door. "Sometimes I think Lock would be happier living in the mountains by himself."

"Yeah, well, he can do that after I retire and Izzy takes over the ranch. Unless you and Calista plan on having more kids."

Gage scratched his head. "I've thought about it. But I'm getting old. I don't know if I can do it again."

He wasn't expecting that answer. He joked with Gage because until recently he was the only one in a serious relationship. Now Kace had joined him at that table, but Kace seemed more likely to have children than Gage, only because Izzy was closer to moving out than elementary school.

"You are the best man I know. Any kid would be lucky to have you as a father." He gripped Gage's shoulder.

"You're just saying that because it's late." Gage choked out a laugh.

"I'm saying it 'cause it's true. You helped raise all of us. We all come to you when we need something.

Look at me. Where did I go tonight? Right to my big brother."

"Can I ask you something?" Gage shoved his hands in the front pocket of his sweatshirt and gave him a sideways glance.

"Sure. Anything."

"You've got this Logan thing all figured out. You didn't show up so late to ask me about that. There's something else you need. What did you really come here to talk about?"

"That was it."

"If you say so. But if you want to change your mind, I can listen."

"Nothing to talk about." He shoved his hat on for the walk back.

"All right then. Night."

"See you." Jett closed the door behind him.

He stared at the door, tempted to knock again. He had come here looking for direction, but he was more confused than before. Not about Logan. He was pretty certain he had done all he could do for the kid.

He was more confused about the woman who drove him crazy.

He lifted his fist but stopped midair. It could wait. Autumn was a story for another time.

Chapter Fifteen

One night had turned into two. Autumn gripped her coffee mug between both hands and contemplated how her father had managed another night. Because he was very good at what he did—that's how.

Quinn had been head over heels when she found out her grandpa was sticking around. They'd played board games that kept her up way too late on a school night. He had picked her up at school the next day and taken her straight to the diner for ice cream floats, which had become dinner, much to her dismay. Then Quinn and Grandpa had shared a blanket on the couch and watched two of her favorite movies.

Autumn fought the emotion trying to surface with persistence, but her father was doing a damn good job of making her daughter happy. Staying mad at him was proving to be difficult when she saw the joy on her daughter's face. Quinn used to do those things with Trent. Trent had been a good father in many ways, probably because he had a severe case of Peter Pan syndrome. *Huh*. Much like her father.

Daybreak tinted the sky a deep pink. Everyone would be up soon. She cherished these quiet moments before the rush of the day hit. A group of four skiers were actually scheduled for the slope. After their full day of skiing, she would be going to Markus's to make dinner for him and Logan. That would require another trip to the store for the things she would need, and hopefully she wouldn't bump into Jett again. Her mother had promised to handle dinner here. Vera relished the idea of cooking for Ives. When Autumn suggested Vera prepare dinner, she had practically twirled in her spot.

Even with the heater working—for now—the house was still cold because she couldn't afford to run the heat above sixty-seven. If she were going to be cold, she might as well be outside where the snow resided and hot breath clouded the icicle air. She took her coffee out to the front porch and dropped into the old rocker with its worn paint and rough wood. Someday she would sand this thing down and restain it. But she could never get rid of it because it had been a Christmas present from Jett. He had found it at a garage sale, sanded it, and stained it for her because he knew how much she had enjoyed sitting on the porch of this very house and dreaming about her future. He had promised her once he would find a second one for him.

An unoiled hinge creaked and groaned as someone opened the front door. Her quiet morning was about to splinter from the invasion.

"Good morning, Snowflake." Her father greeted her with his charming smile. He was already dressed in a red cable-knit sweater over a pair of black corduroys. His eyes danced with energy as if he knew a secret and couldn't wait to tell it. Which he probably did. Like the real reason he was here.

He hadn't called her Snowflake in decades. As a little girl, she had loved the nickname because each winter when the first sign of snow would arrive, they would hurry outside and catch snowflakes on their tongues. He always pretended his tasted of peppermint.

She would try every winter to find the snowflakes that held the magical taste, but she never could. Around the age of ten, she'd figured out he made it up. And she loved him anyway.

She didn't want the warm memory on this cold morning. She needed to stay sharp and alert where Ives Thatcher was concerned. If she relented even a little, she would soften and he would swindle her while her lids were heavy with contentment and her body soft like warm jam.

"You're up early." She pushed out of the rocker to take away his height advantage.

"I thought I'd make breakfast this morning. Do you have a waffle maker?" He glanced past her toward the Ryker Ranch.

She forced her gaze to remain forward, having no need to follow his lead, but maybe having a want or two. She couldn't shake Jett. "No waffle maker."

"Oh. Well, how about some scrambled eggs, then?" Another glance past her.

This time she couldn't let it go. "Are you looking for something over there?"

He straightened his shoulders. "Not at all. Just admiring the beauty of the trees outlined in snow. This property was always breathtaking."

"That's one thing I can agree with. Will you be heading out today?" She was ready to have her life back in its ordinary routine and see Ives slink away under his rock.

He leaned against the railing and picked at a spot of peeling paint. "I think I'm going to stick around in Backwater a few more days. I know you said only the one night, and you were kind enough to give me another.

I won't burden you with any more of my presence here. I've rented a room at the bed-and-breakfast. They fixed it up recently. It's very nice. Have you been over there?"

She didn't want him in town. Backwater was her home, and he dragged trouble around like toilet tissue on the bottom of a shoe. After he'd left town, her life morphed into the quiet kind of existence most people didn't look twice at. She preferred flying under the radar, not worrying about what her father would do next and how it would embarrass her.

She never had a lot of friends in school because everyone in town knew Ives and thought their children might not be safe when he was around. He wasn't always the most attentive adult, and children often found ways to stumble into trouble when he left her and her friends unsupervised.

The affair with Karen Ryker had burned through town like yellow fever. Everyone had heard. Everyone covered their mouths and whispered when she or Vera went by. Vera couldn't take it, and she couldn't pretend that indiscretion hadn't happened—like all the others. Ives and Karen were as juicy as an old Hollywood love affair. Everyone wanted to know what would happen next.

The gossip rolled right off Karen's Teflon back. Who was going to judge a woman who had recently lost her son? Everyone understood her mistake. And it wasn't as if she were the one who was married. Vera, on the other hand, had been tried and convicted as the woman who couldn't handle her man.

"You're going to stay at the bed-and-breakfast? I don't understand why. What's here for you?"

"My family." And yet another glance in the

direction of the ranch.

"And Karen Ryker. You're hoping she'll give you another chance. That's it. Isn't it?" She could think of no other reason.

He stared at her with wide eyes. For once, nothing came out of his mouth.

"You know what? Don't answer that. Just make sure Mom understands you aren't here for her. I don't want to have to pick up her pieces again when you disappear one day because Karen Ryker wanted nothing to do with you. Because she won't."

She had no idea what Karen wanted or didn't want. It wasn't as if they had ever discussed it. She would like to think Karen had more sense than to make the same mistake twice. But then again, Ives could sell snow to a Montana ski area owner in the middle of winter.

Her coffee had grown cold. She left him on the porch, needing to get her day underway. Voices carried from the kitchen. Vera and Quinn chatted around the island as the sulfur smell of eggs hung in the air. Vera had beaten Ives to the punch, unless he had never had any intention of making breakfast and had only used that excuse to come outside and tell her his plans.

A pink flush of color brightened Vera's cheeks as she smiled at Quinn. Neither of them had noticed her yet, giving her a moment to wonder if Ives's presence was putting a little joy in her mother's life. Vera had very little and was about to lose her family's legacy. Life hadn't been kind to Vera, and she had been nasty right back. Autumn pitied her mother for the briefest of moments.

Enough of that. "Good morning," she said into the room.

Vera and Quinn turned. Vera's lips dropped that smile as if it were hot. "Good morning." She turned back to the pan on the stove.

"Hi, Mom. Do you want any eggs?" Quinn held out an empty plate as if it were an invitation to a party.

"No, thank you. I'm not hungry. I can drive you to school today, if you'd like."

"I'm catching a ride to school with Emily this morning. But thanks." Quinn grabbed a piece of toast and trotted out of the kitchen but then came back. "Oh, Coach Ryker canceled practice today. The ski team won't be here, so I'm going to go to Emily's after school to study. Love you." And like a flash of bright lightning, she was gone. Her footsteps pounded up the steps.

"Call your father in from the porch. The eggs are ready, and he's going to catch his death from the cold. The man never wears a jacket." Vera busied herself with arranging a plateful of food.

"He's a grown man, Mom. He can wear a coat or not. It's up to him. And he can come in when he wants. I have to get dressed. I have a busy day."

"You're sending him away." Vera turned and glared at her. She brandished the spatula in her fist.

"I don't want him here. And neither should you. He can't be trusted, but for some unknown reason you dragged the devil out of bed."

"You're being melodramatic. Of course, your father has flaws. I'm well aware of what they are. But he's far from the devil. He was lonely. He wanted to see his family. He isn't getting any younger. None of us are." Vera turned back to the pan and cracked a few more eggs.

Autumn had no idea who the woman was cooking

for because no one else was here, but she stayed silent. Arguing with her mother was pointless. She headed for her room without another word.

Her father came in and brought a blast of cold air with him. He banged his feet and shivered in his sweater. "It's cold."

"You think? It's Montana." She shook her head and dashed past him.

Rummaging through the laundry basket of clean clothes for underwear and socks that matched, she wondered why Jett had canceled practice. She could shoot him a quick text since it was her mountain they practiced on and she had the right to know whether or not to expect them. But Quinn had told her, taking away her excuse. Jett's reasons were his business.

Kissing him had torn open her heart. No amount of stitching it back together would work. She was never going to stop loving him.

She needed another buyer and fast. It was more than time to sell the land and move away so she could forget about Jett and the way her body responded when he was anywhere nearby.

Her father had added a reason to put space between her and Backwater. If he decided to stick around for longer than a week, she might lose her mind.

Moving out of town would crush Quinn, taking her from her friends, her school, and her ski team. She would have to get over it. That's all. Weren't kids resilient?

Autumn would call Dottie Lucier later today, after she got to Markus's, and tell her to hurry up and find another buyer. Any buyer.

****

Jett hesitated outside the diner. Once he went in, he

could not unlearn or unhear what was waiting for him. When he signed up to be coach of this ski team, he'd never dreamed he'd also have to be counselor and secret keeper too. Logan had requested another meeting, and this time he would bring the girlfriend.

Meeting the teenager wasn't going to change Jett's decision to support from the sidelines. But he couldn't tell Logan no. He had even canceled practice to make this happen. Logan had suggested, if anyone asked, that they were discussing Logan's future opportunities in skiing and this afternoon was the only available time. Jett hated lying. Somehow this would come back to bite him in the ass.

On a long breath, he pulled open the door and took a step. Only to stop in his tracks. His mother sat at the counter in deep conversation with Ives Thatcher. Ives leaned near Karen, his lips moved, but Jett couldn't hear what he said.

Karen smirked but pushed Ives away. He slid on the stool beside her, facing her as if waiting for some response. When had Ives returned, and why hadn't Autumn told him? More importantly, what did Ives want with his mother? He was about to find out.

"Coach Ryker." Logan waved from his booth by the window.

Karen spun in her seat. Her blue eyes widened to the size of a cylinder hay bale. She grabbed the cup beside her and walked over to him. "Hi, honey. What are you doing here?"

"I could ask you the same thing, Mom." He eyed Ives over his mother's head. Ives had turned back to the counter.

Logan waved again. Jett gave him the one-minute

sign in return.

"Apparently, Ives is in town for a few weeks. I had no idea until about ten minutes ago. Thank you for saving me. I was trying to get rid of him." Karen lowered her voice.

He hoped that was true. "What did he want?"

"Nothing in particular. I'm assuming he was gearing up to ask me out. Which I don't want." She adjusted her glasses.

"If he bothers you, I'm going to have Gage arrest him."

"Stop that. I can handle Ives."

"Like last time?"

"Jett Lawrence Ryker, I am still your mother. My past love life in all its good and bad is my business. I don't interfere in your or your brothers' personal lives. I expect the same in return."

"Really? Did you not offer relationship advice to both Gage's and Kace's girlfriends about your sons?" His mother always offered her opinion even when it wasn't requested. He almost laughed out loud but would never. The message under the use of his full name was clear. He had walked up to the one line he could not cross with her.

"That was different. Those women just needed a little encouragement to trust themselves. It wasn't as if I played matchmaker. And never mind any of that. I don't want you getting involved where Ives is concerned. I can handle him. You keep your sights on Autumn." She patted his arm.

He bit back the next remark about Autumn accusing him of using her. "I have a meeting with one of my athletes. I've got to go. Just watch your back, okay?"

"I'll be fine. But if for some reason I need rescuing, I will call out to my boys for help."

"Thank you." He would have to tell his brothers about this new development. It couldn't hurt for Gage to keep a watch on Ives just in case the man broke some Backwater law only Gage knew about—or could make up.

She squeezed his arm and walked out. He fought the urge to warn Ives to stay away from his mother, but he respected her wishes and passed him without so much as a word. Instead, he slid into the booth opposite Logan and his girlfriend.

"That was your mom, right?" Logan said.

"Yeah. Sorry about the delay. She had some urgent ranch business to tell me about."

"Coach, this is Maya. Maya, Coach Ryker." Logan beamed at his girlfriend. That kid had it bad.

"Hello," she said. Her gaze dropped to her lap where her hands were. Her dark, curly hair fell over her face. She worked her bottom lip under her teeth. The glass of soda in front of her was still full, but Logan's was mostly empty.

Either she didn't feel the same way about Logan as he did her, or this young lady was scared out of her mind. Jett would vote for the second option because she had agreed to come here, unless Logan had persuaded her. He could be more like his father than Jett realized. Markus was very good at persuading people to do his bidding.

He couldn't be sure, but Maya's chin might have trembled. Logan put an arm around her shoulders, but she sat straight in her seat.

"How can I help you both?" He might as well get

this conversation over with.

Jenna Jones sauntered over, pulling her pad out of her apron. She had a habit of wearing clothes that revealed more than anyone needed to see. Even in the winter, her pink sweater dipped to the valley of her breasts and her black leggings reported her underwear line.

"Hey, Jett. What can I get you?" Jenna said.

"Coffee, please. Black."

"Nothing else?" She glanced between him and the kids.

"Not for now. Thanks."

She rambled off with an eye roll and a shake of her head. He wasn't sure, but she might have muttered something about a bad tip and a waste of her table.

"The waitress is going to be back soon. I'll wait to say why we asked you here until after she brings you your coffee," Logan said.

On cue, Jenna dropped off the coffee and returned to her spot by the counter.

"Okay, Logan. Let's hear it."

"We've made a decision. We're going to elope."

He choked on his coffee. "Aren't you two a little young to get married?"

"We're both seventeen," Logan said. "We can get married in Idaho with parental consent."

"Then you've told your parents." He didn't understand what he was doing there.

"Maya told hers, but I haven't said anything to my dad yet. I was wondering if you would give consent for me to get married. Maya's sister is twenty. She's going to sign the papers as Maya's mother, giving her consent to the marriage."

He did not hear that right. "Say again?"

Maya raised her gaze and held his. Her dark eyes shone with a fierceness. "Mr. Ryker, Logan and I want to get married and have our baby. My parents don't want me to become a mother. They will never agree to allow us to marry, but in Idaho we can get married with a parent's consent. We're ready to have a family."

He shrugged out of his jacket, suddenly too hot. These two weren't thinking clearly. They were kids themselves. "You aren't even out of high school. Have you thought about how you'll support yourselves? Where are you going to live?"

If he could spill this secret, he would grab Cullum Durrell by the collar and shake him until his eyes rolled out of his head for asking him to be the damn ski coach. He figured he would train a few kids, take them to the competition, maybe have to cut one or two and then be on his way. Now he was turning into a parent, a counselor, and what next? Godparent?

He needed something stronger than coffee.

"We haven't worked out all the details yet, but we plan on finishing high school. Maya wants to be a hair stylist, and I'm still going to go to college on my scholarship."

"Once we're married, our parents will have to get on board," Maya said.

"Do you think that's how it works? Your parents are just going to cave because you gave them no choice?"

"Why wouldn't they?" Maya said.

He doubted that would be the case. His mother wouldn't have. Gage wouldn't. "I realize I'm not a parent. My advice might not be the most helpful. Can I bring my brother Gage in to talk to you two? He can give you a lot of insight about being a young and single parent. He raised his daughter by himself because his wife couldn't handle being a mother. It's not as easy as it seems."

"He's just going to talk us out of it. Like our parents," Maya said.

"If all these people tell you it's a bad idea, isn't it worth considering?" How was he going to stop this from derailing?

"Logan, let's go. I told you he wouldn't do it. We'll have to find someone else." Maya pushed Logan out of the booth.

"Coach, would you think about it?" Logan looked down at him with disappointment across his face. "If my mom were still alive, I know she'd agree. You knew her. I can't let her grandchild be in the world without me."

"I thought you didn't want to have the baby." It was a last-ditch effort, and shooting below the belt, but he didn't know what else to do.

"I've changed my mind." Logan pressed his lips into a thin line and shrugged.

Maya shoved Logan again. They hurried out of the diner.

His tongue had turned to dust. What the hell was he going to do now? He couldn't go behind Logan's back and speak with his father. Hell, he didn't want to talk to Markus about anything, least of all his kid. But how, as a coach and a mentor, could he allow two seventeen-year-olds to make a mistake like getting married? He hadn't signed up for this. It might be time to quit.

"Jenna, do you have that to-go order?" A female voice drifted toward him, a voice he often heard in his sleep.

He tossed a few dollars on the table and grabbed his jacket. "Hi, Autumn."

She stared up at him, her face devoid of emotion. "Hey, Jett. We keep bumping into each other."

"Small town. Can I talk to you a minute?" Maybe she would understand his dilemma, and considering they'd been in a similar circumstance once, maybe she would have insight into what he should tell these kids. Of course, the big difference was he and Autumn had been twenty, not seventeen. And though three years wasn't a lot of time, they were legally adults with parents who had supported their decision. Except for Vera. Even before his mother's affair, Vera had never sung his praises.

"I don't have time. I have an appointment." She rummaged in her bag and pulled out her wallet.

He wanted her to look at him, but he was powerless to do anything about it. Staying away from her all these years, as best he could, was how he had survived being without her. All he ever wanted was for her to look at him the way she used to before he had ruined everything and sent her away. If he didn't have to see the emptiness in her eyes when she looked at him, then he would be able to go on with life. But now their lives intersected in a way he hadn't planned, and he had the desire to connect with her in a meaningful way again.

Jenna came out with a large brown paper bag stapled together between the handles. "Here ya go, hon. That'll be sixty-five twenty."

Autumn handed over her credit card.

"Are you entertaining?" What she did was none of his business, but he couldn't help asking. She was in a bit of a financial crisis. Spending a lot of money on takeout might not be her best option.

"Something like that."

He didn't like that answer. Did all this food have to do with her *appointment*? "Can I come by later after your appointment?"

"No. It will have to wait until tomorrow's practice. I'll come out while the kids are skiing. I can talk for a few minutes then. Take care, Jett." Autumn scooped up her bag and hurried out the door.

Jenna arched her brow.

"What's that look for?"

"What's going on between you and Autumn?"

"Mind your own business, Jenna."

She threw her hands in the air. "Sorry to intrude. But you might want to know that she's taking that food to Markus Everett's house."

That news sucker punched him in the throat, and he hoped his face didn't give away his shock. "Why would I want to know that?"

"Old competitions, maybe. I might be taking a leap here, but if you're looking to talk to her about something important, I think you should know what you're up against."

"Well, thanks, but I'm not interested in Autumn's personal life. Haven't been in a very long time. Night."

"Whatever you say."

He pushed out into the cold and scanned the parking lot, but Autumn's truck had ceased to exist. She was long gone to wherever she was headed. He had half a mind to drive past Markus Everett's house and prove Jenna wrong. Autumn wouldn't be having dinner there. She was done with Everett.

Or was it another case of him pushing her away and

straight into Everett's arms? History had a funny way of repeating itself.

And he would get to the bottom of it.

His phone rang from inside his jacket. He dug it out because if it was a call and not a text, something important must be happening at the ranch.

"Lock, what's up?"

"It's Silver Bell. You need to come now."

He ran for his truck.

Chapter Sixteen

Snow drifted in slow sweeps, coating everything it landed on with its thin dust. Little accumulation was expected tonight. For that, Jett was relieved.

Pine trees whispered their goodbyes in the wind. He and Lock stood together with enough light from the snow to see Silver Bell, lying down as if she were asleep.

Any other night, Jett might appreciate the beauty of the open field and nearby trees dotted with white. But not tonight. He fought the emotions churning in his stomach that desperately wanted to be set free in the form of a howl so loud it would reach the mountaintop. He didn't have time to indulge in the pain this loss carried. He had things to do now. Grieving would come later when he was alone.

"Kace is coming with the tractor and the backhoe," Lock said. "He borrowed them from Johnny D who said he can be here with a couple other guys to help."

Lock wasn't saying anything Jett didn't already know. They had plans in place for each of their horses when the time came. Lock needed to fill the space with his rambling noise because he would be fighting his grief too.

They were used to animals passing away. But Silver Bell wasn't any animal. She was family.

"Did you call Mom?" Jett asked. His mother would take this loss hard too. She had been avoiding Silver Bell recently. He suspected it had to do with his mother's avoiding the inevitable. Without Silver Bell on the ranch, they didn't have their last tangible connection to Ajay.

"I called her," Lock said. "She doesn't want to come out here. Said she can't see Bell this way. I didn't argue with her." Lock shoved his hands into his barn jacket. He wasn't wearing a hat. The snow landed on his head, stark against his black hair.

"Better not to. What about Gage?" Gage would not handle this loss well either. They couldn't rely on Gage or their mom to hold them up. It would be his job this time. He was the head rancher. He could take care of the people who would feel the pain the deepest.

Lock scratched his neck. "I wasn't sure Gage should hear it over the phone. I called Calista instead. She said she'd go over to the cottage and tell him in person. He should be here soon."

"Smart. When did you bring her outside?" If Silver Bell had passed in the stall, they would have had to take the stable apart to get her out. Even in her death, that horse looked out for them.

"I suspected we were closer to the end than we had been. I wasn't sure it would be today. I would've called you sooner if I had, but she hadn't eaten all day. It was her idea to come out here. She didn't want to stay in the stall. So I took her for a walk, and that settled her down. She seemed to want to stay outside after that. I left her for a couple of hours to take care of a few guest issues. It was like she knew she was alone now and could go without anyone watching. When I came back and saw her lying down, I knew too."

A beam of light bounced toward them, slicing the dark at angles.

"No, no, no." Gage dropped to his knees, letting the flashlight roll out of his grasp. He ran his hands through his hair and rocked on his heels. He must have run the whole way from his cottage, and he hadn't bothered with a coat. Snow coated his shirt.

"I'm sorry, man." Jett patted Gage on the shoulder.

"It's like losing Ajay all over again. I knew it would be hard, but I didn't think I would react this way." Gage pushed to stand and brushed the snow from his legs.

"She's with Ajay now." He would like to think that was the case. His Kootenai heritage told him that was the case. Hearing that might give Gage some peace, and he wanted that for his brother. Hell, he wanted that for himself.

Losing Silver Bell was the rip in his soul he'd expected. Knowing her time was coming and had been for many months didn't make the pain any less or easier to deal with. She had outlived all the horses bought for each Ryker boy when he was born. She had done them well, and he loved her for sticking around as long as she could to make sure they all made it well into adulthood.

"And Dad. They're both with Dad," Lock said.

Lock had only been six when their father passed away unexpectedly. Gage, Kace, and Jett had shared what stories they knew about their father to help keep him alive in Lock's mind because Lock had so few memories of his own.

"Dad too. They're all together, having a good time because Ajay wouldn't have it any other way. He's probably already saddling up Silver Bell." Gage threw an arm around Lock's shoulders and pulled him close.

Lock leaned his head on Gage's shoulder and for the briefest of moments, Jett could see them as kids again.

Gage always tried to be the strong oldest brother who comforted and supported, and Lock leaned on Gage for that support.

"The ground's frozen. We should wait until tomorrow when the day warms up to bury her." Gage kept his arm around Lock's shoulder.

"We'll bury her out on the edge of the property away from the creek where even if we sell this land someday, no one is ever likely to build there," Jett said. Owning as many acres as they did gave them that option. If they were too close to town or where people might live, they wouldn't be able to bury her there. They would need a service to come and take her.

"Why don't you two go back? I'll wait for Kace and the tractor." Jett wanted to sit for a while out here in the peace and quiet, and he was the one responsible for the animals on the ranch.

"If you don't mind, I would like to stay with her. I need to say goodbye, and Calista went to get Izzy. She wants to see her," Gage said.

"Is that a good idea? Seeing a big horse like Silver Bell, lying on the ground and not getting up, might be too much for her," he said.

"She's a rancher's granddaughter and niece. She'll be fine. It's what she needs to do. I'll make sure she goes inside when Kace is ready to move Silver Bell. But thanks for worrying about her."

"Are you going to be okay, watching that backhoe move her?" Lock said to Gage.

"It's not like I haven't seen a horse buried before. It was my horse we had to put down and push into the grave we dug."

"Yeah, but this is Silver Bell," Lock said.

"I realize I'm more upset than I thought I would be. I wanted her to live forever, but that's not real life."

"She tried to live forever," he said.

"She sure did. So, if you guys are okay with me staying until Kace comes, I'd appreciate it." Gage waited for their answer.

Lock handed Gage the shotgun that had been leaning against a nearby tree. "Just in case any predatory animals get her scent."

Gage took the gun and nodded. They all had been trained to use a long gun from an early age and repeatedly took classes and practiced at the outdoor range. Even Kace, who spent most of his time behind the wheel of a car, was a solid shot, but no one took gun safety more seriously than Gage, considering his line of work.

"Call if you change your mind and don't want to be alone." Jett stuck his hand out to Gage, who shook. Jett didn't want to fall apart in front of his brothers, but each moment out here proved to be more difficult than the last one.

Lock threw his arms around Gage, who patted Lock on the back. "You're going to be okay, big guy," Gage said, using the old term of endearment he saved for when Lock was a boy and needed some male guidance.

Jett and Lock left their big brother out on the hill with another family member lost to them and headed back toward the main house.

"This sucks." Lock shoved his hands in his pockets again.

"It does. But it's the way of life." Still, his heart hurt for this one. He wished he could call Autumn and tell her about it. She would be the person who would know what to say to him.

"Doesn't make it suck less. Never does."

"Nope." He bumped shoulders with Lock to let him know he was there if Lock needed him. They didn't have to say the words. They had been side by side since Jett was four. Lock was his shadow and sometimes had been damn annoying.

Lock was the sensitive one in the group of them. He wore his heart all over his sleeve in a bleeding mess when it came to most things. His heartbreaks were long and hard. He took every death on the ranch personally. And when a woman broke his heart, he almost didn't bounce back.

"Do you ever get tired of this business?" Lock said, hunkering down farther in his coat.

"Not a single day. You?" Jett had plenty of moments when he had questioned his decision to take over the family business, like last summer when they got sued by a guest because of the man's own negligence. Or when feed prices for the horses went up, or they had a slow season, and it seemed no one wanted to come to a guest ranch in Montana. But most days he was the luckiest man in the world to live on this land and be surrounded by the constant of the mountains and the vast sky with his family nearby.

And on those occasions when he missed the soft arms of a woman, he sought someone out to soothe the need. He didn't long for a woman. But there was one woman he wanted, and she didn't seem to feel the same way anymore. His fault. He had taken too damn long to get around to telling her. And might never have if it hadn't been for the ski school needing him.

"When too many things go wrong in a row, then I

wonder what I'm doing here. Like the burglary last summer or that time we gave our guests food poisoning. Or when the roof breaks and the plow dies in the same week. Then I envy Gage and Kace their alternate careers and wonder why I didn't do that too."

"Because you can't be off this land any more than I can. And for the reasons you like being the owner of a guest ranch, the guests who send us letters about their family vacation or how we made them feel like family. We do a good job of making people happy. Giving back feels good."

"Seems strange, doesn't it, that we were never a typical cattle ranch? You think we would've been." Lock blew on his hands and rubbed them together.

"This worked out better. People need their vacations. And we don't deal with the hectic life of raising and moving cattle." The cold was getting to him too now that the shock of seeing Silver Bell was over. He was glad his grandfather had picked people over cattle. Giving a person what they wanted created less worry and easier results than watching cattle prices decrease at auction or an illness wipe out a herd in no time.

"People are hectic too and entitled. We've had guests act as if I'm as dumb as a bale of hay, and they talk to me that way until I slide into the conversation that I'm the owner. Sometimes I wonder what a different life would look like."

"You thinking about leaving?" They arrived at the main house with no word yet from Kace. Jett couldn't lose Lock. They were a team that worked well together.

"Not today."

"Just make sure to give me some notice so I can replace you." He rested on humor to change the subject of something he never wanted to talk about. Someday, when they were too old for this business, they'd have to decide what to do, but he wouldn't worry about the end of the Ryker Ranch until then.

"Yeah, who are you going to replace me with?" Lock poked his thumb against his chest.

"I don't know. Some big dumb lug looking to make a few bucks."

Lock shoved him, and he stumbled back because Lock didn't always know how strong he was. But Jett didn't mind.

"I'm going to walk back to Gage. You don't have to come back. Let me take care of Silver Bell," Lock said.

"It's my responsibility."

"Maybe. But I want to do this for you and for Gage. It's not just strangers I want to help. I want to help my actual family. And whether or not you want to say it, I know losing Silver Bell is tearing you up. You don't need to see them lay her down. I'll come get you after she's taken care of. We'll have a proper burial."

"Lock—"

"No way, Jett. I won't let you try and big brother me into this. And I don't care that your name is first on the deed of this land or on all the contracts we sign. I'm taking care of Silver Bell. And you're going to let me because that's what brothers do."

He opened his mouth to argue but shut it again. Lock was right. And for all his pretending he could handle losing Silver Bell as if she were any other horse, he needed to be alone. At least for now.

"Thanks, little brother." He stuck out his hand.

Lock yanked him into a tight bear-size hug and squeezed him until his feet left the ground.

"Love you," Lock muttered under his breath and ran before he could say *I love you* back.

Chapter Seventeen

In Backwater, word traveled faster than a roller coaster out of control. Autumn shoved her feet into her boots. A phone call wouldn't do this time. What she needed to say had to be done in person.

"Are you going over there?" Ives stood by the front door.

She was pretty sure he wasn't trying to stop her. He had been the one to knock on her bedroom door to tell her that Jett's horse had passed away a couple of hours ago. Ives had been at the B and B when the call came in to Calista, who had hurried out to find Gage. Calista's dad, Andrew, told Ives what had happened. Ives had come straight here and let himself in through the back where the lock didn't work and any random person could come into her home. Good thing she lived in Backwater, Montana.

"He must be devastated." She wound her scarf around her neck. Jett would never admit how upset he would be. He would hold it against his chest and carry it with him until one day he found himself alone, and then maybe he would release his grief.

That wasn't healthy, and he shouldn't carry the burden by himself. That horse was more than a horse for that family. That horse symbolized the life Ajay Ryker lost, and now Ajay would be lost to them for good.

"They all must be," Ives said with a distant look in

his eyes. He would know how much this death would affect this family. He might be a con artist, but he wasn't stupid.

"Stay away from Karen." She grabbed her keys. His heart might be in the right place, but Karen didn't need him slinking around, playing on her vulnerabilities.

"I will. And I'll cover for you if your mother asks where you are."

She paused and looked long and hard at him, expecting to find a smirk of insincerity, but his face was grave and his eyes sad. He could be exactly what she needed him to be in rare moments. Too bad those moments weren't consistent. "Thank you."

"This might not be the best time to bring it up, but I don't want to keep it from you any longer," he said.

"Can it wait?" She wanted to get to Jett's before it became any later.

"It's waited too long. I should've said something sooner, but I didn't know how. I guess the Rykers' horse dying made me think how we waste so much time in this life. Weird for a horse's death to do that, but I guess it has to do with Karen's son Ajay really. He never got to live his life, and here I am an old man now, wasting so much of mine."

"Dad, this sounds like a big revelation coming. Can we talk about it in the morning?"

"We can talk details then. But I want you to know I can save your property if you want me to."

"Excuse me?"

"I can buy the land from you. I have the money now. You don't have to find another buyer. It can stay in the family. For Quinnie. You can pay me back or not. It's up to you. What do you think?"

"I think you're picking the worst time to spring this on me." She had a million questions, none of which she had the time to voice. Jett would need someone to be there for him. She wanted to be that person.

"My timing was always bad." He choked out a laugh. "Just think about it for a few days. We can talk later." He gripped her shoulder, then stepped away from the door.

"Thanks for understanding. We'll talk in a day or two." She slipped out the door without another word.

Her mind reeled from this announcement. Could she possibly sell her land to her father? That would keep it in the family, which she wanted, but did she want to continue to run the ski area? It was becoming increasingly harder each year.

She hurried to Jett's place. Taking the truck was a little longer than walking through the woods. The hour was late and the temperatures freezing. Snow had stopped but had fallen just enough to cover branches that could be sticking out of the ground. She didn't need an injury too.

What would she do if she began a new career? And what would she do if her father owned her land? He could always sell it out from under her without warning. Or gamble it away. But if she sold to him, then she wouldn't have to sell to Jett or anyone else. She could keep her family's land and her pride intact. What would her mother say when she found out? Vera had been thrilled to have Ives around. Ives's owning the land would also mean he would most likely stay in Backwater. Her head spun with all the things to consider.

She parked in the back of the main house beside Jett's truck and knocked on the door that led straight to his apartment upstairs. She didn't want to come in through the front in case anyone was around and wondered what she was doing there so late.

Cold seeped from the cement stoop and right into her boots. She stamped her feet to keep warm and knocked again. No answer.

She sent a text.

—*Are you home?*—

If he didn't come to the door or answer her text in the next two minutes, she would have to leave. He might not even be here. He could be out in the stables—the stables. She prayed Silver Bell hadn't passed away in her stall. Or he could be in the fields dealing with this new loss. She would send another text saying she was here for him. She could always find him tomorrow.

The door swung open. Her finger hovered above her phone. Jett blinked a few times and scratched at his arm. His dark hair was ruffled. His long-sleeve white Henley opened at the neck and revealed a pinch of dark chest hair. The shirt hugged his muscular torso. A pair of blue sweatpants hung loose on his narrow hips. His feet were bare. She had to swallow the arousal climbing up her throat and about to burst out of her mouth in the form of a whistle.

"What's the matter?" he said with gravel in his voice.

"Did I wake you?" She hadn't thought about that possibility either. She had known she had to get to him, and that was it. Logic hadn't factored into her decision to come here at all.

"I fell asleep on the couch. Is something wrong?" He craned his neck above her head and searched the small parking lot.

"That's what I came here to find out. I heard about Silver Bell. I'm so sorry."

"You heard…this damn town." He shook his head. "Come inside. I'm freezing here." He stepped aside and let her in.

She followed him up the steps, trying to keep her gaze off his backside, but those sweatpants outlined his firm butt in all the right places. He pushed open the door but waited for her to enter first. Even half-asleep he was chivalrous.

"Can I get you anything?" He went into the kitchen and popped a coffee pod into the machine.

She hadn't been in this apartment in years. Jett had renovated it. The kitchen gleamed with stainless-steel appliances and a dark shiny counter. The cabinets were a dark wood. Everything in here yelled of masculinity with his leather furniture and wood tables. The large-screen television hung on the wall.

"Isn't it a little late for coffee?" She unzipped her coat and unraveled her scarf. The space was warm, or maybe it was her being so close to Jett indoors.

"I can drink it and fall back asleep." He held up a mug and raised a brow.

"Decaf?" She wandered over to the stone fireplace. It looked like something out of the eighteen hundreds, solid and strong like its owner. The wooden mantel—she was almost certain it must be repurposed wood—was bare without a speck of dust on it.

"Only at Gage's house. I do have hot chocolate." He opened and closed a few cabinet doors. His muscles flexed under the cover of that shirt, which wasn't leaving a whole lot to the imagination.

"You do?" She had to admit she was surprised. She

discarded her coat and draped her things over the chair.

"Izzy makes me keep it for her." He tossed a lopsided grin her way.

Her knees wobbled under its hypnotic powers. "You're good to your niece. You're good to all the kids on the ski team too." So many reasons to adore this man. She needed to stop.

"I try my best. Have a seat." He pointed to the sofa where a red blanket lay in disarray.

She tried not to picture him under it. The image would only make her want to cuddle up with him. Suddenly, she was second-guessing her choice to come here.

"I'm sorry I bothered you. When I heard about Bell, I wanted to make sure you were okay. Clearly, you are. Of course, you would be. You've been preparing for this moment, and it's not like you aren't used to what happens to animals. I'm sorry. I shouldn't have come."

She had to get out of there. Embarrassment burned her cheeks. They weren't a couple. Only his wife or girlfriend would come to him in the middle of the night to help him.

As Calista had done for Gage. She had been envious of Calista in that moment she found out Calista had run to help her man. She and Calista had been friends once, and the four of them had double-dated many times before Ajay died. Calista had left town around the time Autumn and Jett broke up. But Calista had returned to Backwater. She and Gage had made their way back to each other, had righted the past, and were happy and in love again.

She'd wanted that with Jett in the moment her father told her about Bell. Foolish woman, she had forgotten for a split second Jett did not belong to her.

He gripped her wrist, stopping her from reaching the door. "Don't go." His eyes were hooded and glassy. Pain etched itself around his mouth.

She fought the urge to pull him to her and tell him he could let out all the pain he would most certainly deny he felt.

"Okay. I'll stay." She was helpless around him. She didn't trust herself to know what rational behavior was, and that was the reason she had kept her distance all these years. She was powerless against the waves of emotions he evoked in her.

"Thank you." He dropped her wrist and returned to the kitchen.

She followed, her skin sizzling where his hand had been. "Let me make you the coffee. Do you want it black this time, or are you feeling like some milk since it's late?"

He stared at her but said nothing.

"Is that a no to the milk?"

"How did you remember?"

He had posed a very good question. One she could not answer. Not because she didn't have an answer, but because she did. He was a scar upon her mind, as if a cattle prod had come out and hit her when she wasn't looking. All these years later, after one fiancé and a husband, small but powerful memories of Jett would interrupt her day.

She could be driving in the truck, and a song from their past could come on and slam her back in time to the tree trunk by the stream where they sat together and he sang to her. Or she would be pouring coffee in the morning, and the aroma would hit her as if she'd never smelled it before, and she would be sitting at the diner with Jett, studying for finals. He would order a coffee with milk because it was past midnight and he thought it would weaken the caffeine. They would laugh about how silly that idea was.

She didn't recognize that young lady anymore. She had been trusting and sure of herself and believed in her future. But life had been too hard on her and had taken her baby when she was only twenty. Something she thought about every single day and never spoke of because no one seemed to understand the loss she felt.

She had barely been eighteen weeks along. The baby wasn't fully formed. People had told her to get on with her life. The one person who did understand couldn't talk to her. Or wouldn't.

"Autumn, are you okay?" Jett gazed at her with tenderness in his dark eyes.

"I'm sorry. My mind wandered there. It's late. Let me get the coffee going, and you can tell me about Silver Bell, if you want." She busied herself with her task, using it as an excuse to keep her gaze somewhere other than on him. But it betrayed her anyway and slid back to the man she couldn't look away from.

He leaned against the counter and crossed his ankles. "There's something else I'd rather talk about."

"Sure." The machine hissed and gurgled, pouring out hot coffee into the mug. She added a dash of milk and handed it to him.

His fingers grazed hers. That sizzling feeling he had left on her wrist shot over her hand this time. She almost dropped the coffee. He smiled as if he knew what he was doing to her. She returned to the coffee machine and ran hot water through it twice to clean it out and make herself the hot chocolate that she probably wouldn't drink but would be a good device to keep her hands from trying to touch him.

"Why did you bring dinner to Markus Everett's house?"

She froze with her back to him. Her hand was in the middle of tearing open the packet. How did he know that? Jenna must have spilled when she had picked up the food earlier. She had no reason to lie, didn't owe Jett anything, not even an explanation. Her pride couldn't take admitting how much she needed money at the moment. Especially to Jett. And especially because he wanted to buy her land.

"Why are you asking me that?" she said, facing him.

"Are you two dating?"

"When do I have time to date?" She tried to laugh his comment off, but the laughter shriveled up on her lips.

"I don't know. But are you?" He put down the mug and stepped closer to her.

"I didn't come here to discuss my personal life. I came to offer you comfort because your animal passed away and I know what that horse means to you." She returned to pouring the hot chocolate powder in the mug, but he stilled her shaking hands.

"We can talk about Silver Bell till the sun climbs over the mountain. After you answer my question."

"Do you have any idea how bossy you are?"

"Why won't you tell me? It's because it's true and you don't want me to know you went back to him. Is that it? Just say it."

"I try not to repeat the same mistake twice." But here she was in Jett's apartment in the middle of the night making him a comfort beverage. Repeating mistakes might be her thing, actually.

He flinched. She hadn't meant to, but she might have hit home on that one. Did he believe she had included him in that assessment? And if he was trying to get her into bed to buy her land, then it would be a mistake to be with him. But how she hoped that he coveted her and not her land, because she yearned to sleep with him. Mistake number two or three or twenty—she lost count.

"Are you going to deny that you brought him food?"

"Why do you care? Are you worried that Markus will outbid you?" Not that Markus had any offer on her land. Now with her father's proposal still drying like paint on her mind, she would be in some kind of mess if Markus wanted to buy her property too.

Jett closed the space between them, sucking all the oxygen from the air. He smelled of cedar and bourbon and seductive male. His dark eyes smoldered with intentions she would be better off not indulging.

"I don't give a damn about what Markus does. I care about you going to his house with dinner."

"I don't understand. Why? Dinner doesn't mean anything." She sidestepped him to get some air and clear her brain. With him so close, she couldn't think straight.

"Dinner often leads to other things." He pressed his lips into a thin, crooked line.

"You're assuming I slept with him. How could you?" And all she had to do was tell him how wrong he was, but for a minute or two, she wanted him to think that maybe she had gone to bed with Markus. It would serve Jett right for being so presumptuous.

He stepped toward her, closing the space again. She had to look up to see his face and hoped she looked more confident than she felt.

"You're a smart, beautiful woman. Any man would be a fool if he didn't want to take you to bed. I might not like Markus very much, but he's a smart guy. If he had a chance with you, he'd take it."

Her heart stuck on *smart* and *beautiful* and couldn't catch up to the logic screaming in her brain that Jett was not a safe bet. No man was, really, and she had plenty on her plate right now to take care of.

"I don't see how what I do in a man's bedroom is your concern."

"If you're going to be in any man's bed, it should be mine. And not because I put an offer on your land. I don't give a damn about that. I want you in my bed because it's where you belong." His pupils dilated as he ran his thumb over her jaw.

Her knees turned to mush. She gripped his strong arm to keep from puddling on the floor.

"Why did you go to his house?" he said, lowering his voice.

"Not because I'm interested in him in the way you're implying." Her answer would have to be enough for now. If he pushed, she would leave. She wasn't ready to share how she needed any type of job offered to her in order to stay afloat or that Marcus had been the one to do it. Maybe she would tell Jett later—much later.

He cupped the side of her neck. His touch was gentle and warm. "Would you be interested in me kissing you?"

Dear Lord, yes. "Only if you truly wanted to and not because you want me to sell to you."

"There isn't much else I want to do right now. Well, I have a few things in mind, but kissing will lead to that. I also want you to sell to me. But one has nothing to do with the other."

She could tell him her father was buying the land now, but once she said it, the words would become reality. She wouldn't be able to go back on it because whether she liked it or not, she would not lie to Jett.

All her options played tug-of-war. The sexiest man she had ever known was offering her a chance to throw caution to the wind and tangle in his sheets. She could kiss Jett and let nature take its course regardless of how things between them would stand in the morning. He might only want a one-night stand, or he might want any means possible to buy her land. She could walk out right now and stand on the principle that she could not sell to a Ryker. Selling to Jett would kill her mother. Or she could sell to Ives and watch where the chips landed, risking it all anyway.

"What's it going to be, Autumn? Can I kiss you?"

"Kissing you won't change my mind," she said. "I won't sell to you. A Ryker can't own my land. I'm sorry, Jett."

She slipped from his grasp and grabbed her coat.

****

Jett ran a hand over his face. This woman drove him crazy. She'd shown up on his stoop all adorable in her puffy coat and huge scarf tied around her neck, with her pink nose peeking out over the wool. She had come to comfort him. And he needed that very thing. He wanted to be the strong one for his family, but somehow Autumn knew exactly what role he would take with his brothers and mother and still understood how hard losing Bell would be for him.

That had been the biggest turn-on. He had to control himself not to swoop her up in his arms and carry her to bed. But he had to get to the bottom of the Markus thing. He wasn't about to compete with Markus over Autumn again.

She had seemed as if she were more than ready to kiss him a minute ago, except she had allowed her prickly pride to slide right in between them.

"Stop," he said before she could get to the door.

"I don't belong here." She struggled with that oversized scarf.

"Tell me you don't feel whatever the hell is happening between us." He had been trying to ignore his feelings for her for years, then embrace the fact he needed her while he was standing on her mountain and she had somehow become planted in his life. Until she'd called him a pimp. But earlier tonight, when he walked back from the field with Lock, it had been Autumn he wanted to call and talk with about Silver Bell. He wanted to hold her until the pain in his chest subsided.

Instead, he had opted for a beer and the couch where he must have fallen asleep until she texted him, and the buzzing from his phone had sent him jumping off the couch.

"Whatever is going on when you and I are alone doesn't matter," she said, interrupting his wild thoughts.

"It sure matters to me. You think I go around idly wanting to kiss women? When I'm around you, all I can think about is kissing you and touching you and having you under me with your legs around my waist."

Her face beamed red. Yeah, she was damn cute when he embarrassed her. He hadn't meant to. He was being honest about his thoughts. And her tangled up in his sheets was something that had been on his mind a lot lately.

"You have always been direct."

"Character flaw. Say it, Autumn. Say you don't feel the attraction like I do. Say it, and I'll let you go out the door and never bring it up again. But if you tell me you experience it too, then I want to take the few hours of night left and make love to you so I can lose myself in gorgeous you. I've had one hell of day. I need to remember what excellent feels like."

"Is this a one-time thing?" She leaned against the door and tugged at that scarf. Her shoulders dropped for the first time.

"It's whatever you want it to be. One night. One week. One month. One year. But you'll have to choose. And that means dealing with the things you have been avoiding for a long time. Your mother isn't going away, and neither is mine. I can deal with mine. Can you tell Vera we're together? I won't sneak. And I won't hide. I'm not ashamed of who I am or who my family is and the mistakes we've made."

"Will you take your offer off the table?" Her shoulders shot back up to her ears.

"No. It's a good business decision for both of us."

"What if I have another buyer? Do you still want to jump into bed with me?"

She tilted up her chin. He wanted to run his tongue over that chin and then down her neck and lower, but he wasn't getting the signal she wanted the same thing.

"I told you one didn't have anything to do with the other. I wish you understood I'm not like the other men in your life. Who's this buyer anyway?" If whoever wanted her land would do better by her than he would, he would tell her to take the offer. He hated to lose out, but she needed to do what was best for her.

"My father."

"You're going to sell to Ives? Are you sure that's a good idea?" Selling to her father was the worst possible idea. Ives had never done a worthwhile thing with his money or anyone else's. He doubted Ives even had the capital or collateral for a loan.

"Just as good as selling to you." A tilt of that chin again.

He forced back the laugh trying to escape. He would never laugh at her, but the idea that Ives would come in and save the day was ridiculous. "Where did Ives get that kind of money? And what is he going to do with the land? He could sell it right out from under you. Then what would you do?"

"He won't do that."

"I wish that were true. I wish he was the kind of father you have always wanted him to be. He can't be trusted."

"And you can?"

Her words stung. And after the night he'd had, his insides burned with her implications. He took a step forward. "I have never let you down. I have always been honest with you, and for the last decade plus, you have barely spoken to me. How can you stand there and say you can't trust me?"

"You let me down when you wouldn't share the pain of losing our child. I needed you then, and you weren't available. You shut down and wouldn't let me in. And even though you wouldn't grieve with me—I wasn't sure if you grieved at all—I stayed with you anyway only to have you break my heart by leaving me after Ajay died."

He bit back all the words trying to get out. Losing their child had cut him to the core. He had no idea how much pain could rip through his body by someone he had never even met. Hell, at first he hadn't been sure he wanted to be a father. But when the decision had been made for him, he could barely breathe.

But he held it together for Autumn. She fell apart. He held her for hours, lying in bed because she wouldn't get up. He tried to tell her it would be all right, that life had other plans for them. That they were young and could try again.

When Ajay died, he didn't have the strength to be strong for anyone. He folded in on himself, losing his youngest brother. Nothing made sense then. And he lost Gage because Gage imploded and left them all. Jett hadn't been able to lean on anyone.

"If you're still worried I'll leave you again, then you had better go."

"Fine." She tugged at the knob, but the door wouldn't open. She pulled once more, still with no success, then placed her forehead against the door. Her shoulders shook.

He hesitated. If he went to her, he could guess what might happen. He didn't want her turning to him because she felt sad or vulnerable. He wanted her to want him. Plain and simple. He couldn't promise he wouldn't hurt her again. He could try. Would that be enough for her? Life was rarely simple.

His hadn't been from the time he lost his father as a ten-year-old to losing his brother, his child, his woman. Running the ranch was not simple—ever. He didn't shy away from challenges. That trait made him a good athlete. If he wanted to be a good man, then he would have to face the challenge before him now.

He went to her and placed his hands on her

shoulders, bracing himself in case she swung at him. "Hey, I'm sorry."

She lifted her head. "I'm sorry. I shouldn't have said what I did about your grief."

"Would you please look at me?"

She turned, wiping her eyes. Her watery smile wobbled over her lips. Lips he wanted to kiss again. He wanted to kiss away all her pain until she felt nothing but the heat from his mouth on her, doing anything she asked from him.

"I would never deliberately hurt you. I want to take you to my bedroom and forget about the rest. But I don't think that's going to work for you. Sell to me and not Ives. And if you think that I'm only using you to get your property, then you should go. We'll go back to the way things were before. It's up to you."

Chapter Eighteen

She should go out that door and never come back. Her mind screamed for her to put her hand on that knob and twist with all her might. Hopping into bed with Jett would only cause her a world of hurt. She would never really know if he meant what he said or if he was trying to get her land out from under her while she was busy lying under him.

Her body shook as she visualized what being in bed with Jett would be like. She couldn't trust herself, at least not her heart, which wanted her to rip off her clothes and his and forget logic.

He waited for her answer. He wouldn't push her. If she said no, he would back up and let her go—forever. She would not get another chance. She would be making herself very clear in the here and now. He was risking his own heart. She knew it. And she knew how hard it was for him to do such a thing. If she didn't treat him with care, she would never be able to come back from that. Polite neighbors would be the most he could give her afterward—if at all.

She had come here for a reason. More than one reason. She had wanted to comfort him, but she wanted more. He was offering. Could she take the risk?

"I only want to worry about tonight," she said. "I don't want to decide about anything else. Can you live with that deal?"

"I can take things one day at a time if you can."

"This doesn't mean I'll sell to you." Nor would she tell him what she was really doing at Markus's. Her money problems weren't his business even if he knew about some of them.

"My offer stays on the table. You will have to make the best decision you can for you and your family. If Ives can offer you more, then go with him."

But they both knew Ives's offer wouldn't be as good as Jett's because whether she liked it or not, Ives could not be completely trusted. And the timing of his visit was still suspicious. She could think about all of that tomorrow or the next day. For now, she had a decision to make.

"What's it going to be, Autumn?"

She held out her hand. "Take me to bed."

Jett clasped her hand. His skin was warm and rough against hers—his rancher hands. She shivered from his touch. He closed the bedroom door with a click. Light from the moon's reflection on the crystal layer of snow cast a white glow in the room. Plenty to see by.

A king-size bed took up most of the room. Considering he topped off at a good six-one, she wouldn't expect anything smaller. And if memory served her, he also liked to sprawl out when he slept. One side table held a lamp and a charging station, some loose change, and a picture of five men, four of them standing in silly poses except for Jett who stood facing front, arms crossed over his chest. He had wanted his brothers to be serious for five minutes while they took a photo for their mother as a gift. Autumn had been standing to the side by the photographer, trying not to laugh at her boyfriend's frustrations and his brothers' goofiness.

She detected a hint of woodsmoke and laundry detergent in the air. Everything in here fit its owner. Jett was a man of the land, simple and strong. An old-fashioned wooden rocking chair with spindles sat in the far corner. It looked a lot like the one on her porch, but it couldn't be a match. A pile of folded clothes on the seat waited to be put in their rightful place.

"Jett, that rocking chair—"

"Is the twin to yours. Well, almost the twin. I found it at an estate sale a long time ago. I bought it, thinking of you."

She didn't know what to say. All the words tangled with her feelings for him.

"You can still change your mind." He cupped the back of her neck under her hair and riveted her to her spot with his intense gaze.

"My mind is made up, Jett Ryker. I may not know what to do about the land that was in my family for generations or what I will tell my daughter about where we will live in a short time, but I know that standing here with you is exactly what I want."

He kissed her without hesitation. She had given her permission, and he was ready. His tongue pushed her lips apart and sought hers as if his life might depend on it. She matched his determination because she thought her survival might be at stake if she didn't have every inch of him.

He tasted faintly like coffee, but she didn't care. She was with the man she had wanted to be with for more years than she cared to count. All the nights of foolish wondering and imagined unexpected encounters. All the times she'd played out in her mind, saying the things she should have said a long time ago. Each time she'd envisioned this moment—the moment when Jett took her in his arms and held her close. Safe. She had never completely trusted another human. Life had taught her to be leery of others who promised and didn't deliver. And even though Jett had promised once to be by her side, life had broken its promise to him and he had splintered. She should have helped him glue the pieces back together instead of running for the hills.

His lips trailed along her jaw to the soft spot below her ear. His hands slid inside her sweater and over her abdomen. She wriggled against the scratchy trail his touch left. That touch would destroy her, and she wanted to turn to ashes if only to keep his hands on her skin.

She needed to feel him as much as she wanted him to touch her. Her hands slid over his back and lingered on the places where his muscles flexed. She pressed against him, trying to get as close as she could with their clothes on. He gripped her bottom and tugged her against his hips.

"Can we get rid of this?" He eased back and pulled on her scarf.

"Let me." She unraveled the heavy wool and tossed it on the floor.

Jett moved to the king-size bed and turned back the duvet. Even in the dim light, she could tell the comforter was a dark plaid. Something else that was all Jett. He wore plaid shirts open over tees very well.

"You'll be warmer under the covers," he said.

She hadn't given the temperature in the room any thought. He might have misunderstood her shivering for cold when the reason for her trembling was the opposite. Hot desire shook her. She slid under the covers and motioned for him to join her. Wrapping her legs around him would be far easier lying down than standing up anyway.

He took his time kissing her and exploring her body because Jett was never in a rush. He could just as easily amble over to the stables as he could slowly make a breakfast for thirty without breaking a sweat. He could sit on a mountain's ledge and soak in the view without worrying about the hustle of the world.

They used to hike together, and he would find a spot to sit. She would wait off to the side for him to enjoy the view. He would not leave until she sat next to him on the ground, with their legs dangling over the edge of a rock.

She didn't have the patience he did, and on those long hikes, she would be the one to tire of the scenery first. Even now, she couldn't wait any longer to feel his skin against hers and tugged at the bottom of his shirt, trying to set it free.

He sat up and dragged the material over his head, messing his hair a little. "Better?" he said with a devilish smile.

"Much. Thank you." She kissed him this time. While her mouth tried to express how hungry she was for him, her hands took a walk of their own.

His soft chest hair tickled her fingertips. She explored every dip and hill of his muscular torso, creating a trail over his navel with her fingers and stopping at the top of his sweatpants. She wanted to dip lower, but she fought to control herself. They had barely begun. If she didn't slow down, it would be over too soon.

He eased her sweater over her head, dragging his hand over her body as he did and setting her skin aflame. She had another layer under there, and unfortunately, it was her pajama top because it was winter and she hadn't exactly expected to be in his bed. When she heard about Silver Bell, she'd grabbed the sweater, thrown it on, and run for her coat.

She did have a small surprise, though, and hoped he would like it. Sitting up, she lifted the top over her head to reveal she wasn't wearing a bra.

He let out a low growl and eased her back down with her hands over her head. "Don't move," he said. "I want to watch you a second."

"Don't stare too long. Things look a little different twenty years later." She had stayed in decent shape over the years, though each year made it harder to maintain what she had. Her life was mostly physical, and that helped, but when her age climbed into her forties, her body had a good chuckle at her efforts.

He placed a kiss on her shoulder. "Your body looks exactly as it should—curvy, soft, creamy."

Her insides glowed at the compliment. His lips moved to her breast and took it in. He sucked until her nipple ached. His hands left her wrists and trailed her body. She could not believe she was in Jett's bed and could not dream of any other place in the world as wonderful.

He stopped at her other breast to take his time there as well. His mouth descended to her belly and lingered at her hip bone. Slow. Steady. Strong. Everything she wanted in a man and he had been the only one who fit the bill.

She wanted to touch him too, but from her spot she could only reach his shoulders. "Jett, I need to touch you."

He hopped onto his knees. "Don't rush me, woman.

I've got all night."

"I see not much has changed. The ever-patient Jett Ryker."

"You always did have a hard time with that when we were together." He gripped her pajama pants and dragged them over her legs.

She helped him remove them and her socks. She tried not to groan at how unsexy her attire was tonight. Although he didn't seem to mind if his full erection straining against his sweatpants was any indication. She reached for him. Knowing she could arouse him even now, looking sloppy and older, heated her up more.

He stayed on his knees and fisted his hands on his hips. Shy was not a quality to characterize this man. He flashed that devilish grin as she went up on her knees too. With her palms, she slowly pushed down his pants. His gaze never left hers. Once he was free and they both knelt there fully naked, he slipped his hand between her legs, and she nearly came in that second.

From there, even the patient Jett Ryker could not hold back. They became a tangle of hands and tongues, touching and exploring, until they were both breathless. He eased back, panting. "Birth control?"

"I haven't had sex in two years. Haven't bothered."

"You haven't?" His eyebrows shot to his hairline.

"Don't look so surprised. I've had opportunities. I didn't want them."

"This night just got even better." He placed a quick kiss on her lips, rummaged around in the end-table drawer, and presented a condom.

"When was the last time you had sex?"

"We can talk about that later." He took care of the needed business and positioned himself above her. She wrapped her legs around his waist.

He entered her, and all thoughts of his past sex life were obliterated. He filled her up with slow strokes until she was too full to take any more. They rocked together like a small wave on the wet sand, each push and pull growing until the whirl became a tsunami that shook them. Sweat slicked their skins. She would never be cold again as long as Jett loved her just like this.

He held her gaze as the inflamed desire built to an unreachable height. She would never get on the other side of it no matter how high she raised her hips to meet his. He slid his fingers between them, touching the place that pushed her over the edge. He remembered. Tears sprang to her eyes as the release became relief.

He kissed her hard and long as he followed her to the end. His body shook with his own finale, and she held him close until he stilled. His lips found her salty tears.

"You don't have to be sad anymore," he whispered near her ear.

She doubted that was true, because even Jett couldn't stop the sadness that always seemed to wait for her and would find her again. She might want to trust him like before but no longer remembered how. And Jett would not stick around if his woman didn't trust him. Plus, there was still the little matter of her land.

Instead of answering, she kissed him until he was distracted enough from her surge of emotion and only wanted to be inside her again.

Chapter Nineteen

Jett woke with a start. The room was still dark, but the other side of the bed was empty. "Autumn?"

He fumbled for his phone, but it wasn't on the table. He had left it in the living room. He had no use for it the past hour or two. He threw his legs over the side of the bed, then reached for his boxer briefs.

A chill had settled over the room. The empty room. He flipped on the lamp. Her clothes were gone too. Had that woman just made love to him twice and snuck out of his house without a goodbye? He yanked the door open and hurried down the short hall to the living room.

"Are you leaving?" he said to Autumn's back.

She spun around, clutching her hand to her neck. "Jett, geez. You scared me."

"Were you going to leave without saying goodbye?" Had he been the one to be used? That thought had never crossed his mind until this moment. He had believed her posturing about him taking advantage of her. And those noises she made while he had his hands all over were pretty convincing too. But use him for what?

"I have to get home, and I didn't want to wake you."

"What's the hurry?" He grabbed the phone off the table. "It's only three in the morning. Your whole house is asleep."

"I have a child. I don't want her to see me coming in when she's getting up." She slid into her coat.

"You could've woken me." He wanted to say goodbye to her. Maybe even try to convince her to stay a little while longer as long as they were both up.

"Why are you so upset about me leaving?"

"Because you're sneaking out. I told you I wouldn't sneak around. What are you really afraid of besides your teenager thinking you got a little action?" Standing in nothing but his underwear turned his skin to ice.

"I wasn't sneaking."

"Don't lie to me, Autumn. Not that." He fought the pain building in his chest. He could handle almost anything except lies. He would not live like that. If she couldn't be honest with him, they would have no chance.

"Fine." She threw her hands in the air. "Besides the fact that Quinn is only fourteen and I feel as if I should still set a good example for her, I don't know if you and I are a good idea. I can't be what you need."

"You acted as if you were exactly what I needed an hour ago. Why the change? The sex wasn't good enough for another round?" He might have gone too far with that one, but his insides tangled up like fishing line. She infuriated him and intrigued him at the same time.

She flinched. *Yeah, too far.*

"Don't be a jerk."

"I'm sorry. Please make me understand. I thought you were sure you wanted this." He sure did. Being with her had been the only thing he wanted for a long time.

She crossed the room to him and placed a hand on his chest. Her fingers were cold, and he wrapped them in his hand.

"I did want you. I still do. How I feel has nothing to do with real life. And when that sun comes up over the mountain, real life will be waiting with its big pointy teeth to take a bite out of me."

"I can help you with that." He rested his forehead against hers because he wanted to be close to her.

"You think you can, but you can't. You asked me earlier if I could handle my mother if you and I went forward. I might be able to. I don't know. My father is showing an interest in your mom again. Vera won't be able to take it if he ends up with Karen. I can't watch that. And I can't be with you if they're together. And I can't ever sell my land to you because it was her land first. And her father's land and his father's before him. It's not fair that we got caught up in the middle of this battle, but it's real."

"Then don't sell to me. Sell to your father or whoever you want. I'll come up with another business plan." He could always try and buy the land from the new buyer, depending on who and what their plans were. Or he could swallow his damn pride and find another place to send his guests.

"You can live with my decision?"

"I'll support whatever decision you make." He didn't have to like it. But he would rather be with her than lose her over a business transaction. After tonight, he only wanted to be with her.

"There's another buyer on the table. Dottie sent an email last night I didn't see until five minutes ago. The notification popped up while I was trying to leave you a note."

"Good. Who is it?"

"Markus Everett."

He dropped her hand and backed up. "First your father and then Markus? Why does Markus want to buy it?"

"I don't know yet."

"You would sell to him?" His mind raced to try and understand why, when it came to Autumn, Markus was always on his tail. He wanted Autumn to shake Markus loose once and for all.

"I might."

"I don't understand. That man lies, cheats, and steals. He isn't there for his son when his son needs him, and you're willing to sell to him even though he will most likely turn around and sell it to a drug cartel who will build a casino or some such shit. But you won't sell your land to me because our parents had an affair twenty years ago?" He wasn't cold any longer. Fire burned in his veins. This entire conversation was not logical. Autumn was thinking with her misguided guilt and not that smart brain of hers.

"It's complicated."

"No, Autumn, it isn't. We're not twenty-three anymore. It's time to tell your mother to mind her own business and let you live your life." The fire in his veins boiled red-hot anger in his belly. He gritted his teeth to hold the emotion in place but was quickly losing the fight. After what they'd shared, the feelings he had for her, she would turn around and hand over her family's legacy to Markus Everett because she still didn't know how to tell Vera Thatcher that her grudge wasn't Autumn's.

"Why can't you understand what your mother did destroyed Vera and because of that my mother makes my life a living hell even now?" Her face bloomed red, and her voice climbed to the ceiling as she shook her fists in the air. "I can't sell her land to a Ryker."

"No, but you can fuck one."

211

A loud crack as if wood snapped inside a fire registered before the sting of her palm against his face.

****

Autumn wrapped up the dinner with aluminum foil and put the dishes of burgers, salad, and sliced tomatoes in Markus's refrigerator. Traces of hot oil and fatty beef permeated the air, making her nauseous. She hadn't eaten in a couple of days. Not since her awful fight with Jett. She had been avoiding the ski team at all costs every day at practice. Quinn had asked her to watch today, but she couldn't go out there and stand beside Jett as if nothing had happened.

She should have stayed the course and kept pretending they were nothing more than neighbors. She had been doing that for so long it was rote. But after sleeping with him and dredging up all the old, good feelings, she didn't know how to put the pieces of that puzzle back together. How was she ever going to move on without moving out of Backwater?

She should never have hit him, and she would apologize for that when he had enough time to cool down. He would have every right to blast her. He would never hit her back. Jett wasn't built like that. He was a gentleman to the core even if he had used words that stung as much as her slap did. Her hand had hurt for a full day.

She wiped the quartz counter free of crumbs and steak juices. This kitchen was right out of a fancy social media app where the appliances gleamed and the island was clear except for the decorative glass bowl of lemons. The stove vent was ornate and shot to the high ceiling alongside white cabinets that stretched and yawned so far away she needed a ladder for the third shelf.

If she hurried, she could be gone before Markus came home from work. Logan had ascended to his room the minute he arrived without so much as a hello. Not like the boy at all. The furrowed brow and the dark circles as well as the decline of a snack indicated something was wrong. Whatever his problem, it was none of her business. But what Jett had said the other night stuck with her. Markus wasn't there for his son. What did Jett know? She certainly couldn't ask him. He would never want to speak to her again. She still couldn't believe she had hit him.

He had made what they shared sound vulgar, and it tore her in two. She had never been so open with a man in bed. Not even with Trent who would ask her to do things and she would turn him down. But God help her, when it came to Jett, she couldn't keep her hands or her tongue off him. The more he claimed her body, the more she wanted to give him. What they shared was special, not some tawdry act to belittle.

The kitchen was suddenly too hot. She left a note for Markus with reheating instructions, located her purse and coat, and headed for the door to the garage. Before she could grab the handle, Markus pushed open the door. Both of them halted in their tracks.

"Oh. Did I get you with the door?" He ran a glassy-eyed gaze over her. His dark hair was thick and oily, not a hair out of place. He wore an expensive suit, but his rail-thin frame couldn't carry the material. His wool coat hung on him as if he had borrowed a wider man's jacket. What had she ever seen in him, looks-wise?

"Nope. Jumped out of the way in time." She hoped he didn't want to make small talk tonight. The past couple of evenings, he'd tried to keep her longer by asking a lot of questions about nothing in particular.

"I'm glad I caught you still here. I picked up a bottle of wine on the way home. I think it's your favorite. Would you like to have a glass before you go?" He pulled out a bottle of Shiraz and held it for her to see. The bold red wine was her favorite, but she wasn't in the mood.

"Thanks, but I have to get home and make dinner for my crew." No one was home tonight. Vera and Ives had driven to Bozeman with Quinn for a fancy dinner and a movie. They wouldn't be back until after nine.

"Oh, that's too bad." He stepped around her and removed his coat. "Are you sure you can't have just one glass? I wanted to talk to you about your land for a minute."

"Not much to talk about there." She still hadn't accepted his offer. Time was running out, and she would be without a buyer once the bank took hold of the land for good. She was spiting herself with all her dawdling, but she wasn't ready to give up her property.

"Dottie was kind enough to tell me I have the highest offer. She's waiting on you to decide. I thought maybe I could help you. You know, if you have any questions for me, I don't mind answering them." He grabbed two wineglasses from the butler's pantry and poured into each, ignoring her decision to decline and the fact she was still wearing her coat and standing near the door.

Saying she had no questions would be so easy. But easy didn't seem to be her thing. "Why do you want the land?"

"To develop on it. What else?" he said with a shrug and a smirk.

"What would you put there?" Her stomach knotted.

Markus would turn her beautiful property into something ugly and smarmy. More of Jett's warnings echoed in her head. Damn that man for being right all the time.

"I thought a bigger ski resort maybe. I could expand your house to make it a real lodge. Upgrade the lift and add one or two more. Where your property comes to the street would be a good place for some shops. You know, give those Rykers a real run for their money. Finally." He eyed her over the rim of the glass.

"That would take a lot of money." She forced her voice to remain neutral. Showing her emotions would do her no good. Markus didn't understand what that land meant to her and how much it hurt that she was losing it.

She put on a good face for everyone, but deep inside her the pain was unbearable. She had let down generations of people, including her daughter. Even though she would have no say as to what a new buyer did with the property, knowing Markus already had a plan to divide it up and make it a spectacle twisted her in knots. This mess was her own fault for ever trusting Trent to handle the money. She had never learned her lesson when it came to men.

"I have capital and investors ready. I'm not the only one in this town ready to take the Ryker family down a peg or two. It's about time. Don't you think?"

"What did the Rykers do to you?"

"They sit up on that ranch and stare down their noses at everyone. Gage Ryker thinks he's better than everyone else because he's the sheriff. As if he's untouchable. The other brother, the race car one." Markus snapped his fingers.

"You mean Kace?" As if Markus didn't know Kace's name. She tried not to roll her eyes.

"Yeah. That one. He's nothing but trouble, but his family always saves him. And Lockwood is plain not right in the head. The mother is promiscuous. Sorry. That slipped."

She doubted Markus's sleight of tongue. "Karen isn't like that."

"Whatever. Logan won't stop talking about Jett. Coach this and Coach that." Markus tipped his head from side to side and heightened his voice. "I'm sick of hearing how great Coach is. He doesn't know the first thing about being a father. The whole family thinks they own this town. I want to show them they don't. You gave me the perfect opportunity."

"How is Logan?" She ignored his last comment because there was no point in arguing. Markus would believe what he wanted, though he could learn a thing or two from Jett.

"He's a teenager. Stays in his room most of the time. Gives me one-word answers, if he bothers to answer at all. Spends a lot of time at his girlfriend's house. Which is fine with me. Gets him out of the house so I don't have to deal with his mood."

"Do you think he's having any problems? He seemed a little off to me the past two days."

"No clue. He wouldn't say even if I asked. He's killing it on the ski team. I doubt that's it. His grades are good. He's got everything he could want." Markus waved his hand as if to point out the grandeur of the house. "If he has a problem, it can't be much. Not compared to real problems anyway. I wish I had half his good fortune as a kid."

Her heart ached for Logan. His mother had been a sweet woman who Markus had snowed with his charm, but who he never really cared about. After she died, Logan was basically on his own. Markus was too self-centered and self-absorbed to raise a child. She had half expected Logan to end up in boarding school. If she had to guess, because Logan appeared to be well-liked, attractive, smart, and athletic, Markus kept him around to show off.

She would have to ask Jett what he meant about his *Markus not being there for Logan* comment. If Logan was hurting, Jett would help him. And someone needed to check on that poor kid.

"I really have to go, Markus. I'll see you tomorrow."

"One more thing." He poured another glass of wine and took a large sip. "Can you come over Saturday and make dinner?"

"I think so. I'll double-check and get back to you."

"I need you to be here. I'm entertaining. But I don't want you to just stay in the kitchen. I'd like you to be my date."

"No, I'm sorry. I'm not interested in a date." She should have known this was where he was heading. Making dinner and nothing more was too good to be true, but she had been desperate, and Markus had promised to keep her employment a secret, which he had.

"The way I see it, you need the money, right?"

"It's not just about the money. I wouldn't want to mislead you. I'm not interested in getting involved with anyone." Except for the man she'd recently assaulted, who most likely hated her now.

"It's only for one night. All I need you to do is put on a nice dress and let me drape my arm over your shoulders once or twice. The clients I have coming expect to see me with a date."

"There must be someone else you could ask." She couldn't imagine what kind of client would insist he have a date. Either he made that up to guilt her, or these clients were barbarians from another time who still believed women were property. Either way, the bile in her stomach rolled.

"I want you to do it."

"That's very nice of you, but I have to politely decline the date. I can make your dinner, even serve it if that helps, but I will not sit beside you and pretend we are a couple. For anyone."

"Then you're done cooking for me as of now. And I'll make sure everyone in town knows you've been here cooking and whatever else I want them to think. You wouldn't want the good old coach to hear those rumors, would you? Because rumor I heard says you and he are working things out."

She couldn't breathe. How could anyone know about her and Jett? Had someone seen her coming out of his apartment at three in the morning? A guest could have been outside. Or it could have been Ives. She sank against the door. Had her father told someone she went to Jett's after the horse died? Or had her mother been gossiping to her friend again?

"What do you say, Autumn? It's only one date. Unless you want it to be more. I'm game for a jump in the sack for old times' sake, but that's not necessary for Saturday."

She couldn't find her words. Markus didn't make idle threats. He would do exactly what he said. He'd go into town, whisper in the right ears, and have everyone thinking she had come here for sex and he had paid her right up to and including the purchase of her land.

"It's a win-win. You get to keep your secret job and your reputation." He took a healthy swig of wine.

"Why are you doing this?"

"Because this is a client I can't disappoint. That would be far worse than you having to eat a meal with me for one night. After that, we can be done. You'll want it that way, I'm sure. Though I'd be thrilled if you proved me wrong. I'm not so bad, Autumn. You and Quinn would have a good life with me. You could move into my house, have all the money you want. We could put your mother in a home, and you'd only have to see her on holidays."

She bit back bile. She wouldn't sleep with Markus again if her life depended on it, and she sure as hell wouldn't move in here. He had been a selfish lover and companion. She had been so sad and desperate for love when their paths crossed after she and Jett broke up. She had been willing to take anything to wipe out all the memories of the love she and Jett shared. But that theory hadn't worked. At all.

"One dinner. Nothing more. No trip down memory lane, no future relationships. Just one night. Then I quit."

"Fair enough." He raised his glass and drained the rest. "I'll see you Saturday."

Chapter Twenty

Jett stood between Gage and Kace with Lock on the other side of Kace. No one had told them to line up that way near the grave dug for Silver Bell. They had simply found their birth-order spot because they understood each other in a way only brothers who were close could.

Dusk slipped into the blue sky as the sun dipped behind the mountain, taking all the color with it. A cold wind picked up and snuck under his barn coat. With a stern slap, the breeze reminded him of the hurt he swam in. Winter suited his mood lately. Cold. Gray. Empty.

Gage said a few words about Silver Bell and Ajay. Lock placed flowers from the local florist on the mound of dirt. Eventually, the ground would even out, and only the small boulder would be left to show Bell's final resting spot.

They all walked back to the horses waiting for them. No one spoke. They rode to the ranch in silence, where their mother had made dinner for the family. Jett offered to put the horses away, but his brothers wouldn't hear of it.

"We take care of each other," Gage said.

He figured Gage needed to feel useful and didn't argue. When the horses were tucked in, they followed each other into the house.

Tara and Calista helped Karen set the table as they entered the kitchen. Smells of sauce and warm bread met them. Izzy helped Royce, Tara's son, with his homework at the island. The kitchen was filled with love and family.

Jett had to pause a minute. Seeing Kace grab Tara from behind and swing her around, both of them laughing and causing a ruckus, made his heart ache. Tara planted a loud kiss on Kace's lips. The two pressed against each other as if no one else was in the room. His mother swatted Kace's arm and shook her head. That didn't stop Kace from whispering something into Tara's ear that had her cheeks blooming red.

Gage slid behind Calista standing at the sink washing lettuce. He stopped by her side and placed a kiss on her lips. She smiled up at Gage with love written all over her face. Without saying a word, Gage joined her in cleaning the food, their motions in complete sync.

Jett missed Autumn. She would fit in with his family like a good saddle oil.

But then he remembered the slap on his face. He'd deserved it, but that didn't mean he was in any big hurry to run over to her and let her do it again. He hadn't seen her since that night. He had wanted to call or text, but each time he tried, he relived that moment and put the phone away. He was being a coward, but that would have to do for now. She didn't trust him. She was spending time with Markus. She was right. They couldn't work out their differences. Their differences defined them.

It was high time he let the past go and move on. Find himself another woman to share his life with so he could have what his brothers had. He was tired of being a bachelor. Maybe he'd like to be a father someday if it wasn't too late for him. Maybe he was just kidding himself.

"Mom, I just remembered some bills that need

paying. I'm going to make a plate and take it upstairs."
He grabbed a dish and plopped a kiss on his mom's head.

"But I thought we were going to have a family dinner tonight. Aren't we?" Karen turned, staring at him as he scooped and dumped food on his dish.

"The rest of us are here," Lock said. "Do we really need him?"

"Lockwood, that's enough. I want to have dinner with all my boys, their loved ones, and my two grandchildren."

Just like his mom to make Tara's son part of their family without blinking. Kace gave their mom a nod. Tara rested her head on Kace's shoulder. Yeah, he'd seen enough.

"Next week. I promise." He rushed out before anyone could say another thing. He couldn't watch all that happiness. Not tonight. The pain of losing Bell was too raw. The pain of losing Autumn was as powerful as a blizzard.

He took his plate out back to the firepit. The night was freezing, but the thought of being inside made his insides twitch. One of the employees had lit the pit for the guests, but no one had braved the cold. He didn't mind. Montana winters were in his blood.

He dropped into one of the chairs and ignored his food. He wasn't hungry. He had nowhere to go and no one to check in with. He would sit there until the fire burned out, and then he'd go inside, pour himself a beer, and fall asleep on the couch.

Nice life, Ryker. He needed to make changes to his personal life. Working the ranch had consumed him. Normally, he didn't give it a second thought, but today and recently, he wanted more. A wife. A family of his

222

own.

What would become of him if his brothers moved on with their own families? Gage had plans to build a house on the far corner of their land. Kace had been itching to get off the ranch. Jett suspected Kace and Tara would announce another child was on the way at some point, and if that happened, they would certainly want to live somewhere other than the employee cottages. Lock's unexpected conversation about life as something other than a rancher shook Jett to the core. He needed to start thinking about his future in ways that didn't just include the ranch.

"Jett?" A female voice drifted over to him. And not just any voice.

He pushed out of the chair and faced Autumn. "Howdy."

She wore that oversized scarf again. It swallowed her up, and he liked how cute it made her look. Her puffy coat went down to her knees. She was so small compared to him, but not weak. Still, he wanted to protect her, keep her safe. When she wasn't slapping him.

"Am I interrupting anything?" She kept her distance.

"Just having dinner." He wished she would come closer.

"Out here by yourself?" She searched the area as if someone else might appear.

"Too many people in the kitchen, and I needed some air. What can I help you with?" Her arrival had to be something about the ski lift, or she had finally decided the ski school should practice somewhere else.

"You always liked being outdoors." Her lips pressed into a thin line.

He wished she didn't remember so much about him. Her knowledge only made the pain worse. "Why are you here, Autumn?"

"I understand. No small talk. I came to apologize for the other night. I should not have hit you. That was wrong." She dipped her chin below the scarf.

"I'm sorry too. I shouldn't have said what I did about you and me." He wanted to say more, but he clamped his mouth over words of love and long-term promises. At least she didn't enjoy hitting him. He had wondered about that.

"Thank you. What we shared…it was special to me. I need you to know that."

"Okay. Was there something else?" He couldn't hear about how important being with him was if she insisted on pushing him away for reasons that made no sense to him. She wasn't ready to take the stand she needed to, and she didn't trust him. How could they be together if there was no trust?

She shifted her feet and shoved her hands into her coat pockets. She looked as if she wanted to say something else but shook her head.

"The other night you said something about Markus not being there for Logan. Did you mean something specific?" she said.

He didn't remember much of what he'd said during their argument except where he accused her of fucking him and made her sound like a morally questionable person. He would always regret that.

If he had said anything about Markus and Logan, and he probably had, he did have a specific incident in mind. Something he had wanted to talk to Autumn about that night he bumped into her buying dinner for Markus.

He wasn't sure if he should mention Logan and his pregnant girlfriend now.

"Jett? Did you hear me?"

"I did."

"Well, did you mean something specific about Logan? I'm concerned about him. He's been acting strange lately."

"You're still spending time at Markus's." It wasn't a question. She had no other way of knowing about Logan's behavior. It wasn't as if she came to the ski practices. He wished she would, but what would that change? She was here now, though.

"That's not what's important. I'm worried about Logan. He's not been himself. And Markus doesn't seem to want to get to the bottom of it. What if something is really wrong? I can't stand by and not do something for him if he needs help."

"Logan will work it out." He would keep Logan's secret, mainly because his athlete trusted him but also because Autumn didn't.

"So you know what it is?" She sank deeper into her coat.

"We've spoken about it." He hadn't heard from Logan since that day at the diner. But the kid had shown up at practice each and every time, doing his best. Logan skied with so much intensity Jett wondered if the kid was trying to punish himself.

Logan had been short tempered with his teammates. Jett had hesitated to say much to him, knowing he was under a lot of stress, but the team couldn't suffer for Logan's moods. They had a shot of winning their division, and Jett wanted that to happen for them. If Logan was bringing that mood home, Jett might have to say something after all.

"But Markus doesn't know what Logan's problem is?" She moved closer to the fire, probably for the warmth.

"I don't know what Markus knows." He would gladly grab her a blanket and wrap it around her to keep her warm, but he remained where he stood. She would have to make a move if she wanted his help or attention.

"Can you help Logan?"

"I've done all I can." Not exactly the kind of help he wanted her to ask for.

"Which isn't much from the sound of it. Are you staying out of it because it's too emotional for you?" Her voice seemed to tighten as if the words might be an effort to say. Or she was controlling her temper.

"Don't start again. You made yourself clear about your feelings for me when you swung at me. I will leave you alone. You can have Markus." And if she wanted to sell to him too, Jett had no way of stopping the sale unless he upped his offer. That wasn't even a guarantee.

He might have to richen the pot just to piss Markus off. Markus didn't deserve Autumn. He had done nothing to prove himself except have a lot of money he flashed around. If he had to bet, he'd say Markus came gunning for Autumn because Markus suspected she was involved somehow with him.

"I don't want Markus." She held her hands out to the fire. "You are the most stubborn man I have ever met. You want everything your way. And don't deny it. You're used to being in charge and people following your orders, including your brothers—except for Gage. Gage is the only person you'll listen to."

She knew him too well. He had made a habit of

keeping his emotions close and his words few because he didn't see the point in spreading either all over the place. What good did it do? Things happened in life. Bad things. He chose to move forward because he couldn't undo what had been done. But she could read him like a billboard on the interstate. It infuriated him and made him love her more.

"I'm not the only stubborn person here. You want things your way too. Listen, it was very nice of you to come over to ask me about Logan and offer him some help. You don't have to worry about him. He'll figure out his problems. He's resourceful."

"What kind of trouble is he in?"

Her stubborn streak was a mile long. She wouldn't leave this topic alone. He dropped back in the chair and let the heat of the fire wash over him. This day had worn him out, and he was tired of fighting with her. He had come outside for some peace and quiet. Instead, he got this determined and obstinate woman who wanted to do right by everyone except herself.

She came and sat beside him, making it hard for him to resist her. He caught a whiff of her sweet scent, and his mouth watered. She had tasted incredible the other night. He hadn't been able to get enough of her as his tongue roamed over the curves of her body. He shifted in his seat to keep his erection from growing. He embarrassed himself.

"I'm sorry, Jett. I'm so sorry for everything. I'm sorry about Silver Bell, about my mother, about our fight. All of it." She placed her hand on the arm of his chair but didn't reach any farther for him.

He kept his gaze on the fire. "Are you sorry we made love?"

"Never," she said barely loud enough for him to hear her.

He fought the urge to scoop her into his arms and make love to her by the fire until she begged him to stop. She was in his blood, under his skin. He needed to get loose of her somehow. But he didn't know how. The horse was out of the barn, as that stupid saying went.

He turned to her and held her gaze. He could tell her what he had wanted to talk to her about. He wanted to hear what she would say. They had been in the same predicament all those years ago. She might have new insight on what he should do as a coach and as a man concerned with the choices of the young man he cared about.

"Logan got his girlfriend pregnant, and they want to get married. He asked me to pose as his father and give my consent."

"Oh my. I hadn't expected something like that. What did you say?"

"I told him no to the parent thing. I've also told him I would support whatever decision he made, but he needed to tell his father. I'm concerned they're going to go through with the marriage and make some big mistakes they won't know how to undo."

"They're too young to get married and raise a family. They should give that baby up to a set of parents in better circumstances to care for it."

He expected her to say they should keep the baby. Wait to get married until they were older, but that baby deserved to be with its parents even if the parents were young. She had wanted that for their baby even when he had asked her to consider other options.

"They aren't much younger than we were." His life

would look very different if nature hadn't decided the timing was wrong. He might have a slew of kids with Autumn. Or they would be divorced, shuttling kids back and forth between two houses. And arguing over who would get the kids over vacations.

"Those few years make a difference. And honestly, we were too young as well. Sometimes I think Mother Nature knew better than we did."

"That's not how you felt back then."

"I was practically a child myself. So were you. We thought we were in love and wanted to spend our whole lives together. Look how that worked out."

"And us breaking up was my fault, right?" He could not undo the past, and she refused to let it go. If he could go back, would he make different choices? Maybe. Maybe he'd been too young, even at twenty-three, to be in a committed relationship. He'd had no idea who he was back then or what he wanted.

She stood and stared down at him with fire in her eyes. "You left me. I didn't leave you."

He stood too. "You replaced me in minutes. How much did you really love me?"

"You don't know because you wouldn't let me in to show you. You kept shutting down every time life got hard. After Ajay, you were impossible to reach."

"Show me now."

"Excuse me?"

"Show me now how much you love me." He was almost positive she still loved him. She had given him doubts, but recently, especially since they had slept together, he was less doubtful about her feelings for him. Autumn didn't trust her own feelings.

She stepped away and shook her head. "Find

someone whose life isn't a tangled mess like mine. You deserve to be happy. I want you to be happy. But I'm not the person for you anymore. I'm not that young lady who wanted your child more than anything in the world. Logan's girlfriend probably wants to keep her baby too if she loves Logan half as much as I love you."

He closed the space between them and gripped her arm. "You said love. You do still love me."

"Loved. I meant to say I loved you. I don't feel the same way anymore. We're wrong for each other. Life is too complicated for us. I'm tired of life being so complicated. I want something to be easy for once."

He turned, fighting the rage rattling inside him. He would not react again and say something he would regret. She didn't trust him or her feelings for him. Maybe she was right, and they were wrong for each other. Maybe he had been holding on too hard to something that wasn't real. Being around her stirred up all the old memories when life had been easier. The past was just that.

"Jett, wait," she said.

He couldn't stay and dashed inside without responding. He slammed the door shut, shaking it in its frame, then took the steps to his apartment two at a time. He paced the small space, trying to understand what had happened. She had come to ask him about Logan, and he had misread her. He had been misreading her for weeks. So why sleep with him? What was her goal? And damn it, he had fallen for it. Maybe she did want him to buy her land, and this game playing was all part of her plan.

He stormed into the bathroom, turned on the water, and stripped. He would need ice in his veins to forget the heat she caused. And he would stay under the water until she was long gone from his memory.

****

Autumn didn't move. The fire burned down to embers. The wind picked up, no match for her coat. She should go home. Jett had walked away from her, thinking she had no real feelings for him. She never lied about how she felt, but she had to deny it. Then she could say she was over him, didn't think about him, didn't want him anymore. But none of that was true.

She was freezing, but returning home held no appeal. Quinn wasn't there, and Autumn didn't want to spend time with her parents. If she continued to stand on the patio of the Ryker's main guest building, staring up at Jett's apartment, someone was bound to come out and ask questions. Her messed-up, confusing life tortured her.

Her phone rang from deep in her coat pocket. She dug it out, hoping it was Jett. Instead, her mother's name scrolled across the screen. She swiped the screen and walked toward her truck in the parking lot.

"Hi, Mom."

"Where are you? We got home about thirty minutes ago and expected to find you here."

"I had a few things to take care of." And she'd taken care of nothing except upsetting Jett again.

"You aren't over at the Rykers', are you?"

"Where I go is my business. I'll be home soon." She stopped with her hand on the truck's door. She had nowhere to go. Her friends had moved on without her. Sitting in a bar alone held no appeal. It was too cold for a long walk. The absence in her life echoed over and over.

"That man is manipulating you, Autumn. He doesn't

care about you. That kindness when he invited you to his house was just guilt talking. He's trying to get the land. That's the only thing he cares about."

"Stop it. I don't want to talk about Jett anymore."

"Fine. But don't say I didn't warn you. The house is freezing. I think the heater broke again. You have to come home right now and check." Vera clucked her tongue.

"Where's Quinn?" Her daughter was her only concern.

"She went to Emily's. Your father is dropping her off now. It's too cold for her here, and we didn't think you'd mind."

She was actually grateful Quinn wasn't home at the moment. She would send her a quick text to make sure her daughter was okay and to stay at Emily's until Autumn came to get her. No one else.

"Mom, hold on a second."

She switched her phone to the text app and shot off a note to Quinn.

—*Are you at Emily's?*—

The writing dots popped up.

—*Grandpa dropped me off. Grandma said you said OK.*—

—*Is the heat broken at home?*—

—*I don't think so. Can I stay?*—

—*Yes, have fun. Don't stay up late. I'll grab you before the competition tomorrow.*—

She didn't normally approve of a sleepover before a competition because the girls would stay up all night giggling and Quinn wouldn't get the rest she needed to ski her best, but she wouldn't let Quinn be hurt by another of her mother's deceptions.

"Autumn, are you still there?" Vera's voice scratched through the speaker.

She was done with her mother and her manipulations. "I don't have time to deal with the heat at the moment. But I do need you to tell me why Dad came back to town."

She walked back to the patio and craned her neck to see the window of Jett's living room. A light was on. Her mother would always get in between them, if Autumn allowed her to. Vera would tell story after story if it meant that she could keep Autumn from Jett, and Autumn was not going to put up with it any longer.

"Oh, that. I asked him to come home," Vera said.

"I know. Why did you do that?"

"Because I want him to buy my land and keep the Rykers away once and for all."

"Your land? Don't you mean my land?" Autumn had received the property from her mother before Vera passed because Vera hadn't wanted to deal with the pressures after Autumn's dad left. Vera had fallen apart, losing her husband for good, and had been unable to function. She had handed over the land as if it were a nuisance.

"No, sweetheart. It isn't. Not on paper. On paper it still belongs to me."

"I don't understand. You gave me the land when Dad left."

"Autumn, you never signed anything. I never signed anything. I told you the land was yours because I was in a bad way, but I never made it official. And you've been doing a good job taking care of it until the last two years. I had no reason to correct your errors. But since you've managed to lose our family's legacy, I had to step in and

233

take over. That's why I called your father."

"Why would you lie to me like that?" The world spun in front of her. Everything she believed was a lie. Her whole life had been built on mistrust and hurt. And she had been dumb enough to send away the only person who had been honest and truthful to her.

"It wasn't a complete lie. You would've inherited the land when I died anyway. What was the harm in letting you think it was yours sooner?"

"Because I've been trying to make the mortgage payment alone for the past two years. You haven't helped at all."

"How was I going to do that when I had my cancer scare?"

A scare that had ended up not being much of a scare at all, but Vera had milked it for over a year. Autumn dropped into the chair and put her head between her legs. She didn't care who came outside now and found her sitting uninvited on the patio.

Her mother continued to speak as if this were a regular conversation. "I admit I should've stepped in sooner and showed my hand, but I didn't want to hurt Quinn any further. She had lost her father and found out about his gambling problems all at once. I suppose if I had told you two years ago you didn't own the land, we could've called Ives back sooner to save us."

"Dad is not going to save us. He doesn't have that kind of money."

"He's doing fine. He'll be able to get the loan that you can't. I had hoped you would decide to sell to your father on your own, then you would never have been the wiser about my little indiscretion. But you had to go and get yourself involved with that Ryker boy again. I can't risk you selling to him."

"*Boy*. He's a middle-aged man who runs a very successful business and is well respected in this town. He doesn't lie. He takes care of the people he loves." Her stomach burned. She had never been able to give him the credit for taking care of his loved ones because he had left her. She had never allowed him to be human and young. She had been the selfish one.

"Whatever, dear. I can't allow a Ryker to own my property. Not ever. I'd rather die first. I had to get involved. So I called your father. He was more than happy to return."

"What's in it for him?"

"Nothing. Except to be around his family. That's all he wants."

"He's lying to you, Mother. If you sell to him, you'll regret it."

"I doubt that. I know what I'm doing, Autumn. I fooled you, didn't I? When are you coming home? You need to fix the heater."

"I'm not coming home tonight." She might never return.

"But the heater," Vera said.

"Fix it yourself." She ended the call and stole another glance at Jett's apartment.

The light in the bathroom was on. She needed to do what she should have done earlier and let herself in.

Chapter Twenty-One

Cold water streamed over his head and down his back. Jett rested one hand on the tiled wall and let the other hang by his side. If he stayed in the shower long enough, maybe the cold water would freeze off the part of him that wanted Autumn so badly.

And she wanted Markus. That was one thing he did not understand. In fact, he didn't understand women at all. Plain and simple. His earlier thoughts of finding someone to spend his life with circled the drain along with the cold water. He had no idea how to pick the right woman. How Gage and Kace had done it was beyond him.

Someone knocked on the door. *What the hell?*

"Lock, if that's you, go away." He didn't care what was wrong downstairs. Mrs. Crosby could have spilled a glass of wine on the white couch in her room, or Mr. McCarthy could have stuck his foot in the wagon's wheel, or Mrs. King could have broken off her room key in the lock and couldn't get inside. He wasn't coming downstairs to fix a thing. Any one of his family members could handle whatever problem was on fire. Hell, even Kace's girlfriend was an employee. She could put out a fire too.

The door cracked open.

"I swear, Lock, if you try to throw another snowball in my shower, I'll beat the shit out of you while I'm naked."

"It's not Lock." Autumn came around the door. She still wore her coat and scarf. A grave look crossed her face.

Her appearance in his bathroom put him in a tough spot. Well, she'd already seen him naked. No point in trying to cover up. The water hadn't steamed up the glass, and he had to lean out of the shower to grab a towel. If she wanted an eyeful, she could have one. He had nothing to hide. He turned off the water and stepped out.

"What are you doing here?" He wrapped the towel around his waist.

"I needed to talk to you." She held his gaze.

"It couldn't wait until I was out of the shower?" If she was rethinking her decision to come in, too bad. She'd have to deal with him in this state.

"I'm afraid not."

"Then I guess you better get to whatever it is that's bothering you." Thirty minutes ago the woman told him she wasn't in love with him, and now she stood in his bathroom. This was why he didn't understand women.

"Do you want to get dressed first?"

"Nope. My bathroom. You barged in. I can stand here all night like this."

"Then maybe I should join you." She smirked and removed that scarf. Her coat hit the floor next.

"Autumn, what's going on? I'm not up for any game playing." Or having his heart broken. Loving someone— anyone, including animals—was hard. When they left and took a piece of his heart too, he wanted to rage against the world. He had spent his whole life trying not to be angry with the losses. He didn't always do a good job of it. He wanted to do a better job now.

"I'm sorry for what I said tonight. I've been afraid to ask for what I want. Maybe because I didn't think I deserved it." Autumn took a small step closer.

"And that's changed?"

"My mother told me something a few minutes ago that finally made me see I've been handling this thing between us all wrong. I truly am sorry. I'm sorry about everything I've put you through lately. I've allowed my mother to get in between us. That won't happen any longer. I promise." She pulled her sweater over her head, revealing her creamy skin and deep-blue bra.

"You keep taking your clothes off, and I'm going to think you're here for one thing only." Temptation stirred low in his belly. He wouldn't be able to resist her much longer, especially not standing here in the damn towel.

"I'm here for a few things." She kicked off her boots.

"Stop and tell me what you're up to, please. What do you mean about not letting your mother between us?"

"She just revealed something to me that has me mad enough to do something drastic. Something I should've been brave enough to do without that information. I'm sorry I wasn't."

"Are you going to tell me what that information is?"

"I'll tell you all about that later. I promise. But now I want to focus on us and how we make each other feel. I want to make you feel as good as you make me."

She crossed the room and put her cold hands on his already cold skin. "Can you forgive me?" She looked up at him.

"She must've said something big for this change of heart from twenty minutes ago."

"Do you want me to go?" She narrowed her eyes.

"Not a chance. But I'm not going to take you to bed so you can change your mind again in the morning. Tell me."

She ran her fingers over his pecs and down his abdomen. His brain misfired for a second. Her touch drove him mad. He grabbed her hands and stilled them before she could remove his towel. And all his leverage would be gone.

"Please trust me, Jett."

"I want to." He also didn't want to regret this. If she stayed and they made love again, he wouldn't bounce back too quickly if she rode away with his heart.

"I will tell you everything later. I can stay all night." She laced her fingers through his. Her hands were so small compared to his.

"All night?" He squeezed her hands and glanced at their grip, her fair skin against his darker one. They fit and contrasted at the same time.

"If you want me to." She gazed up at him through her lashes.

He leaned down and placed a kiss by her ear. "I want you to," he said, hoping she felt as turned on as he was. "But I need to know what happened."

"Later, Jett." She moved her hands to his shoulders, slid her fingers down his spine, and rested them on his backside. "I will tell you everything later. Right now, I want to forget about all the bad things in my life and think only about you and me and getting rid of this towel."

His heart took control. He would no longer be safe from the hurt if she chose to leave him. He wouldn't be able to keep the pain under wraps if she walked away.

He did as she wished and dropped the towel.

Then he took her on the bathroom floor.

****

Jett pulled Autumn to him and rested his chin on her head. She smelled like winter snow and honey. She tasted like sweet cream, and he wanted more. The bed was warm, and they were tucked under his comforter. The wind howled outside, long moans that threatened another storm. Right now, he didn't have a care in the world. *Let the skies open up.* Life could spin all around them. As long as he was here with Autumn, everything else could wait.

After the bathroom, they'd come into his bedroom and made love again under the covers, slowly and deliberately, never taking their gazes off the other. He had entered her, clasping her hands above her head, holding her stare, and moving back and forth in a deliberate rhythm that had her begging him to pick up his speed. But he'd waited until he was certain she was ready, and then had given the woman exactly what she wanted.

He grinned into her hair with pride at his ability to hold it together long enough to make sure she was satisfied before he followed her to the finish. Twenty years ago he wouldn't have been able to do that. Age had its benefits.

"There is no place in the world I'd rather be," she said, wrapping her leg over his and snuggling against him.

Her heated core rubbed his thigh, turning him right back on. The wind howled again. He had to agree. A howl was somewhere deep in him too.

He could lie there all night, never having to say a

word. Just hold her. Love her. But they had issues hanging over their heads, and he wasn't one to leave what needed to be done for tomorrow. Too many things required tending on his ranch. He preferred to deal with his problems head on.

"I think we need to discuss a few things."

She pushed up on her elbow and stared down at him. "Now?"

"Yes, ma'am. Right now."

"Can't we enjoy what we shared?"

"I'm enjoying this just fine. You can climb back down and curl up against me while we talk. I don't mind. Or you can go on giving me that glare, but either way, I need to know what had you changing your mind earlier and barging into my bathroom."

A surprise he would never complain about.

"It's awful." She sat up and pulled the covers around her.

"How does something awful get you inside my house and wanting to have sex with me?" He sat up to see her better. He hadn't been expecting *awful* as her answer.

He brushed back the hair that had fallen over her face. Tears brimmed the rims of her eyes. His instincts yelled to protect her, to find out what the hell Vera had done now. He waited, but she kept her head down.

"Autumn, darlin', what happened?"

She finally turned to look at him. "Somehow I don't own my land. My mother told me tonight that she still owns it. I don't know how I missed that. Stupid, I guess. Gullible maybe. She said I never signed anything. And I don't think I did. The conversation about me taking control of the property happened so long ago. I don't remember."

"I don't understand. That seems impossible." At least in his world, it was. He was completely transparent with his family about the running of the ranch. He and Lock had control of the everyday activities. His other brothers and his mother were a part of any major changes affecting the business. He owned the ranch and its acres equally with his brothers. No one could sell off a piece without the others' agreement. When Kace had tried to sell his portion without family consent, he had almost destroyed their relationship.

"I thought so too. But I can't remember exactly what happened when she gave me control. It was when my dad left. She wasn't in her right mind, and honestly, I wasn't either." Tears spilled down her cheeks. She covered her face with her hands.

"Hey, now. Let's think on this for a minute. What does the monthly mortgage statement say?"

"It has her name on it. I didn't think it was a big deal that only her name was on the mortgage. I thought my name was on the deed."

"Have you seen the deed?"

"Not in forever."

"You need to get a look at the deed. Your mother could be lying to you." The official document would tell them the truth. He wouldn't put it past Vera to make up the whole business of her still owning the property just to control Autumn. He would have words with that woman if he found out that she had stooped so low.

"Why would she lie about that?" She looked at him with pain in her eyes.

"Because you're with me, Autumn. She doesn't want you involved with me. She'll do whatever she has to in order to keep us apart." He didn't want to see her hurt. If he could keep her from ever feeling pain again, he would. She deserved better from Vera.

"Why is she so cruel?" Autumn fisted the sheet.

"Darlin', I have no idea. I am sorry, though. Your mother has it in her. I hate to say it."

"What do I do?" She began to cry again.

He gathered her to him and held her close. "You aren't any worse off than you were before."

She eased back, wiped her face with her hand. "How do you mean?"

"You were going to lose your land. You had to sell it. She still has to sell it."

"But she'll never sell it to you. She thinks my father is going to save her."

"I'll up my offer."

"Jett, she isn't going to sell to you. And I don't have anywhere to live or raise my child. I don't have a career anymore. I can't even go back there tomorrow and look at her."

"You can work for me. You and Quinn can stay on the ranch. I can make Lock stay with me. You can take his place for now."

"I'm not throwing your brother out of his house. But thank you." She placed a kiss on his cheek. "I need to fix this on my own."

"You're not going to let me help you."

"There isn't anything you can do."

"I just offered you a job and a place to live. Even if they're temporary."

"Please let me do this on my own. I don't want to feel as if I owe you. I want to be with you without any strings. I will not burden our relationship by relying on you to clean up my mess. I've relied on too many people my whole life, and it's gotten me into a ton of trouble."

He didn't want to argue. He didn't see the point. She had her mind made up. His stubborn woman would forge her own way, and he would have to stand beside her as she did it. If she needed him, he would jump in.

He only hoped whatever she had to do to make things right for herself didn't scare her away from him. He wouldn't do this dance for a third time.

Chapter Twenty-Two

"I have to go." Autumn placed the mug in the dishwasher and turned to Jett.

Dawn had barely rinsed out the sky. A splash of pink outlined the mountain in the distance. He stood before the window, smiling at her. The edges of his hair were still wet from the shower they'd taken together. Her thighs shook as she remembered how he'd pressed her against the shower wall and thrust into her from behind. For a man who said little and expressed his emotions less, he had an expert way of showing her what she meant to him.

She could stay with him all day, would love to climb back into his bed, but she needed to get home and figure out her next move, a place to live, a job, taking care of Quinn.

He crossed the room and pulled her to him. "Do you want me to come with you? I can stand guard while you pack a bag."

"Thank you, but not yet. I need a plan of some kind. Then I'll pack us up and move us."

"Can you come back tonight?" He kissed her neck.

"I'll try. After Quinn settles into her room for the night."

"Are you going to tell her about us?"

"I will. She loves you. She isn't going to mind that we're together. She is going to be upset about having to move out of her house. Give me a few days, okay? Then I'll sit her down and tell her all of it."

"I can wait a few days."

He kissed her, pushing her lips open. Her body melted against his. Even a simple kiss made her weak for him. His hands shot up her shirt and cupped her breasts. She reached for the button of his jeans, then stopped.

With regret, she eased out of the kiss. "Jett Ryker, we won't get out of this kitchen if we keep this up."

"Kind of the plan, ma'am." His lips returned to her neck.

She pressed her hands into his shoulders. "Later. I want to get home and get started on my plan before I have to pick up Quinn."

He arched a brow. "Okay. I get it. No more fooling around."

"Thank you for understanding."

"I still think you should move onto the ranch."

"I can't. I'll text you later, okay?" She scooted away from him and grabbed her coat before she could rethink her decision to stop his advances.

"Hey, after the ski competition today, do you want to go out to dinner? A real date. I hear there's a new restaurant on the highway, not far from here."

Today was Saturday. The night she had agreed to help Markus. She couldn't explain to Jett now about her agreement. He would probably think Markus was up to no good. Just like Markus always thought the worst of Jett. Their competition would never end. And she was tired of being the supposed prize Markus always tried to win.

Markus was only wrapped up in his own world. He didn't really want her. He only wanted to beat Jett. She could handle Markus. And she didn't want to cancel. She needed the job working there. At least she didn't have to keep the job a secret and worry what other people would think about her working for Markus. Now she was openly with Jett. Later tonight, she would come clean with Jett about Markus and working for him. When they were in bed, happy, and with no need to rush.

"I'm meeting a friend for dinner. Can I take a rain check on that date?" She avoided his gaze. He would know she was lying—well, not telling a complete truth—and grill her. Markus meant nothing to her, but she didn't have the time for the discussion and the persuasion she would need to make Jett understand what she was doing.

He narrowed his eyes. "Yeah, sure."

She kissed him again. "I'll see you later tonight. Good luck today."

"Thanks."

She ran out the door. If she had more time, she would have told him the whole story, but she did need to get home and look at her personal finances and job prospects and then pick up Quinn before the competition.

She stopped at the mailbox at the edge of the driveway. The wind whipped the truck's door from her hand. Last night the wind had been so strong she thought the roof of Jett's place would come off. If a storm was on its way, it hadn't arrived yet.

Yesterday's mail filled the box. Some of it was wet. She wiped her hand on her leg. The mail carrier must have dropped it in the puddle by the edge of the road. Luckily, most of it headed straight for the recycle bin. One long white envelope caught her attention. The address label was smudged, but the return address was crystal clear, as was the stamp on the front reading *foreclosure papers.* The bank wanted their money. Time was up.

Her breath caught in her throat. Someone would own this property soon. She couldn't deal with that loss at the moment. She shoved the letter in her purse and drove up to the house. She'd look at the papers later. Or better yet, she'd give them to her mother to deal with. Since she was the owner.

Unless Vera had lied as Jett suggested. But that was too much even for Vera.

Ives came out onto the porch as she hopped out of the truck.

"Good morning," he said, raising his mug.

"Hi, Dad. You're up early."

"I could say the same about you." He eyed her over the mug, one eyebrow reaching for the top of his forehead.

"I'm a grown-up. I can sleep where I want."

"Do you have to be involved with Jett? Isn't there another man in a twenty-mile radius you could fall for?"

"No. And I don't care what Mom thinks. What you and Karen did was a long time ago and between you and Mom. I shouldn't have to sacrifice my happiness because of what you did. I've done that for too long."

"Your mother is in rare form this morning because you didn't come home last night. You might want to steer clear of her."

"Why are you here, Dad? Why do you keep coming back and putting up with her?"

"I miss you and Quinn. And you needed my help. I want to save your land for you."

"You're not saving me. You're saving Vera. She says it's her land. Told me last night." She brushed past her father and went inside.

He was fast on her heels. "What are you talking about?"

"Ask her. I have some things to do before I have to grab Quinn." She hurried into her laundry room slash office and locked the door. Let Ives and Vera deal with each other for once. She wasn't going to be in the middle any longer.

She sat at her computer, reviewing her situation and researching a new one. Every click brought her no closer to a better answer. She might have to ask Markus for a few referrals and start cooking for other wealthy families in town. Or take Jett up on his offer to work on the ranch. What would his family say when they found out she and Jett were together again?

She suspected they would be okay with it, but would Karen? No matter what Jett said or believed, his mother might have a problem with her returning to the fold. Autumn and Jett being together would mean their families would have to cross paths.

For most of her life, she had tried to love other men. But in the end, her heart belonged to Jett. Everyone else would have to get on board. She wasn't going to deny her own happiness for others any longer.

Her phone buzzed with a text from Quinn.

—*Where are you? I'm going to be late!*—

She saw the time and jumped from her chair. She grabbed her purse, then dashed from the room.

"Autumn, wait. I need to talk to you." Vera followed her down the hall.

"Not now. I have to get Quinn." She flung open the door, and a blast of wind met her.

"But the heat."

"Is working fine." She slammed the door behind her and went to get her kid.

****

Jett waited in the ski school's parking lot. Gray clouds filled the sky. He had hoped for a better day weather-wise. Snow would make the course more difficult for some of the kids. He had also hoped to have left thirty-five minutes ago. He checked his phone. No texts. No calls. Where was Logan? Five more minutes might not hurt.

All the athletes were on the bus, also waiting to leave and getting more anxious by the minute. Jett had tried to reach Logan several times, but the texts were never delivered. He even tried a call, but it went straight to voicemail. He was worried. It wasn't like the kid to go dark like this.

"Hey, Quinn, could you come here a minute?" he said from the bus steps.

She hurried down the aisle onto the asphalt. She looked a lot like her mom at that age. He could still remember Autumn in high school with her red earmuffs and leg warmers, standing out by the student parking lot laughing with her friends. He'd had a huge crush on her back then. He would never have guessed they'd be where they were today and all the hills and valleys in between high school and now.

"Hi, Coach." Her smile was wide. She was a good kid who tried hard. She wanted to please everyone.

He hoped she still liked him after she found out he was dating her mother. He would have to ask Kace how Royce had done when he found out Kace was dating his mother. Royce was only five, so maybe the situation was a little different with a teenager. And Kace and Tara had no history.

"Has anyone heard from Logan?"

"I don't know. I could ask around."

"Would you do that? We need to get on the road, but I don't want to leave without him."

"Sure. No problem." Quinn hopped back on the bus.

And without Logan, the team didn't stand a chance to win. This was an important competition. Finding Logan was more important.

Logan was letting his teammates down, which also wasn't typical behavior for him. That led Jett to suspect he knew where Logan might be, and he didn't like it. He should have said something to Markus sooner or pressed his opinion harder on why getting married and having a baby at seventeen was a huge mistake.

Darren Scott trotted off the bus, holding his phone. Darren was tall, dark, and from what Jett could tell, well liked by the others. He had some speed on the slope and a healthy attitude about winning. He was one of Logan's good buddies.

"Coach, I don't know where Logan is. I've tried him like a hundred times. He's not answering. Do you think he's sick or something?"

Or something. "Probably. He wouldn't leave us hanging otherwise." He had no idea if Logan had told anyone else what he was up to, but he wouldn't spill it.

"Should we call the hospital?"

"I'll call his father. Get back on the bus where it's warmer. Thanks for the help. I'll be right there."

He searched for Markus's number in the paperwork. Every athlete had to give a parent's information in case of emergencies. He dialed. The call went to voicemail.

"Everett, it's Coach Ryker. We have a competition

today. Logan hasn't arrived. If he's okay and planning on attending, tell him to meet us at the slope. The bus has to leave now. If he's sick, I hope he feels better. But can someone get back to me and let me know? Thanks."

He made one other call.

"Sheriff Ryker," Gage said when he answered.

"It's me. I need a favor." Still no sign of Logan. The bus driver gave him a palms-up sign. He flashed a one-minute back at him.

"Sure, what's up?"

"Can you take a ride past the Everett place and tell me if anyone is home?" He wanted Logan to be there, lying in bed with a fever instead of on his way to Idaho.

"Everything okay?"

"I think Logan might've left town today to get married."

"You're kidding?"

"I wish. I'm hoping he's just home sick and forgot to call me." He could wish all he wanted, but Logan had been determined that night at the diner with Maya by his side. Logan had changed his mind about not wanting the child to eloping and raising a family.

"I'll knock on the door and see if anyone's home. I'll call you back."

"Thanks, man."

"No thanks needed. Besides, it's a quiet day in Backwater."

"When isn't it?"

Gage hung up laughing. Out of options, Jett climbed onto the bus without Logan, and they drove off.

Chapter Twenty-Three

Autumn willed herself to get out of the truck. It was a simple dinner. Nothing more. It didn't matter that Markus had sent a text earlier, saying he was having food brought in and she didn't have to cook. He was just being nice. So why was her stomach braided into a rope? Because she still hadn't told Jett the truth. His day had fallen apart. She didn't have the heart to drop more stress on his shoulders.

Jett had called her at the end of the competition. From the moment he said her name, his troubled voice concerned her. Her man was overwrought. The team had lost. Quinn had come in last and burst into tears, which Jett didn't know how to deal with. He had tried to make her laugh and then tell her it was no big deal, but Quinn hadn't let it go. If it wasn't for one of the other mothers consoling Quinn, he might have had a stroke trying to make Quinn feel better. She appreciated his attempt to help Quinn. Even Autumn struggled to do that at times. He had wanted Autumn to know Quinn was okay. She loved him for that.

Jett revealed that Logan had never shown. Markus had never called Jett back. Jett was more worried than Markus seemed to be.

Her phone buzzed with a call. Jett again. She let it go to voicemail. She needed to get this night over with. Then she could make love to her man and tell him about her day.

Markus opened the front door and waved her in. He rubbed his arms and shivered, then went back inside, leaving the door open.

Now or never.

She closed the front door and leaned against it. The warmth of the house wrapped around her. A fire burned in the hearth. Bach played softly through the house speakers. The table was set for three.

"Why were you sitting outside?" Markus took her coat. "You look nice."

"Thank you." She had opted for a green sleeveless dress even though it was cold out. The dress showed off her shoulders and shimmered when she walked. The skirt flared out, offering her middle section a little forgiveness. It was also the nicest thing she owned and often her only choice for special occasions.

"Why is the table only set for three? I thought your client was a couple." She kept her voice low in case the other person was in earshot.

"He came alone. He's in the bathroom. Do you want a drink?" Markus put a hand on the small of her back and led her to the bar set up in the living space.

"Just a seltzer, please." She needed to keep her wits about her and slipped away from his touch. A hand on the shoulder was one thing. The low back was something else. "How's Logan feeling?"

Markus gazed at her with confusion painted across his face, as if she had arranged her words in the wrong order. "He's not sick. He's been at his girlfriend's all day."

"Didn't you get Jett's text or call?" She feared Jett might have been correct about Logan's intentions.

"I forgot my phone at the office. I didn't realize it until about an hour ago. I hate being without it, but I didn't have time to run and get it."

"You weren't home when Sheriff Ryker stopped by?"

"Sheriff Ryker? Why would he come here?"

"Well, hello. This must be your lovely lady. I'm Brian Anderson. It's nice to finally meet you. Markus has gone on and on about you." A short man with a shiny head and a goatee stuck his hand out.

She slid hers in for a firm shake. His gap-toothed smile seemed genuine. He was casual in a tweed sports coat and white button-down shirt tucked into a pair of navy-blue stiff-looking jeans. His loafers gleamed from the overhead lighting.

"Hello. It's nice to meet you." She turned to Markus. "You really shouldn't go on about me like that, dear." She plastered a smile on her face but hoped her eyes shot the daggers at Markus she wanted him to see. Talking about her as if they were a couple was not part of the deal.

"Dinner will be ready soon," Markus said. "Yvette will be ready to serve at seven. Why don't we have a seat near the fire?"

She took the single straight-backed chair, leaving the sofa and another chair for the men. Markus handed her the seltzer. At least she had something to do with her hands. She had to assume Yvette was the caterer or someone Markus had hired to serve. The job she would have performed—and preferred—if he hadn't begged her to pretend to be his date.

"So, Autumn, Markus here tells me you own a ski area." Brian took a sip of his whiskey. The light from the lamp beside him caught the etchings of the glass and spun color on the coffee table.

"A failing ski area." That wasn't hers at all. The foreclosure papers were still in her purse. She would have to deal with those first thing in the morning. And dealing with them meant handing them over to her deceitful mother.

"I'm sure with a few tweaks things could turn around." Brian winked at her.

Her chest tightened. She leaned against the back of the chair, trying to put space between her and creepy Brian.

"Sweetheart." Markus grabbed her hand. "What Brian is trying to say is he has ideas for your property."

She eased her hand away and wrapped it around her drink. "Really? Are you a ski expert? Or maybe you own a resort?"

"I have skied a black diamond. Once and badly." Brian chuckled. "My expertise is in the rehabilitation of an area. More than...let's say sports. I leave the gold-medal winning to my friends like Markus."

Markus had never won a gold medal, but he had been quite the athlete in his younger days. He had gunned for Jett all through high school. In skiing he couldn't touch Jett's abilities. She assumed Markus's push to make Logan a stellar athlete was Markus's way of reliving his glory days. Poor Logan. No wonder he was in a mess.

"I've tried to teach you." Markus clinked his glass against Brian's. The men shared in the humor.

She wanted to go home. *Home.* She had no home. She lived in a house built on lies and fragile enough to collapse in a good wind. Jett had offered her a home and a place to stay. Refusing him because of her pride might have been a mistake. She would ask him tonight if his offer still stood.

"I brought you two together because Brian would be a good fit to buy your property," Markus said, yanking her from her thoughts.

"I'm sorry. What did you say?"

"I'm a developer." Brian handed her a card. Her trembling fingers dropped it. Brian retrieved it and handed it back. The card read *Anderson Development Corp.* "Markus mentioned to me that your land was for sale. I did a little research, just a quick analysis, and knew right away I could really turn your place into a full ski resort with a hotel, more lifts, and shops. I'd like to make an offer tonight. We can take care of the paperwork on Monday. If you say yes, of course. But I don't see how you'd turn it down. I will top any offer on the table by fifteen percent."

She stared at Markus. His smile didn't reach his cold eyes. Why hadn't she noticed that before? Everything about him was for show. His home, his car, his life. Even his son. His sweet son who hadn't been home all day. Markus wasn't concerned because he stood to make a fortune on this.

"You benefit from this too," she said to Markus.

"Well, sure. I will put up a strip of stores at the base of the property near the road. Not far from the entrance to the Ryker Ranch. This way, I can get the people coming from the south who are just driving by, and I can benefit from any of the guests that continue to stay there. But with what Brian has in mind, that ranch won't stand a chance. In five years, they'll go under."

"How could you?"

"It's a win-win. You will walk away with a little money in your pocket so you can start over. The town will get some much-needed industry. And the Rykers will finally get what's coming to them."

"Why do you hate them so much?"

"You know why."

"Because Jett is a better man than you are?"

Brian choked out a cough.

"In fact, all of the Rykers are better men than you are. You didn't ask me here to help you out with a client who preferred a man involved in a relationship. You asked me here so I would sell my land to your friend and you could make a killing. The win-win is you don't have to buy my property outright. You don't care at all about the fact that land has been in my family for generations. That my daughter lives there. All you care about is money."

She pushed herself to stand and faced Brian. "I'm sorry that Markus lied to you. I'm not his girlfriend. I'm his ex-fiancé who felt sorry for him and was in a desperate situation this past month. If I had the power to turn your offer down, I would. You don't deserve that beautiful piece of Montana so you can build something large and ugly on it. It breaks my heart to say this, but I don't have the power to stop you. The bank will sell to anyone." And she had the papers to prove it.

She turned back to Markus. "And shame on you. Shame on you for thinking money was more important than people. And shame on me for once again feeling sorry for you. I truly need to learn my lesson. If you two will excuse me."

She hurried for her coat and tore open the front door and stopped in her tracks. Jett stood on the porch with his hand hovering near the bell. He wore his black cowboy hat and barn coat. His navy-blue flannel shirt hung out over his jeans. His chin was dusted in a day-old beard. His sexy look halted the breath in her lungs.

"What are you doing here?" He gave her the once-over before resting his gaze on her dress and bare legs.

"Why are you here?" Her heart climbed into her throat. The situation must look awful, and she would have a lot of explaining to do. Whatever had brought him here, and she could guess it had to do with Logan, had him fired up. He wouldn't show up unless he had a good reason. Seeing her here dressed this way was bound to rile him more. She had been dishonest with him.

"I need to talk to Markus. Why are you here and dressed like that?" He stared at her with hurt in his eyes.

She could have handled anger. But not hurt. "Jett, let me explain."

"Well, look who's here," Markus said, rounding the corner. "What brings the great and powerful Coach Ryker to my door on a Saturday night?"

"Where is Logan?" Jett brushed past her.

Both men stood inches apart, their gazes held as if a force beyond this room controlled them.

"My son is none of your business when he's not on the ski slope."

"You don't seem to know his business. I'm here only because I think he's put himself in trouble. It's my duty as his coach to inform his parent. I believe your son and his girlfriend crossed the state line to get married today."

Markus flinched. "That's crazy."

"Logan came to me with a problem. A big one. His answer to it was to get married. I tried to talk him out of it. I don't think he listened. You need to find your son and help him."

"He came to you?" Markus said. "My son is a fool to listen to anything you told him. If he's in trouble, it's because of you."

Jett fisted his hands.

She stepped in front of him before he did something he might regret. "Markus, Jett told Logan to come talk to you. It was the right thing to do."

"I don't need the coach telling me how to take care of my son. Logan has his whole future in front of him. He wouldn't throw it all away on some girl and get married... Wait a second. Is she pregnant? Did Logan get some tramp pregnant?"

Jett took a step forward.

She slapped her hand against Jett's chest, hoping to keep him from pummeling Markus. "Jett, he's not worth it."

Jett stepped back and ran his gaze over her again. His lips curled in a snarl. "You seem to think he is." Jett pointed at Markus. "Find your son." He marched out.

"Jett, wait."

"Don't run after him, Autumn," Markus said. "He doesn't deserve you."

"I can't believe you. You will stop at nothing to get what you want. For once, do the right thing and take care of Logan. He needs you. And forget about me. My life is with someone else." She hurried after Jett.

He hitched his leg into his truck and slammed the door. She waved with both arms, trying to get his attention. His gaze fell on her. His face was as stoic as ever. He would not give her an inch because she had broken his one rule.

He looked back over his shoulder. The truck bucked as he shifted gears, but then he gazed at her again. His face was still impassive. He tossed his hat on the seat and wiped a hand through his hair.

"Roll down the window." She mimed the gesture and then shoved her arms into her coat. She would freeze to death out here dressed the way she was. Even the nylon inside the jacket was cold.

"Not now," he said more as a bark than a statement. A proclamation. A demand.

"I need to talk to you. Can we go for a ride?"

"I'm not in the mood to talk about why you're at Markus Everett's dressed like you're off to a wedding. You kept this from me. You laid in my bed and lied to me."

"Jett, I'm sorry. I can explain."

"Your reason doesn't matter." He shook his head. "I'm not up for any emotional showdown right now. Give me my space. I have a lot of thinking to do."

"I need you to understand. I came here as a friend." A friend who had been fooled again and again. That was her legacy. Not a ski area to hand down, but a line of men behind her with the ability to persuade her to do their bidding.

"I don't care who your friends are. I care about the truth you wouldn't share. You never told me why you brought him dinner. Now tonight I find you here with him instead of with me."

"Are you going to end this thing between us?" She needed to brace herself for the inevitable. Without any warning, she might not survive the impact of losing him again.

"You may have already done that. I need to go."

"Say you'll call me tomorrow." She gripped the door, as if her small hand could hold him in place. As if anyone could hold Jett Ryker anywhere he didn't want to be.

He looked at her. She held her breath.

"I'll call you tomorrow. Do you have a way home?"

"I drove myself." She wrapped her coat tighter around her.

"Well, get to it, then. Or go back inside."

"I'm not going back in there. I was a fool to think Markus was anything other than he is."

He nodded and pulled away, leaving her standing in the frigid air wearing her pretty dress and uncomfortable shoes. Cold settled in her bones.

She might never be warm again.

Chapter Twenty-Four

Autumn poured coffee into her oversized mug. She hadn't slept a wink last night. After Jett had driven away, she had climbed into her own truck and driven around town for an hour or more before succumbing to the fact she had nowhere to go.

She had picked up her phone a dozen times to text or call Jett, but each time she had put it down. Jagged-edged fear kept her from reaching out to him and giving him the chance to say things were over. He would say it soon enough.

Almost her entire life she had placed her trust in the wrong places. A long time ago she had lost trust in Jett when he walked away, her heart broken and battered from his departure.

She had trusted Markus and then Trent. Each one had disappointed her. Even her mother had let her down by allowing her to believe she loved her enough to give her the family legacy.

Her cheeks were wet with tears. Her coffee grew cold. She needed to pull herself together. Quinn would be downstairs soon, and she would have to tell her sweet daughter they would be leaving their home—maybe even their town.

"Good morning," her father said, sauntering into the kitchen. A whistle played on his lips.

"You're chipper today."

"Had myself a pleasant night." He pulled down a mug and poured a cup of coffee. "You look a little tired."

"Ha. A lot tired is more like it."

Quinn bounded into the kitchen. Her oversized faded sweatshirt hung to her knees. Her hair was tied into a knot on the top of her head. "Mom, do you have a charger I could borrow? I think I left mine at Emily's."

"In my purse. I think. I'll look." She slipped out of the kitchen, relieved to have a reason to be alone. Her purse was still in her room.

The green dress was crumpled on the floor. She never wanted to wear that thing again. She'd burn it first. She grabbed her purse. Instead of the charger, her hand circled around the foreclosure papers.

She had almost forgotten about them. Her fight with Jett had given her little else to think about. She grabbed the charger too and returned to the kitchen. Quinn and Ives sat at the table, laughing over something on her phone.

"Here you go." She handed Quinn the charger.

"Thanks. My phone is about to die."

"What do you have there?" Ives turned in his chair. "That envelope is in pretty bad shape. Looks like it got caught in the rain."

"It's from the bank." She flashed the front to him, then tore open the envelope. Even though this place was no longer her problem, she had to see the letter.

For the past two years, she had worked to save this place. Her blood was in the ground, the beams, the air. All that time and energy spent was for nothing now. She could have built a different life.

But then she wouldn't have had these past weeks with Jett. To have loved him once more would take her through the rest of her life. She was grateful for the few moments together. To have seen him look at her as if she were the only person in the room could give her the strength to face what waited for her. No one had ever looked at her that way. And no one probably would again.

The letter read with typical rhetoric about foreclosing on the land. In three days, the property would belong to the bank. They would have to remove themselves from the premises.

"What's it say?" Ives said.

"What's going on?" Quinn looked between her and her father.

"I have some bad news." She flipped to the second page and stopped.

A copy of the deed was included. Her heart picked up speed. Heat flushed over her body. Her hand trembled.

"Autumn?" Ives stood beside her and read over her shoulder. "I don't understand."

"The deed says I own the land. Me. And only me." She waved around the paper. "Jett was right. She lied to keep me from him. She stooped to the lowest possible place because I wanted to be with Jett."

"Your mother did something," Ives said.

"She told me she owned the land. Not me. She also told me she asked you to come back so you could buy the land and sell it back to her. Not buy the land and help me. But buy the land and sell it to her. She wanted to get my land out from under me, and she was prepared to use you to do it." Her voice jarred the ceiling. Anger shook her whole body.

"Vera is the queen of manipulation," Ives said.

"What's all the hollering about?" Vera ran into the kitchen.

"How could you?" She shoved the papers at Vera, who didn't take them. "How could you lie to me like that? You're a snake. My own mother is a snake."

"Now, Autumn, let's stay calm. I did it for your own good."

"What are you saying right now?"

Vera's face crumpled. Tears sprang from her eyes. "I had to do what was best for my family. I had to save you from the Rykers. They aren't any good for you. You wouldn't listen to me. If you would only listen and take my advice when I give it. I had to lie to you about me still owning the land so you wouldn't stay with that man."

"That doesn't make any sense," Autumn said. "You still need to sell. Someone had to buy it."

"But not the Rykers. I needed a little time to prove to you Jett Ryker was all wrong for you. He would only control you and make you do what he wanted. He would never consider me in any of it. I'd be left all alone. I had to save us all."

"So you lied," Autumn said. "You hurt me so you could have your own way."

"Selfish comes to mind," Ives said.

Vera kept her gaze on her. "It wasn't much of a lie. It was just a stall tactic. You found out, didn't you? Now we can go back to the way things were."

"The bank owns the land now." She shoved the papers at her mother again. Vera's shaky grip sent the papers to the floor.

"Why did you bring me into this, Vera?" Her father's face was filled with pain. For the first time, he looked old, and her heart ached for him. He had his flaws, many of them, but he had never used her in the way her mother had.

"You know why." Vera waved her hand in the air.

"To use me too? I came back thinking you missed me. I did want to consider another chance with you because we always had something together. But you only wanted to use me."

"Oh please. As if you haven't used me a hundred times over the years. Whenever you get lonely, you call me. And when you're living high on the hog, you forget about me. I called you so I could show my daughter how all men are pigs and can't be trusted."

"You're the one who can't be trusted, Grandma. Mom was right about you. And you're wrong about Coach Ryker. He's a good guy. He's helped me so much these past weeks. He cares about the team. I can't stay in this house. I'm going to Emily's. I'll ride my bike."

Autumn pulled Quinn into a hug. "I'm sorry. I'm sorry for so many things. I promise to make our lives right somehow."

Quinn eased out of the hug. "I know, Mom. We'll figure it out. I hope."

"I'll give you a ride," Ives said, then turned to Autumn. "I'm going back to the B and B. Call me if you need anything."

"Dad, can you stay here instead? I'd like the company."

"I would love that. Vera, if I were you, I'd pack a bag and get out."

"I'm not going anywhere. This is my home."

"Actually, it's my home. I have to run out. I have to take care of something that can't wait. I want you gone within the hour. And if you're not gone by the time I get back, I'm going to call Sheriff Ryker to have you removed from the premises."

Vera huffed. But for the first time, she said nothing at all.

Autumn scooped up the papers and ran from the house. She had to find Jett.

****

She threw the truck in park and raced into the Ryker Ranch's main house. She bumped square into Lock and landed on her butt, as if she'd collided with a brick wall.

"Geez." She shook her head.

"Sorry about that. I didn't see you." Lock held out a hand and helped her to her feet. "You okay?"

"I think so. Is Jett here?"

Lock took a bite out of an apple. "Haven't seen him all morning. Did you text him?"

She hadn't bothered. She needed to see him in person and show him what she had discovered. She also needed to explain what had happened with Markus. "Where can I find him?"

"Try the stables."

"Thanks, Lock. I've got to run."

"Good luck."

She ran to the stables, passing guests who gave her strange looks. Her breath came in quick spirts, and her lungs hurt. She bent at the waist to gulp in air. The stable doors were open. A few of the horses were in their stalls. Most of the stalls were empty. On a Sunday, guests would be taking the horses for a ride. Jett could be with them.

"Can I help you?" A male voice drifted from behind her.

She turned.

"Oh, hey, Autumn. Are you looking for Jett?" Kace ambled farther into the stable. He looked so much like Jett in his jeans and sweatshirt.

"I am. Do you know where he is?" She needed to find her man, if he still wanted to be.

"He took a horse out for a ride. Not sure when he'll be back. You can wait if you want." He grabbed a rope from the hook.

"Is he with guests?"

"He said he needed to go alone. One of the employees, Paulie, took the guests out. Jett's in a bad mood. Just want to warn you."

She choked out a laugh. "Thanks." He would probably be in a worse mood when he saw her.

But she couldn't very well run around the ranch until she found him. She could be gone for a day or get lost in the mountain where the hiking trails were. She didn't even remember how to get to the cute little cabin they had set up for hikers who needed to take a break while out.

"I'll come back. But if you see him, will you tell him I was here? I have something I need to talk to him about."

"Sure. I'll tell him, but why don't you just text him?"

"This needs to be said in person."

"Did my brother say something stupid?"

"Kace, don't talk about your brother that way." Karen Ryker walked up the middle of the stable. Her face was grim, and she shook her head.

"Mom, have you talked to him today? He's acting like a grizzly."

"Never mind that. Hello, Autumn." Karen turned to

her.

"Hello." The stable was suddenly too warm. She had no reason to be nervous around Karen, but she still was. Jett was close to his mother. If Karen had any idea about the problems between Autumn and Jett, she would be telling Autumn to stay away from her son.

"I'll leave you two ladies to whatever it is you're going to talk about. I have to get back to my garage." He hugged his mother and sauntered away.

Karen watched as Kace disappeared around the corner. A smile the size of Montana delighted her face. "A mother never stops loving her children even when they're all grown men."

Karen turned back to her.

"I don't suppose she does. At least that's how I feel about Quinn." Her love for Quinn had only grown over the years, and if a man ever treated her badly, Autumn would stop at nothing to right that wrong. She suspected Karen felt that way too and was about to tell Autumn to take a hike.

"My son is struggling with his feelings for you."

"I know. I'm sorry about that. I didn't mean to hurt him." As she suspected, Karen was gearing up to send her away.

"Do you love him?"

"Very much." More than any other man before or after.

"Then you need to fix it."

She stared at Karen, waiting for her to say more, to say she wanted Autumn off the ranch, to find a rock and crawl under it, that Autumn would never be good enough for her son.

"I'm not sure how. I want to, but maybe I ruined us."

"He's so much like his father, and he doesn't even know it. John was a man of few words. In fact, all of my sons are that way. Except for Ajay. He had been the talkative one. Jett tries the hardest to keep his emotions to himself. He wants to be like Gage. Always has. Since he could walk across the room and chase his brother."

"That's sweet." She enjoyed picturing Jett as a boy toddling around. Hard to believe her rugged and deliberate man had been a little boy, but she still liked imagining it, imagining what their little boy would have been like too.

"I love how close my sons are. But sometimes Jett trying to be like Gage gets him tangled up the most. He has to work through those emotions he's got. You need to give him some space. A day or two. Maybe a week. I don't know what happened yesterday. He isn't going to say. Not to me. Maybe to Gage, but not now. He'll find you when he's ready."

"I don't know if I can wait. I only have three days."

"Three days?"

"It's a long story. And one I want you to know. But I do have to find Jett. This is important. Even if he and I can't work our differences out. I have information he needs."

"Autumn?" Jett stood at the entrance of the stable, his horse beside him.

"Looks to me like you had your prayers answered." Karen stole a glance at the ceiling and smiled. "Good luck." She patted Jett's arm as she went past.

He led the horse to the stall but didn't put it inside. Then he came to her.

"What are you doing here?" He kept his distance and leaned against the stall door. His eyes were hooded, and his beard was thicker. Instead of his cowboy hat, he wore a gray knit cap on his head. He was gorgeous and strong and off-limits.

"You were right. My mother lied." She pulled the papers out of her coat pocket, unfolded them, and handed them to him.

He glanced at them, then at her. "I'm sorry she lied to you. But now you can decide what to do."

"I want you to buy the land. We have three days to make it happen."

"I don't want your land anymore."

"What? Why? It's a perfect business decision for you."

"It was. But not anymore."

"Why? Because of us? Don't be foolish and allow your feelings for me to get in the way." She had to convince him. He was the best person to take care of her family's legacy. She had been too caught up in her own demons to see her way clearly.

"I can't buy your land and see you every day. And I can't go back to pretending like we've done for so long. You wrecked me. I don't know what to do to get back to my old self."

"I'm sorry."

"We've been saying 'sorry' a lot lately. I don't know if love is supposed to be this hard." He pulled off his hat and scratched his head.

"We aren't perfect. We're going to mess up. All the time. We're going to get hurt. I can't promise I won't hurt you again. And you can't promise that either." She wanted to make him understand a love for a lifetime would come with joy and pain.

"I know what it's like to be hurt, Autumn."

"You don't do hurt. You avoid it. You think if you love someone, they're going to leave you. Your father left you. Your brother left you. Our child left us. I married someone else. I never stopped loving you. I made a mistake. Lots of them. And your father didn't die because he loved you. And Ajay didn't die because he loved you. And Silver Bell didn't die because she loved you. She lived because she loved all of you."

"Why did you lie to me? That's what I can't live with."

She had to touch him and crossed the space to him and placed her hands on his chest. He didn't push her away. He looked down at her, and all the hurt she had mentioned pooled in his eyes.

"I was afraid. I needed the money, and Markus offered me a job cooking for him. That was how it started. I didn't want the whole town to know I was over at Markus's. Especially not you. And then he asked me for a favor. He pleaded with me. And I fell for it. Stupid. Gullible Autumn. Fell for it. But all he wanted was a way to get a piece of my land without buying it and make a ton of money. As soon as I knew that, I left. That's when you showed up. I'm sorry. I planned on telling you everything last night."

He laced his fingers through hers. "You're not stupid or gullible. No more talk like that. You're kind with a big heart. You want to believe the best in people. It's why you've given your mother so many chances."

"Not anymore. I threw her out."

He barked out a laugh. "You did?"

"I did."

"That's my girl."

"Am I, Jett? Am I yours?"

"If you'll put up with my stubbornness and my competitiveness. If you'll understand I want to protect you even when you don't need it. I won't share you with any other man. I will always want the truth even when I don't want to hear it. If you can live with that and all my other flaws, then you are mine and I am yours. For good this time."

"I will tell you the truth always. I will tell you when I'm scared. I will lean on you when I need help."

"I believe we have ourselves a deal."

Then he kissed her.

Epilogue

Two months later

Winter would not let go of her hold on the weather no matter how hard spring fought for control. Another storm had landed four feet of snow on Backwater. Autumn was never gladder to be stuck inside.

She couldn't believe how much life could change in a short time. Last year if someone had told her she would be engaged to Jett Ryker and planning a wedding, she would have laughed so hard she would have split her jeans.

But here she was, sitting at his table in the kitchen of the main house with Quinn and Karen head-to-head in a bridal magazine. A Christmas wedding was on the horizon.

She and Jett didn't see any point in waiting, and Christmas was her favorite time of year. Jett wanted to run to the justice of the peace, just the two of them. As much as she loved the spunky woman in town who married those couples seeking non-clergy, Autumn wanted to give Quinn a chance to be a part of a real ceremony built on love, and that would take some time to plan. So Lisa, the justice of the peace, would marry them in December on the ranch with their loved ones surrounding them. And Ives would walk her down the aisle.

He had rented a house in town and started working at the hardware store. She liked having her father back in her life. He still wanted to take Karen out on a date. She still said no.

Vera had moved out of the house. Gage had shown up as Autumn had promised and helped Vera pack her things. He'd driven her to her sister's house in Wyoming. Autumn would eternally be grateful to Gage.

And Jett had purchased the land. They had arrived at the bank the next morning after their conversation in the stables. Well, they had done a lot more than talk that day. He had taken her into the loft and made love to her twice under horse blankets. She'd pulled hay out of her hair for days.

They had made love almost every day since. She hoped they would go on that way for as long as the universe would allow it. She could never get enough of her man.

Her man. She sighed.

"Everything okay?" Jett said, coming from the office side of the building. He took the mug from her hand, placed it on the table, and kissed each of her knuckles.

"Perfect." She tipped her chin in the direction of Quinn and his mother. "They've been at it all morning."

"My mom is thrilled to have a wedding to plan since Gage and Kace haven't done the deed yet. She's hoping they'll get on the wagon now."

"I hope so too. Wouldn't it be fun if we all got married at the same time?"

"If that's what you want, darlin', that is what you will have," Jett said. "I spoke with Logan. He and Maya chose the couple to adopt their baby. Looks like things will work out for them."

"Giving the baby up and not getting married was the best option. They'll see that someday." She had checked in with Logan regularly too. He struggled with his decision to break up with Maya and move forward. They had made it to the state line when he turned the car around that day. He hadn't wanted to be married. Autumn wanted to be there to give him support. Markus dropped the ball too often.

"I hope so."

"No one would guess you're a worrywart, Jett Ryker."

He arched a brow.

"How are the renovations coming?" She wrapped her arms around his neck and pressed against him. Maybe not the best behavior in front of others, but too bad.

Her house had been gutted and was being renovated for a ski lodge with gym and sauna. Jett had plans for locker rooms, a bar, and a café. And two more slopes. He was also going to clear the trees between the properties and provide shuttle service. Business was looking up. He was already booking for next ski season.

In the meantime, she and Quinn had moved into his apartment. After the ski lodge was complete, they would build a home on the ranch's property. Right next door to where Gage planned on building a house for him and Calista.

"Do you think we could sneak away for an hour?" She rubbed against him, and he responded in kind. Maybe make a baby of their own.

"I can take a break before anyone needs me." He turned to Karen and Quinn. "Mom, I want to show

Autumn something at the lodge. Will you two be okay here for a while?"

Karen waved him away. "Quinn and I have a whole day planned. Don't worry about us."

Her heart melted because Quinn had the kind of grandmother she deserved. And they both had a whole family to love them.

She looked at Jett and smiled. "Thank you for making all my dreams come true."

He smiled back. "Same."

A word about the author…

Stacey Wilk wrote her first novel in middle school to quiet the characters in her head. It was that or let them out to eat the cannolis, and she wasn't sharing her grandfather's Italian pastries.

Many years later her life took an adventurous turn when she gave birth to two different kinds of characters. She often sits in awe of their abilities to make objects fly, make it snow on command, and remain dirty after contact with water. She does share the cannolis with them for fear of having her fingers bit off if she doesn't.

Because of the extraordinary characters now in her home instead of in her head, including a king who surfaces after dark and for coffee, she writes novels about family: those that we are born to and those that we pick up along the way. You can find her message in her middle-grade fantasy novels as well as her women's fiction novels. Family are those that love you when you need them.

When she's not creating stories in make-believe places, she can be found hanging with the cast members of her house, or teaching others how to make make-believe worlds of their own. Stop by for a visit and make sure to bring some cannolis. www.staceywilk.com

Thank you for purchasing
this publication of The Wild Rose Press, Inc.

For questions or more information
contact us at
info@thewildrosepress.com.

The Wild Rose Press, Inc.
www.thewildrosepress.com